SURVIVAL IS A MATTER OF CHOICE

HERA'S
CURSE
SHAUN GRIFFIN

BOOK ONE OF THE AMERICAN NOIR TRILOGY

To Jane, Kyle & Claire for all your support.

HERA'S
CURSE

One could say life is only a matter of the choices we make. That our day-to-day lives amount to nothing more than a finite combination of those choices. If this is true, if our lives are the sum of these choices, are we not then masters of our own destinies? Free to say yes or free to say no, and in so doing, free to take our lives in any direction we choose?

There is, of course, the other point of view: that the path each person's life takes is preordained. Set before us at birth. That we have no choice but to walk that one path, forced to follow wherever it leads until, at last, we come to its inevitable end.

Perhaps Joe da Silva was reflecting on this as he scrambled down the dirty alleyway, his rasping breath echoing off the graffiti-covered walls. He could hear his pursuers gaining on him but did not look back, worried that in so doing they would be closer still. The thought injected a new energy into his shuffling run.

The pace of the men following quickened, too. Joe looked over his shoulder and stumbled into some trash cans. He almost lost his footing but regained his balance and forced his aching legs on. Up ahead, a high brick wall blocked the way, but Joe could see the alley leading off to both right and left in front of it. He had seconds to make his choice.

He turned right, glancing back as he did. The men chasing him were close, the light glinting malevolently off their long-barrelled silencer pistols. Joe took a few more steps before realising the way he'd chosen was a dead end. He pulled up, blinking stupidly at the wall that blocked his way. Large black garbage bags were heaped carelessly at its base, some split to spill their rotting contents into the alley. Sweat trickled down his face. He licked his lips nervously and tried to focus on what was happening behind him. His pursuers had stopped running and Joe could hear their steady footsteps as they strode calmly toward him. His left hand groped for the .38 tucked in the waistband of his baggy jeans.

"Put your hands where we can see them, da Silva!" demanded a voice from behind.

Joe's hand closed around the .38's grip.

"Hands where we can see them, Joe," urged the voice again.

"Give us Manny Mendez and we let you walk," offered a second voice reasonably.

Manny Mendez was not the kind of man you crossed. Joe knew what would happen if he did. On the flipside, he wasn't even sure these men would let him live, should he talk. This, if anything, decided it for him. He wrenched the .38 from his waistband and spun about.

The men fired repeatedly before Joe could even pull the trigger, the cough of their silenced pistols echoing loudly off the brick walls. He staggered back as the rounds hit him and slumped down onto the heap of garbage bags, the .38 slipping from his grip. The two men walked up to where he lay propped, a beggar-king hunched on his sagging throne of garbage. They held their pistols casually; Joe da Silva was no longer a threat.

"Now that wasn't very friendly of you, Joseph," said the shorter man with mock surprise.

Joe squinted up at the two strangers standing over him.

"Who the fuck are you?" he stammered.

"We ask the questions," grunted the taller man.

He lifted his pistol and put a bullet through Joe's left knee.

Joe screamed.

The two paused to allow Joe a moment to collect himself.

"Now, tell us where we can find Manny Mendez?" enquired the shorter man.

Joe grimaced in reply.

"Don't know him."

"Whenever a person wants to insult someone, you ever wonder why they call them a dick, or a cunt, or an asshole?" began the shorter man. "You know, when you think about it, all those are useful body parts. I mean, the body just can't function without them. The appendix, on the other hand, now that's pretty much a useless appendage. It just hangs out in your body until one day it ruptures, poisons you, and then you end up dying because you didn't get to the hospital in time. So, what are you, Joseph? Are you a cunt or are you an appendix? You gonna help us out, or does my friend here have to get creative with his pistol?"

"You talk too much," retorted Joe with feigned braggadocio.

"Fuck this," spat the taller man.

He raised his pistol again and shot the prone man's other knee. Joe uttered another high-pitched scream, and then in a tumble of words proceeded to detail everything he knew about Manny Mendez.

A short while later, the two men exited the alley onto the quiet city street, one carrying a sports bag. They strolled past a hooker, her ample ass on display as she bent forward to rest her elbows on the open car window of a potential john. Neither noticed the two men walk by as they continued to negotiate her price. The men continued toward the black sedan parked farther up the street.

"You think he told us the truth?" asked the shorter man.

"No reason to believe he wouldn't," replied the taller. "Stupid fuck actually thought giving up Manny was gonna save him."

"Suppose we'll find out soon enough," mused the shorter man.

"Of course, if it doesn't check out, then killing him might appear a little shortsighted."

The taller man scowled.

"Say what?"

"Manny's been lying low for over a month now, correct?"

"Yeah, and?"

The shorter man shrugged.

"Well, considering this is the first decent lead we've had on where he's been hiding, I just thought it might've been prudent to keep the source of that information alive," replied the shorter man. "Besides, he wasn't the target."

The taller man snorted.

"Are you going soft on me, John?" he asked.

"No, Matt, I'm just making a point."

"What?" retorted Matt. "That we should let all drug dealers live?"

"No, that we should stick to the job we were given."

"He told us to eliminate Manny," said Matt. "He didn't say how we should do it. Besides, it's a bit late for you to grow a conscience now, isn't it?"

"I'm in this, same as you, Matt," said John. "I remember why we volunteered for it. Maybe it's just that I don't take as much pleasure from this as you seem to."

They stopped by the car and John walked round to the driver's side, opened the door, and got in.

Matt laughed as he slid into the passenger seat.

"We're all going to pay the piper sooner or later, John," he observed casually. "Joe just got to do it sooner."

John answered with a contemplative look which, had Matt been more observant, he would have recognized as a signal of the growing rift between them. They had walked one road, but now, perhaps enticed by some unseen power, each had turned to follow their own path, neither man understanding the awful fate each choice held.

Moments later, their black sedan pulled away from the kerb, leaving the world no poorer for the loss of one Joe da Silva.

◊ ◊ ◊

Manny Mendez was across town at that moment. He had just finished filling the tank of his purple Cadillac and was waiting for his change from the gas station clerk. His swept-back black hair, chiselled features, and olive skin had caught the eye of many women, but the more perceptive would have noticed a certain malevolence in his studied swagger. Manny took a long draw from his cigarette and exhaled slowly. He noticed the full cash register and made a casual mental note.

The clerk's nose wrinkled at the acrid smell. He coughed and opened his mouth to launch into a speech about second-hand smoke but thought better of it. Something in the coal-black eyes of the individual opposite him was unsettling. Manny's lips curled back into a predatory grin and the clerk's gaze faltered under Manny's malevolent stare.

"Have a good day," the cashier offered weakly along with the $1.50 change.

Manny took the money.

"Give me a pack of Marlboro," he said.

The cashier hesitated.

"Excuse me?" His voice wavered nervously.

"A pack of Marlboro. Give me a pack of Marlboro. You stock them, don't you?"

There was a hard edge to Manny's voice now.

"Yes, of course. Sorry, I... I'll just get them for you," stammered the cashier.

He turned his back reluctantly on Manny to unlock the cabinet behind.

Manny didn't smoke Marlboros, preferring the stronger taste of his own hand-rolled cigarettes. He just enjoyed watching the cashier squirm, a dog lying on its back offering its belly to the dominant alpha male.

The cashier turned back with the cigarettes.

"That'll be $6.00," he said.

He pushed the pack as far forward as the counter would allow.

Manny snorted derisively. "$6.00?"

The cashier took an involuntary step backward.

"You know what? I've changed my mind. You can put them back now."

The cashier hesitated.

"Stupid fuck," Manny sneered, then turned and left the store.

He strolled over to his Cadillac and reached into his pocket for his keys. At that moment, a silver minibus rolled quietly into the gas station and stopped at the pumps opposite him.

'The Whitby Foundation Finishing Academy', it read on the side of the bus.

Seated behind the driver were six young women. Manny's interest quickened, his eyes roving over the young women and examining each in turn. They appeared identical—styled blonde bobs that finished just above their navy-blue blazers; cool porcelain skin; long eyelashes and pinched noses perched above full sensual lips. The young women stared ahead in silence, apparently oblivious to the world outside. They were out of his league.

Manny whistled softly. He'd pimped young women from time to time over the years. Most had been teenage girls with drug habits who owed him money and had run out of options. The others were those he'd coerced using more forceful methods. His eyes lingered on the young women. Having one or two of these girls work for him would sure turn a handsome profit.

But not before he'd sampled the goods first. Nothing quite like getting in the saddle and breaking a young filly in. He smiled at the thought.

The nearest young woman turned suddenly and looked at him, her pale, ice-blue eyes moving over his body, studying him. Manny smiled wolfishly. She returned the smile with a slight curve of her lips, then lowered her eyes demurely and turned back to face her front. A sudden hardcore vision of him penetrating her writhing naked body popped into his head.

Any thought of introducing himself was quickly quashed at the sight of the man that suddenly exited the driver's side of the bus. He was a big man in a black suit which just managed to contain his heavy, muscled body. A black chauffeur's cap was pulled low over his bald, dome-shaped head. The man proceeded to fill the minibus with fuel.

Manny's pornographic mental imagery quickly evaporated.

No hope in hell, he decided.

His gaze strayed back to the young women for one final look. The one who'd made eye contact before was looking at him again. She raised a tube of red lipstick to the bus window. The young woman wrote in reverse without a hint of hesitation, so that to him the numbers appeared in their correct order.

Phone number, he thought, and reached for the cell phone in his pocket.

He quickly punched in the numbers then glanced back at the chauffeur. The man continued to fill the gas tank. Manny opened the door of his Cadillac and slid behind the wheel. He inserted the key into the ignition and the engine turned over with a satisfying rumble. He revved the engine gently, looked over at the blonde, winked, and slowly pulled out of the gas station.

2

The spent sun hung low in the sky, a blood-red orb sinking slowly behind the smoggy horizon of the sprawling city. The black sedan rolled smoothly down the street of one of the city's tougher neighbourhoods. According to police stats, crime was down for the area, though that still meant it exceeded the state average, so it was little comfort to the more law-abiding who lived there. In this neighbourhood, double-bolted doors, bars on windows, and ownership of a handgun or two were not a matter of choice—they were necessary, desperate solutions to a problem an overstretched police force could not afford to tackle.

The car slowed to a stop outside a house, the flaking fascia-boards and grubby walls of which made it almost indistinguishable from any of its equally ill-kept neighbours. The two men in the car sat for a moment and looked around at a street that appeared deserted. They got out of their car, looked up and down the street once more, and strode purposefully up the cracked pathway toward the front door. The sinking sun's light stretched their shadows into distorted caricatures which slithered ahead of them up to the waiting house.

John pressed the door buzzer as Matt stood carefully to one side. It took two more attempts before they were rewarded with the noise of someone approaching. The door creaked open the width of an eye.

"Can I help you?"

The nervous voice belonged to a young woman.

"Good afternoon, ma'am," greeted John. "We're here to see a Manny Mendez."

"Sorry, he's not in," replied the young woman quickly.

She moved to shut the door. A violent shove sent her sprawling to the floor as the two men forced their way in, their pistols drawn.

Matt ignored the girl as he moved down the hall, his pistol trained on the first room. John closed the door behind him and looked down at the young woman as she attempted to cover her long white thighs with the cheap dressing gown she wore. He squatted down beside her and noticed the bruised welts on her legs. She looked at him uncertainly.

"Don't be frightened. We're not going to hurt you. My name's John, what's yours?" he said softly.

"Faith," she said carefully.

"You look like you've been through a lot, Faith. Here, let me help you up. Let's find somewhere more comfortable where we can talk," he said.

He extended his hand.

She looked up at John, and after a moment's indecision, took his hand. He led her into the sitting room while Matthew continued to check each of the rooms in turn.

"You seem kinda out of place here, Faith," said John.

"What do you mean?" countered the girl carefully.

Did her eyes betray fear or was it something else? John could not tell.

"I mean, Manny," he said. "How did you end up here with him?"

"You mean, how was I stupid enough to get myself in this situation?"

He detected a note of defiance in her voice.

"Getting caught up in the wrong decision doesn't mean you're stupid," said John. "It just means things didn't turn out the way you thought they would."

He smiled.

Faith chewed her lip nervously as her eyes searched his. She was hesitant at first but once she began the words spilled easily from her lips, as though in speaking she were exorcizing some inner demon.

Her story unfolded much like a badly scripted B-movie plot. She, a nineteen-year-old suffocated by the limited prospects of her small Midwest town life, is seduced by the cinematic Hollywood glow of the flickering screen in the local movie theatre. Reasoning that somewhere in the City of Dreams is a star with her name on it, she leaves home. Somewhere down the line, she finds herself on the street, destitute and too proud (or scared) to return home. The constant battle to survive coupled with the condescending looks on the passing faces of respectable wage-earners slowly sap all remaining self-respect and self-belief.

Then one day a kind face emerges from the wall of spiteful looks.

"Down on your luck?" asks the face. "Never mind, girl, ignore these people. They just never had it hard. Now me, I know different. Come with me and I'll make sure you get a hot meal, a bath, and a warm bed."

The voice is warm and reassuring.

"The cost? Never mind that. We can talk about that later. Right now, let's concentrate on getting you on your feet again, looking beautiful like I know you can be."

Clutching at this one last hope, the young woman goes with the face. There is no happy ending.

Faith finished her story and began to cry, relieved to have finally spoken of her lonely descent into the hell of being trapped with Manny.

"He said if I ever left him, he'd find me," she sobbed. "He'd find me and kill me."

John placed a reassuring hand on her slim shoulder.

"That's not going to happen. I promise."

Matthew's tall frame appeared in the doorway.

"He's not here," he said.

John sat back on the stained sofa.

"Now that's a real pity, because right now I'm itching to have a little word with him."

"A little word?" chuckled Matthew. "Is that what we're doing now?"

"You know what I mean," replied John patiently.

"Yeah, does she?" quipped Matthew.

"I think the circumstances have changed a little, don't you?"

"Let's just focus on the job, John. You can play white knight another time," growled Matthew.

"I think I know where he's gone," said Faith.

Had she tried to analyse her true intentions, Faith might've decided that she'd volunteered the information as an act of self-preservation, either because she hoped these men would rid her of Manny or because she thought they might kill her if she didn't talk. The fact was that Faith had done what she always did: She had gone with her gut-instinct, which to date had admittedly not served her well. A pair of expectant faces looked at her.

"Manny phoned someone earlier. He wrote something down. It's in the bedroom..."

Faith walked through to the bedroom. Her body was tense, aware of the two figures following her closely. Her nervous hands searched through the unkempt clutter on Manny's bedside table. Her face brightened.

"Here it is. Manny wrote down this address, then he went out."

She handed the crumpled piece of paper to John.

"Looks like we have our lead," he smiled.

Matthew grunted but made no move to leave the room.

Faith looked at the men, attempting to gauge their intent, and breathed an inner sigh of relief as they turned to leave. In a strange way, she was glad these men had forced their way in. Being able to speak to someone had finally made her face her situation. Sure, she'd have to go crawling back to her aunt and that asshole she was living with, but even that was better than this. Her one hope was that these men would get rid of Manny—she'd feel better knowing he wouldn't be around to hunt her down and kill her like he'd threatened.

John stopped at the bedroom doorway and looked back at her.

"You don't need to be here anymore. Why don't you put some clothes on and come with us?"

Did the offer cloak a hidden threat? Their way of getting her to go with them, to take her to a more convenient spot and eliminate her like they would Manny? She wasn't sure. So why go with them? Was it because she wanted to know for sure Manny had been taken care of? Or was it because the only other alternative was going back to the viper pit that was home? Faith was never one for analysing her decisions too closely, and so, for the second time in as many minutes, she went with her gut.

3

The old mansion's Georgian architecture blended easily with its stately neighbours. Like the others, it was set back from the street behind a set of imposing iron gates. Remote cameras located above ornate iron railings and an intercom sited in front of the large stone wall provided what was, for this street, the standard welcome.

For the third time that evening, the purple Cadillac cruised quietly down the street. This time, the car pulled up to the kerb, stopping just beyond the light of a streetlamp. Manny's eyes strained as he peered into the inky dark. He was attempting to get a feel for the grounds that lay couched in the darkness beyond the muted light at the gate.

Being a suspicious man, Manny's cock-stiffening euphoria at the gas station had quickly given way to some serious doubts. The first had been the legitimacy of the phone number. But when he'd dialled the number later, he'd been rewarded with a young woman's sultry voice.

"Hi, you must be the guy from the gas station."

"Could be. How would you know?"

The young woman had chuckled seductively.

"Call it an educated guess."

"Let's say I am that guy. You always give your number out to strangers?"

"It depends."

"Depends on what?"

"On whether I see an opportunity."

"Opportunity?" Manny had snorted. "An opportunity for what, exactly?"

The young woman had responded with a knowing laugh.

"Oh, I think you can figure that out for yourself."

"That depends, girl. I can figure a whole lot of things. Things that might be outta your league."

"Maybe, maybe not. But then I guess you'll just have to find that out for yourself."

"You got a name?"

"Bethany. What's yours?"

"Manny."

"Well, Manny, what do you say?"

"Say to what?"

"Why, to a nice, quiet visit. Just you and me, and maybe one or two of my friends."

Giggling female voices had chorused in the background, "We're bored, Manny."

"Maybe you are. Or maybe, you're just a bunch of rich chicks with nothing better to do than jerk a man around."

"We never joke about a good fuck, Manny. The question is, are you man enough to handle what we've got?"

"I think you already know the answer to that," Manny had said.

"Then say it, Manny," Bethany had purred saucily. "Say 'I'm man enough'."

"I don't have time for your little games, girl," Manny had growled. "Now, you either tell me where we can meet, or you hang up."

Bethany had responded with another sultry chuckle.

"I'll send you the details now, big boy."

Then she'd hung up.

A few seconds later Bethany had sent a photo of the lower half of her body. Her dress had been raised to reveal her shaved crotch. Written neatly above the cleft of her sex was a three-digit number and the letter M. She'd sent a text message a few minutes after that.

'A clue to where we're at. Phone me in two hours if you're serious and I'll give up the rest', it had read.

◊ ◊ ◊

He'd gone home after that, mainly because he'd needed more speed, but also so that he could take his frustration out on his latest girl. He'd found Faith living on the streets a few weeks back. By now he'd normally have put her to work on those same streets, but he'd held back, in part because he wanted to enjoy her first, but also because he'd sensed an inner strength he knew he'd have to break. Given time, she would break. They always did. When it came to women, Manny was always in control. Always.

Now, sitting in his car in the dark, he played out that earlier phone conversation again in his head. If this was the cops doing some entrapment gig, then they'd gone to a whole lot of trouble for a small-timer like himself.

'Anyway,' he reasoned to himself, 'female cops wouldn't send crotch-shots. That would be grounds for entrapment. Could be a hit? I go in and I never come out. The house is located far back from the street. Shots inside would probably never be heard. Especially silenced ones. Fuck!'

His stomach tightened at the thought. The gang war between Carlos da Silva and the Mortagua brothers had made a lot of people nervous, but he belonged to neither gang. Of course, he'd had dealings with da Silva's brother, Joe. Lots of people did. But surely nothing that'd be worth killing for—besides, it'd be much easier to just walk up on the street and gun him down rather than all this bullshit. To his mind, that just left one alternative. The girl was legit.

"Fuck it," muttered Manny.

He opened the car door and slid out from behind the wheel. He closed the door carefully to keep any noise to a minimum.

'No need to alert nosey neighbours,' he thought.

A quick look up and down the street and a few short steps, and Manny stood in the shadow of the stone wall. He turned and reached up to grip the top of the wall. It was easier than he had at first supposed, the protruding stones in the wall allowing enough purchase even for his expensive heeled boots.

Manny dropped to the ground on the opposite side of the wall with a dull thud. He straightened up and looked around. The darkness made each tree and shrub he saw appear more menacing. Beyond the trees stood the mansion. Silent. Brooding. Ominous. Not at all as inviting as he'd first imagined. He slunk nervously through the trees towards the house, his senses sharpened by that most basic of human instincts: the primeval fear of the dark. He soon found himself at the edge of the trees. An exposed stretch of neat lawn and rows of flowerbeds stood between him and the mansion. Manny licked his lips nervously, still not completely able to shake the fear this might all be a trap.

'You will find a door at the end of the east wing,' she had said.

East wing? He looked up at the imposing double-storey structure. High brick chimneys bookended what he supposed was the main part of the house. A single-storey level extended from either end of the main building. One of these had to be the east wing, he reasoned, but which? The building, with its ivy-covered-brickwork and rows of narrow windows, stood mutely and offered no clues.

Light suddenly pierced the dark, spilling onto the lawn from one of the windows set at the far end of one of the mansion's extensions. Manny moved along the edge of the trees until he stood opposite the finger of light.

A naked young woman stood at the window. Pale white skin, heavy upturned breasts topped with soft pink nipples, shaven sex between long thighs—a Bouguereau nude framed by the open curtains.

His eyes drank in every detail before the naked woman closed the curtains. The vision was gone.

Manny crossed the expanse of lawn like a man in a trance, his legs moving of their own accord. He found the door easily enough. It was open. He stepped inside and waited for his eyes to adjust to the dark. A strip of light beneath a door to his right cast its invitation to paradise onto the polished wooden floor of the hallway. He moved quickly toward the door, and after a brief moment's reservation, opened it.

Manny blinked as his eyes adjusted to the light. A large Victorian-style four-poster bed dominated the room. Three young women had draped themselves over the bed, naked bodies moving languorously over each other. The young woman from the window stood in front of him.

"I knew you would come," she said in a low sultry tone. "I'm Bethany. Come in. Let me introduce you to my friends."

She took Manny's hand and pulled him deeper into the room. The women, seemingly oblivious to their nakedness, uncoiled themselves from the bed and moved toward him.

His primal inner sense prickled.

'Something's not right. I can feel it. Get out! Get out now, while you still can!'

But it was too late. The women were upon him, restless hands pulling him back onto the large bed as he struggled to comprehend what was happening. Their nubile forms slithered over Manny's rigid body as they deftly removed his clothing. His mind, confused by the conflicting sensations of cold fear and hot lust, seemed unable to regain control of his spread-eagled limbs. Three pairs of hungry lips caressed his body. Bethany straddled his hips, her long fingers raking through the thick hair on his chest. He could feel the moistness of her sex against his lower belly. She raised her hips and pushed back, slowly impaling herself on Manny's engorged penis.

A low moan escaped her lips. Bethany's thighs flexed as she rode him, Manny's penis sliding within her sheath. She pushed down again, then up, down, her hips settling into a grinding rhythm, moving her towards orgasm. All the while the others continued their caresses. Bethany arched her back and shuddered, her pink nipples erect on her marble breasts. She threw her head back to release a low animalistic moan, then bent forward, her hands sliding over his chest to rest on his shoulders.

"Nothing like a good fuck to give a girl an appetite!" she growled huskily.

Her cold blue eyes bored into Manny's as her lips curled back to reveal long, pointed canines. A predator and her prey.

Adrenaline surged through Manny's body as his survival instinct finally kicked in. He strained impotently against the unseen force that pinned him to the bed, a helpless insect on a specimen board. The nightmarish face descended toward his. He could smell the metallic scent of blood on her breath.

"Don't worry, lover, you won't suffer long!" Bethany moved quickly then, her long canines sinking violently into his jugular as one hand covered his mouth to stifle his screams.

Manny's muffled screams reached a new pitch when three more sets of fangs pierced his flesh.

It was at that moment that Matthew and John chose to make their entrance. The door burst open under the impact of Matthew's boot. The two men and the vampires stared at each other in surprise. It was Bethany who moved first, an angry hiss escaping from her blood-drenched lips as she launched herself toward the waiting men.

But Matthew was quicker. He flicked the switch of his G18C to fully automatic and let off a long burst, hitting Bethany in mid-lunge. The force of the high-powered rounds sent her spinning back over the bed.

Howls of indignant anger issued from the remaining vampires. They quickly detached themselves from Manny and hurled themselves at the intruders. The girls darted forward quickly, moving from side to side as they evaded the gunfire. The men kept their fingers depressed on the automatics' triggers, stocks kicking back into their shoulders as they sprayed the room with death. The girls' attack wilted under the volume of fire as each vampire was hit multiple times, bullets ripping through flesh and bone. Despite their horrific wounds, the women came on, dragging torn limbs behind them, intent only on ripping apart their enemy. An obscene collage of sight and sound followed, spattered gore interlaced with the staccato reports of the silenced weapons and the vampires' screams of impotent rage. It took another thirty-three-round clip in each weapon to finally kill the vampires. The smell of blood and cordite hung in the air.

"You believe this?"

John spoke loudly, his ears ringing from the noise. The silencers had been surprisingly loud in the closed confines of the bedroom.

Matthew nodded mutely, ejecting the empty magazine clip from his weapon.

"Think he's still alive?" he asked, nodding in the direction of the bed.

"I'll check."

John stepped over the broken body of one of the dead vampires.

It was this moment that Bethany chose to attack. The virus which made her a vampire meant her body had begun rapidly repairing her wounds as she lay feigning death while her sisters were being murdered. She leapt over the bed, hitting John full in the chest. He staggered back, fell over a corpse, and his pistol went skidding across the bloody floor. Bethany ignored him, her only focus the man who'd shot her. Matthew parried her first strike with his empty weapon, but she evaded his desperate counterblow and wrapped herself about him in a deadly embrace.

The pair staggered about the room until Bethany wrestled him to the gore-strewn floor. She sat astride the struggling man, naked thighs coiled around his waist, squeezing the breath from him. Her fingers dug into his wrists as she forced his arms down to bring her fangs closer to the pulsing vein in his neck. Matthew jammed his weapon under the chin of the vampire as he frantically attempted to stop her.

John sat up in a daze and looked around desperately for his weapon. He could hear the uneven struggle behind him as he spotted his pistol six feet away. Matthew's laboured grunts added to John's urgency as he scrambled toward the weapon. Bethany's breath was hot against Matthew's neck, her fangs now inches away from their mark.

"Get off him you, fucking bitch!"

Bethany looked up, her eyes widening in dismay and then her face disintegrated in a roar of shotgun fire. Faith pulled back quickly on the slide action of the Remington Tactical and fired the next twelve-gauge round into the chest of the vampire, lifting her off Matthew. Two more shots followed in quick succession. She was taking no chances.

John walked over to Matthew and offered a hand-up.

"And you said she'd be a dead weight!" he smiled.

Matthew stood unsteadily on his feet. He brushed himself off and looked over at the slight young woman cradling the shotgun.

"Thanks," he muttered.

John cocked his pistol and walked over to the bed.

"Matt, take a look at this," he said.

He had expected to find Manny dead, or at least close to death, but what he saw was something else entirely.

"What the hell do you think is happening to him?"

The bloodied figure of Manny lay curled in the foetal position. His eyes had rolled back. Blackened lips were pulled back in a pained grimace and foam dribbled down his chin, but his skin was what most caught the men's attention. It appeared translucent, the blackened veins clearly visible beneath the skin, each writhing as the body transformed itself under the unseen spell of the virus.

"I don't know, but I'm sure this'll stop it!"

The silenced pistol burped loudly as John emptied a full clip into Manny. The body expired with a long sigh. Manny Mendez was no more.

"I think we better get outta here now. Shotgun shots must've been heard," said Matthew, looking about the room.

"That, or the screaming," said John. "It's time to go."

The pair turned from the bed and walked quickly from the room, Faith in tow, the shotgun clutched tightly to her chest.

◊ ◊ ◊

The trio sat silently in the car as they drove away, their numbed expressions alternately exposed in light or hidden in darkness as they passed each streetlamp. The tempo of light and dark quickened as the black sedan gathered speed, turning out of the leafy suburb toward home.

Matthew finally broke the silence.

"What'll we tell him?"

John shrugged.

"Don't know yet. A lot has happened tonight. I'll figure it out later."

"What about her?"

Mathew didn't bother to lower his voice.

"Let's worry about that in the morning, okay, Matt?" replied John.

There was a slight edge to his voice. He liked the girl. She had a quiet strength about her. A light within. He just needed to convince the others, he decided. He pressed down on the accelerator again and they merged with the flowing traffic on the busy highway.

Faith sat quietly in the back. The hopelessness she'd felt these past months had been replaced by a quiet determination. She had discovered her purpose.

4

"Murderers!" spat Anastasiya.

She stood at the doorway to the blood-spattered bedroom. Her gaze moved over the withered remains of her acolytes. Two females and a tall, heavily muscled man followed her into the room. If Manny had been alive, he'd have recognized the man as the big chauffeur from the gas station.

Anastasiya moved with a natural elegance, her tall, lithe figure wrapped in a clinging black evening dress that opened to reveal her long white legs when she moved. Ice-blue eyes, high cheekbones, and full lips betrayed her Eastern European origins. She had pulled her long blonde hair back into a chignon to accentuate her slender neck. The dress's plunging backline revealed more pale skin, a long-strand pearl necklace tracing the line of her backbone. She appeared to be about thirty, yet her eyes hinted at someone infinitely older.

Anastasiya knelt beside one of the corpses. Muscle and internal organs had disintegrated so that the skin was stretched over the skeletal remains like yellowed parchment. She was all-too-familiar with the inescapable fate of her kind—they were a product of a struggle between a lethal alien bacterium and the virus it had inadvertently released within its host. If the virus could successfully modify the body's cells and continually repair them, it could control the deadly bacteria. She was not familiar with the cellular biology, but she knew that when severe injury caused the virus to lose control of this delicate balance the unchecked bacteria quickly ravaged the unprotected cells. She stared intently into the hollow eye sockets of the corpse.

It was Bethany.

"Wilful girl. You deliberately disobeyed my rules. And for what? For a night's illicit pleasure? All it has brought you is death and invited evil into my house. How are we to survive if we do not remain in the shadows?"

Her words, though directed at Bethany's remains, were meant for her surviving acolytes. She stood up and turned to one of them.

"I am disappointed, Eden. Disappointed with Bethany's deliberate attempt to undermine my authority, and with you for not alerting me to her plans."

Anastasiya extended her hand. Her long fingers traced the line of Eden's cheek to her red lips.

"Tell me you knew nothing of this?"

Eden had been her trusted companion for close to fifty years; the question and its implied threat were not directed at her. The other younger acolyte lowered her head. Was her reaction due to guilt or fear?

"I knew nothing, and in that I have failed you, Countess."

Eden's tone hinted at the talk she'd have with the other girl later.

"I believe you, Eden," said Anastasiya.

She looked pointedly at the other acolyte before turning to the man.

"Lotho, dispose of the remains. Ensure the room retains no hint of this night. Girls, you will help him. Use this time as an opportunity to learn the price of disobedience."

She turned and left the room, closing the door behind her as she did.

Anastasiya stood in the darkened hallway. In her mind's eye she saw the bullet-chipped walls. She saw the contorted bodies scattered carelessly like forgotten dolls over the bloodied floor. It was a scene familiar-yet-different from that which lay behind the closed door.

It was a memory of a distant time and place. A memory which had threatened to overwhelm her in the room and shatter her composure. Of course, she had not allowed that to happen. There could never be any sign of weakness, especially in front of her acolytes. But now she stood alone, and the memories rushed back.

She was no longer the Countess. She was Anastasiya, born into the nobility of the Ostoja, and her father's favourite. He was a powerful count with the privilege granted the szlachta. The power to rule over the towns and villages of the land granted him by his birthright. He was master of all those who worked his lands and who lived in his villages. But then the Russians had come, and, like the comet which three years before had stolen her humanity and killed her mother and sisters, they had come to destroy her father. Naturally, he had resisted, and so the soldiers had come. To rape and pillage, murder, and burn everything.

Anastasiya stood alone in the dark, a girl of seventeen, covered in the gore from the pile of bodies she had clawed her way out of. Her wounds had miraculously healed. The same disease which had cursed her with a need for human blood had also blessed her with the gift of seeming immortality. However, even though the virus healed wounds, it did not grant invincibility—the dead girls in the room beyond where she stood attested to that. The continued renewal of her body's cells by the virus also meant she'd aged incredibly slowly. By human count, she was nearly one hundred and seventy years old but looked to be a woman of about thirty. That made her almost immortal to humans.

Almost, but not quite.

She'd not understood the limitations of her cruel gift then, of course. All she could see was that her wounds had miraculously healed, and she had been made immortal. But even if she had known the truth, she doubted it would have stopped her from taking her revenge. So, she had left the burning ruin of her home and tracked the soldiers to a nearby village. Twenty men billeted in the homes of luckless villagers who had been forced to find refuge against the bitter cold of the night in some other place. Drunk on the liquor and excesses of the day, most of the soldiers had passed out, and so had been ill-prepared for her attack. A whirlwind of bloody revenge, the girl of seventeen had moved relentlessly from house to house. She had spared no one.

When it was over, and after she had gorged herself on their blood, she had taken their heads and stacked them in a pile in the village square. Then she had disappeared into the night, leaving the villagers to the inevitable retribution which would follow.

She would find the men who'd murdered her acolytes. Of that, Anastasiya had no doubt. She would find them and she would bathe in their blood.

◊ ◊ ◊

An hour later, Anastasiya was staring intently at her security monitors. The cameras in the garden had recorded the earlier intrusions, each grainy black-and-white image captured faithfully at twenty-four frames a second. She had watched a man sneak across the lawn, then two more, then finally the girl.

The girl had intrigued her. She was obviously connected to the two men yet her every movement betrayed something else: the nervous walk, the clumsy handling of the weapon. These were so different from the confidence of the men before. Eden had brought her the wallet of the first man. The driver's licence belonged to a Manny Mendez. It was he who Bethany must have lured to the house, and his body Lotho was now disposing of. There was no way of knowing when and how Bethany had met the man. Not that it mattered at this stage—the damage had been done. Her world had been compromised.

Anastasiya paused the video on an image of the girl. A frightened face looked directly up at the camera. How was she connected to the others? Why had these two men ventured here, armed as they were?

Had they known of this place? No, she decided. If they had, they would have come more prepared. Their attack would have been timed to ensure she and all her acolytes had been destroyed.

Anastasiya scowled. To think she had been exposed in this way. By amateurs! She had lived in this country for more than a century without ever coming close to being discovered for what she was: Vampir. The stuff of legend. The stuff of nightmares. Each time she had feared discovery, each time she had felt it necessary, she had simply disappeared. Immersed herself into the mass of humanity that was America only to resurface later someplace else and as someone else.

So if they had not come for her, they must have been after the dead man. The one whose body they had left behind without a hint of remorse. They had come here for him. Had they meant to kill him? Probably. How had they known he would be here? Bethany? No. The girl? Perhaps she was the link between the two. Perhaps, or perhaps not.

Anastasiya's long fingers rapped incessantly upon the chair arm. She had no way of knowing who had murdered her progeny, or what they might say to others, and whether they would return. This frustration was a feeling she was not used to—she had always been the one in control. She, the girl drenched in the blood of the soldiers she'd slaughtered. She, seeing the fear and awe in the eyes of the cowering villagers. Then, as now, she was master of her own destiny. Her face hardened into a look of grim determination.

'I will not be forced to leave this place. These amateurs will not be allowed to destroy all I have created. Nor will they escape my vengeance. Not for what they have done.'

Anastasiya leant toward the screen. The girl was the key. She was the link between the dead man and the killers. All that was required now was a way to find her.

"Anastasiya?"

Eden hesitated at the doorway. That Anastasiya was upset was understandable. They all were. But Eden had never seen her mistress and lover so unsettled.

"Come in, Eden," replied Anastasiya.

Eden looked at the young woman on the flickering screen.

"Is she one of the killers?" she asked.

She walked up to the monitor and studied the young face.

"She just doesn't seem capable, somehow," she said finally.

"Anyone is capable, Eden, given the right motivation. You know this."

"Yes, I've been with you long enough to know exactly what people are capable of," replied Eden quietly. "Still, I don't think she came here with the intent to kill."

Eden's unique position meant she could be frank with her mistress, but only to a point.

"You are correct," said Anastasiya. "The fact is that none of these people knew about us. They were after the other man—Manny Mendez."

Anastasiya handed the licence to Eden.

"I assume you came to inform me that Lotho has located Manny's car?"

"Yes," nodded Eden. "He found it parked a little way down the street. I think he might also know where Bethany met this man."

"Tell me."

"He noticed the same car earlier today, at a gas station. The visit to the Museum of Contemporary Art..."

Eden's voice trailed off.

"You were with them today, weren't you?" reminded Anastasiya.

Eden looked down at the floor.

"Yes. I'm so sorry, Anastasiya," she said. "But I didn't notice Bethany speaking with anyone at the gas station. None of us even left the bus. I can—"

"It matters little now," interrupted Anastasiya. "The damage is done. I assume Lotho will dispose of the car?"

"Yes, he's doing that now."

"Have you searched their rooms?"

"Not yet."

"I think you will find either Bethany or one of the others had a cell phone."

"But where?"

Eden frowned, and then it occurred to her.

"The art gallery! She must've stolen it from someone there."

"Bethany appears to have been every bit as resourceful as I'd have expected from any of you," said Anastasiya and turned away from Eden.

Eden understood what was really at stake. If the virus which infected them were ever allowed to run unrestrained through the population, mutating as it spread, it could mean the end of everything. Anastasiya had shared this fear with her once in an intimate moment.

"I know I've disappointed you, Anastasiya. I know I should have been more aware. It's just that Bethany never gave any hint of being unhappy," replied Eden.

"Perhaps we've all become too comfortable here," mused Anastasiya. "Perhaps we've all become a little too complacent."

Eden sensed Anastasiya was also annoyed at herself. Considering she was their leader, their teacher, their life-giver, this was understandable. Anastasiya, more than anyone, should have noticed the change in Bethany, yet she hadn't.

"You think it's time to move again?" enquired Eden.

"No, not this time. And certainly not because of these fools."

"Do you think they'll attack again? I mean, now that they know of our existence?" asked Eden.

"No. If they do decide to attack, they will want to consider their options. We have time yet."

"How are we going to find them?"

Eden never doubted that her mistress intended to hunt down the killers. The only question was how.

"The girl!"

Anastasiya pointed to the face on the monitor.

"She is the link between the two men and Manny. She is the key. If we find her, we will find them."

"Find her? How?" asked Eden.

"We will require the services of someone familiar with investigation. Someone who knows how to find people who do not want to be found."

"A private investigator?"

"Precisely."

Anastasiya wasn't entirely happy with the idea but knew she had little alternative. She'd created the school to be their sanctuary—a place they could exist without interference from the world outside, a place they need only venture from when they wanted to feed. But the violation of her house had forced her to acknowledge the bitter fact that in creating her sanctuary, she'd also lost touch with the outside world.

This meant she would require the aid of someone more familiar with the way the world worked now. Someone who would know how to find the girl. All she needed to do was decide who that someone would be.

5

5 Years Ago

"Your mother was a murdering whore!"

"That's not true!" screamed Faith. "You're just saying that! You're just saying that because you hate everyone. That's why Mike left. He was tired of putting up with your bullshit!"

"You little..."

Her aunt raised her hand to strike then stopped herself. It was not because she knew better; she'd hit Faith many times in the past. It was because she realised the girl now standing resolutely in front of her was not the same. Something had changed. The girl was now a teenager, and with that came a new self-awareness. The compliant little girl had been replaced by someone who refused to be intimidated.

"Fourteen years old and you think you got it all figured out, don't you?" she sneered. "Think you're all grown-up now. Well, then, maybe it's time for a few home truths. Mary Ann was about your age when she met Danny. Up till then, your mother had been sweet as pie, always ready to help her big sister. Then Danny came along, and it was Danny this and Danny that. She loved to tell me about how they fucked, saying how maybe if my face ever cleared up, boys might wanna fuck me too. Your mother turned into a spiteful little bitch. And then she got knocked-up. Ma insisted they get married, and Danny agreed. Hell, it was either that or a statutory rape charge. Your father, the rapist."

The aunt paused with relish and waited for a reaction from the obstinate teen. But Faith refused to be goaded. She'd always believed her parents had died in a car crash when she was very young. That's what Aunt Louanne had always told her. Now her aunt was telling her something different, and despite how awful it sounded, she realised she wanted to know more. She was like one of those spectators watching a terrible accident unfold, unwilling to tear their eyes away. In her heart she knew her aunt was lying, but in the pit of her stomach, she felt the truth.

"Seven months later she popped you out," drawled Aunt Louanne. "Didn't take long for the happy couple to start fighting. Of course, your father wasn't going to take any lip from the little slut. A couple of good slaps and he soon put her in her place. I wasn't surprised when I heard she'd started screwing around. Trying to hook the next Mr Right. Wasn't long before your father found out. He got mean-drunk first, then went home to confront her. That's when she shot him. You were there, Faith, you know that? Eighteen months old. She shot him dead right in front of you. Next thing I knew, she was standing at my door, holding you. She handed you over like you were a package and then she was gone. She never even looked back. Just disappeared into the night."

"You're lying!" shouted Faith. "You're just mad because I said I liked Mike."

"So, the apple doesn't fall far from the tree after all," sneered Louanne. "Just like your no-good mother. What? You think just because you've grown a little moss on the landing strip, a man's gonna look at you?"

Faith's face reddened.

"Fuck you!" she yelled.

She shoved past her startled aunt and ran from their mobile home.

Faith didn't go home that night. She went to Jonah, her only refuge. Jonah lived in another mobile home in the trailer park. He was her age and he understood. It wasn't because his life was like hers. His parents weren't drunks like Aunt Louanne, nor did they beat on him. They were just ordinary people struggling to keep a roof over their heads. If they were guilty of anything it was that they were never around, which was understandable, considering they both worked long shifts in their thankless menial labour jobs. They always seemed to be one paycheque away from being evicted, and Jonah sometimes went hungry, but they loved him in their own way, and that's all that really mattered.

Jonah's parents had already left for work by the time Faith woke up the next morning. They didn't seem to mind her sleeping in the same bed as their son. Either they trusted there would be no funny business or they were too tired to care. Faith could never tell. Not that it mattered. She didn't think of Jonah in that way—he was just her best friend. Her only friend, really.

She could hear the TV on in the living area. Jonah would be eating his cereal now. They hadn't talked about her fight with Louanne the night before. One look at her face and he knew to give her the space she needed.

Faith tarried a while. She didn't want to get up. She didn't want to go back and face Louanne. Not because she was scared, but because she hated the thought of the smug look on her aunt's face. She had nowhere else to go and they both knew it.

Faith threw back the bed covers and got up. She slipped out of the T-shirt and baggy shorts Jonah had loaned her and pulled on her own clothes.

"You gonna have breakfast?" asked Jonah when she walked in.

Faith shook her head.

"Too early," she said.

She slumped down next to him on the old sofa. He was watching an old rerun of TMNT. They sat in silence as he ate.

"She was drunk again," said Faith finally. "She talked some shit about my parents. She called my mom a whore. I mean, I know it must be all bullshit, but it hurt, you know? I guess I shouldn't've pushed her about Mike, but I was pissed off. I mean, he was a good guy. He really cared. Not like those assholes she usually hooks up with, especially the creeps. Always trying to feel me up. Mike wasn't like that."

"What you gonna do now?" asked Jonah quietly.

"Don't know. Go home, I suppose," sighed Faith.

She shook her head.

"You know, it was the one time I really thought she'd gotten her shit together, Jonah. These last few months with Mike being around, everything felt almost...like normal."

Jonah snorted derisively.

"Normal? What, in this place?"

Faith thumped him playfully on the shoulder.

"Don't be an asshole," she said. "You know what I mean!"

They went back to pretending to watch TV, Jonah chewing thoughtfully on his breakfast cereal. He shot her a quick sideways glance.

"So, you think maybe she kicked Mike out because she was jealous of you?"

Faith thought a moment.

"Nope. I think she got scared," she said. "Louanne's been fucking her life up for so long, the moment it looked like it was going good, she just freaked out."

Jonah nodded sagely, not because he really understood but because he wanted Faith to believe he understood.

"What you gonna do now?" he asked carefully.

Faith shrugged.

"Go home, I guess."

She looked down and picked distractedly at the chipped black nail polish on her fingernails.

"I'm gonna leave this place, Jonah," she said. "Sooner or later. I've got to. Either that or I end up like Louanne."

"You could always stay here, you know. I mean, for good," he said hopefully.

Faith offered him a brief smile and got up from the sofa.

"I better get back, then."

She walked over to the door and opened it to leave.

"Faith."

She turned to look at him.

"Yes?"

"See you tomorrow?"

Faith smiled.

"Sure," she said, then stepped outside and closed the door behind her.

6

Warm tentacles of the dawn's light crept across the city. The dark relinquished its reign sullenly, retreating to the places the light could not go. John stood in the doorway of the bedroom and watched the girl sleep. The morning light shone through the threadbare curtains and bathed the room in a twilight glow.

She looked so innocent—long dark hair spilling over the pillow in untidy curls, eyelashes touching her lightly freckled cheeks. Her features were almost elfin, he decided.

Faith's eyes flickered open. She looked at him warily and sat up, clutching the bed covers.

"Good morning," said John. "I didn't mean to disturb you. There's breakfast if you want it."

He felt like a voyeur who'd just been caught and blushed instinctively.

Faith clutched the bedcovers close to her chest.

"Morning," she replied.

An uneasy silence followed, the two strangers eyeing each other, each wondering how to respond. John broke the silence first.

"I should leave you to get dressed. Matthew and I are in the kitchen. We can talk some more once you've eaten."

He turned to leave, then stopped.

"Look, I know things got a bit weird last night and I understand if you're just a little freaked-out, but we can help. You just have to trust me."

He smiled briefly then turned and closed the door quietly behind him.

Faith lay back on the bed and stared up at the ceiling. Cobwebs littered the corners and the white paint had yellowed with time. Trust! How could so much depend on such a small word? 'I trust you'. 'Don't you trust me?' 'It's all a matter of trust'. 'Trust is a two-way street'. Easy for some to say, especially if they held all the cards. And in this case, they did hold all the cards. But could she trust them? Did she even have a choice?

She thought back to the previous night. It seemed like some surreal dream, made even more unreal by the banal normality of the room around her. Weird? Definitely. What really got her was how she felt that somehow this was all meant to be. The hand of fate? God's will? Whatever.

'Or maybe you feel this way and believe this to be your true path because it's all you've got left. You've fucked up your life so good that your only choice is to hitch up with these two killers,' a voice sneered in her head.

How come that voice sounded so much like her aunt? Always ready to drag her down, pick her apart, and chip away at what little self-confidence remained? The line of her mouth hardened, and her eyes narrowed. No! She had a choice. Whatever the alternative, there was always a choice.

She threw back the bedcovers and got up. Her clothes lay in a heap on a nearby chair. She took off the T-shirt she'd slept in. It was probably John's, she decided. She had found it laid out on the bed after she'd come back from her shower the night before. She pulled on her jeans. No bra. Not that she needed one, she thought to herself, inspecting her small, pert breasts in the full-length mirror.

'You'll have to work hard to please the johns with tits like that', sniggered Manny's voice in her head.

Now who's laughing?

She smiled grimly and pulled on her own T-shirt. It was black with a picture of a fortune teller on the front. The band's name printed above the picture had long-since faded. She put on a pair of socks, her sneakers and finally tied her hair back into a ponytail. She inspected herself in the mirror.

All that I possess in this world.

Faith walked down the passage but hesitated before entering the kitchen. The two men were talking. She stood quietly just outside the doorway.

"I still don't like it. We know nothing about her," said Matthew.

"So what are you saying? We just throw her out?"

There was a hint of irritation in John's voice.

"Maybe," replied Matt. "But that all depends."

"Depends on what?"

"Well, for one thing, do you think she'd go to the cops?"

John shook his head.

"No, she'd have too much to lose. She's a runaway. I think the last thing she wants is to be packed off back home. Besides, I don't think she'd want the cops involved, especially seeing as she's now linked to a dead man."

"Dead man?" Matthew snorted. "Only we know that for sure. You really think anyone's gonna miss that jerk? You think whatever the fuck is in that mansion is gonna call the cops over to investigate?"

He continued, mimicking a heavy Bela Lugosi accent.

"Good day, Officer, vee vere about to suck ze blood out of some unlucky asshole ven zese two men burst in and started shooting up ze place! Vee demand you arrest zem now!"

John shrugged.

"Maybe we killed them all," he said hopefully.

Matt snorted derisively.

"Jesus Christ, John, do you really think those things we killed last night are the only ones around? That's bullshit and you know it."

"Okay, so let's say there are more of these things creeping around. That's all the more reason to keep her with us, don't you think? And don't forget, she saved your ass last night, Matt. So now you want to throw her out on the street?"

"Who said anything about throwing her out?" said Matt.

His voice had a cold edge to it now.

There was a chilling pause. Faith stood out in the passageway with her breath caught in her throat. It was obvious what Matthew really meant.

"You're one cold fuck," said John finally.

"You might want to think that about me," responded Matthew, "but I'd like to think I'm just being careful. After all, we haven't lasted this long just through dumb luck, now, have we?"

"No, I guess we haven't," said John. "Though I don't know what else you could call what happened to us last night. Which kinda proves my point. If she hadn't come in packing that shotgun when she did, we both would've been well and truly fucked. So I say Faith stays. After what she did, it's the least we can do. If it makes you any happier, I'll run it by the old man today."

Faith chose to make her entrance before Matthew could respond.

"Good morning," she said breezily.

Her voice betrayed no hint of fear.

She took the chair nearest John. Two fried eggs and a slice of bacon looked up at her from the plate. Her stomach was a knot of emotion. Would she be able to keep the food down? Faith cut the bacon into smaller pieces, then the eggs, spearing a piece of each and lifting them to her mouth. She hesitated, fork hovering. The men were looking at her.

"I'm sorry, is there something wrong?" she asked.

"We usually give thanks before we eat," said Matthew.

His tone was condescending.

"Give, thanks? Oh...pray," replied Faith, her fork still in midair.

"Don't worry about it. Not like it's a mortal sin or anything. Just a habit we learned in the Home," interjected John smoothly. "Please, keep going, food's gonna get cold otherwise."

He smiled at her. Faith smiled back, the fork completed its journey, and suddenly things didn't seem so bad.

The meal proceeded in silence, the pretence of eating much easier than the pretence of small talk. Things needed to be said. Each person seated at the table knew that. It was just a matter of finding the right words.

"Thanks for breakfast. Can't remember the last time I had eggs and bacon," said Faith softly.

She placed the knife and fork carefully on the empty plate. She'd made herself eat everything, forcing the food past the tightness in her throat.

"Think nothing of it," said John.

He smiled again. Matthew grunted and kept on chewing. He'd barely looked in her direction the entire meal.

Faith took a deep breath.

"Look," she began. "You got me away from Manny's. You took me along with you last night. I know I was supposed to wait in the car. I know things would probably be a whole lot easier for you now. If I hadn't seen those things, you could've just dropped me off somewhere this morning, me being none-the-wiser. But somehow, I don't know how, I just knew something was wrong. I knew I had to go in after you. So now you're wondering, what do you do with me, and can you trust me?"

John opened his mouth to speak but Faith cut him off, the stream of words continuing without a pause.

"Well, you can," she said. "I could've snuck outta here last night, but I didn't. I chose to stay. Besides, if there're any more of those monsters out there, then being with you is safer than most anywhere else. At least that's what I think."

Her voice trailed off.

Matthew chuckled derisively.

"Well, you got that right," he said. "Being here is probably safer. Just don't get too comfortable, because neither one of us have the final say about your situation."

He pushed his chair back from the table and got up.

"Think I'll see what's on TV."

He stopped at the doorway and looked over his shoulder at Faith.

"You really want to be useful to us? Then how about you wash those dishes? There's a good girl."

Faith resisted the urge to give him the finger, instead promising herself next time she made the coffee she'd spit in his. She got up and started clearing the table.

"Here, let me help you," said John.

He got up and placed his plate in the sink. The TV came on in the lounge room and a disjointed collage of news commentary, Sesame Street, shopping channels, and sport highlights ensued as Matthew flicked idly through the channels.

"I'll wash, you dry and put the dishes away. You'll have to get to know where everything goes sooner or later."

He smiled at her and she smiled back. He had kind eyes, she decided.

◊ ◊ ◊

It had been two hours since breakfast. The trio were in the black sedan driving down a leafy suburban street. Matthew and John sat up front and Faith in the back. She watched the endless procession of middle-class houses go by, each with the same façade of picket-fences, neatly tended lawns, and shuttered windows. They'd been driving for nearly an hour and she still had no idea where they were going. Faith looked at the two men. Both wore the same combination of comfortable chino pants, white open-collared shirts, and tan shoes: in outward appearance, a pair of respectable young men on their way to work.

The car slowed and pulled up to the kerbside. Faith frowned. A church? Matthew pulled up the handbrake and turned off the ignition.

John turned back to her.

"We're going to confession. You'll need to come with us," he said.

Faith looked back at the church. It looked pretty much like the kind of building one would expect, she decided: a large sandstone structure with stained-glass windows arranged along high walls, and near the front, a set of solid timber doors. The doors stood wide-open, an invitation to the faithful.

Faith followed the two men into the building. It had been a long while since she had last been inside a church. When she was a young girl, her aunt had insisted on dragging her to every Pentecostal revival that hit town. Faith could never understand how her aunt could praise God one day then indulge in almost every vice imaginable the next. Children tend to accept the way of things, but teenagers generally do not. It was inevitable, then, that the teenage Faith eventually rebelled against the hypocrisy of it all.

Faith had never been inside a Catholic church. She looked about with interest. A statue of the Madonna presided over a small font of what she presumed to be holy water. She imitated the men as they went through the motions of dipping fingers into the water and making a sign of the cross.

They walked through a doorway into the main area of worship. Another statue of Mary, this time surrounded by small candles, stood to the rear of rows of pews. Matthew and John took a seat near the back of the church, Faith sat down next to them, and the three sat in silence. The two men were obviously waiting for something or someone, she realised. The minutes ticked by and Faith looked about the interior. There were pictures on the walls, and she recognized scenes of the crucifixion in some. Statues depicting angels or saints stood within niches along one wall. At the front, looming over the altar, hung a large crucifix. Faith looked at the figure upon the cross—head bowed under a crown of thorns, blood streaming from nailed hands, feet, and wounded side. He seemed so lost and helpless, she thought.

The rustle of a curtain being drawn back startled her. An old woman to her right appeared from an opening in the wall and walked by quietly with her head bowed.

John got up and made his way to the confessional. He drew the curtain behind him and knelt upon the padded knee-rest.

"Bless me, Father, for I have sinned," he said.

"You're late!"

The voice behind the screen sounded annoyed.

"I'm sorry, Father, but there were some complications," replied John.

"Complications? Were either of you hurt?"

There was a note of concern in the priest's voice now.

"No."

"But you say there were complications. Did things then not go according to plan?"

"Yes and no."

"What do you mean?"

"We took care of the business, but we needed help."

"Help? From whom?"

"A girl. She is here with us now," answered John.

He sensed movement beyond the screen as the priest leant over and pulled back the curtain slightly to look at the young woman seated next to Matthew.

"Why did you bring her here, John?" the priest asked with a note of irritation.

"I felt it the best thing to do under the circumstances. Besides, I think she might be a good addition to the team."

"A good addition to the team? That might be your opinion, John, but it will be for me to decide."

The priest's tone hardened.

"I assume she is not the complication you're referring to?"

"No, Father. There were others."

"Others?"

"Yes, but..."

John hesitated as he searched for the right words.

"They weren't human," he said finally.

"Not human?" the priest asked, perplexed.

"What exactly happened last night, John?"

"It is hard to explain, Father. It all happened so fast. We barely had time to think. Maybe if we could talk later, Matthew and I can better explain what happened last night."

There was a pause.

"Perhaps tonight would be better, then," agreed the priest finally.

He sounded frustrated, but both knew this was not the place to go into detail.

"I will pay a visit tonight. Expect me around eight."

"Thank you, Father."

John pushed himself up from the knee-rest. He pulled back the curtain to go.

"One more thing: You are to say nothing of our work to the girl," ordered the priest.

John nodded then left.

◊ ◊ ◊

Father Samuel O'Connor sat back in his chair, stroked his chin, and stared into space as he mulled over John's troubling words. Though certainly a complication, the girl appeared to be least of their worries. 'Not human'? What had John meant? And why be so cryptic? Father O'Connor frowned. He could not help feeling annoyed at the boy for bringing this troubling news to him here and now. Why had he not simply waited till later? Now he'd have to spend the day attending to his church duties whilst wrestling with whatever wild speculation his mind could conjure.

'But what did you expect him to do?' he thought. 'He was only following the protocol you set for them. What had the boy said? *Not human*. And, if not human, then what? Animal? Perhaps that was what he'd meant. Then again, perhaps not. So, if not animal, then what? Demon?'

O'Connor shook his head. No, it could not be demon. He had long-since given up belief in the spiritual world, whether demon or angel or God. There had to be a more rational explanation for whatever his boys had encountered the previous night. The question was, what? 'Not human', John had said.

O'Connor's fist thumped his chair.

"Goddamn almighty!" he exclaimed.

"Father," enquired a nervous voice from behind the screen. "Is that you?"

Father O'Connor blinked. He had been so lost in thought, he had not heard one of his parishioners come into the confessional.

"Yes, it is me," he said softly. "I must apologise, my dear, for allowing a minor frustration to get to me."

"I'm sure you have much to feel frustrated by, Father. Maybe you'd prefer to hear my confession later?"

Father O'Connor allowed a brief smile. Tracy-Anne Jenkins, a bored housewife in her late-fifties. She had a decent-enough husband but his job as a shift-worker coupled with the many hours of overtime had slowly eroded their relationship. In the past few years, she had flitted from affair to affair, mostly as part of some ill-conceived attempt to rekindle that part of her life lost to caring for a husband and three children, now adults who had long since flown from the nest.

O'Connor cloaked his voice in the approachable tone he saved for his flock.

"No," he replied. "Now is the proper time. Please do continue."

"Thank you, Father," said Mrs Jenkins.

Father O'Connor sat back as the woman began, giving the appropriate responses when required, whilst all the while his mind struggled with a more pressing problem.

7

Don Stone listened carefully to the woman. She spoke very good English but with a foreign accent. Russian? Polish? He couldn't be sure, but it was certainly Eastern European. Though not to his taste, he could appreciate her beauty. Angular features, slim frame, uptown poise. Nope! Big tits, generous hips—that was more his style.

He took notes as she spoke. She was the headmistress of an exclusive finishing school for girls. The girls were all from very wealthy families. In many cases these young women had been sent to the school because the anonymity afforded by its controlled environment allowed them to deal with personal issues that had generally landed them in some sort of trouble. Alcohol, drugs, shoplifting—the usual vices of bored, rich teenage girls. On occasion, however, a girl would prove more difficult to tutor than her peers. The girl in the photo was just such a case.

Don picked up the photo of the girl. The grainy image, which had been enlarged and cropped, showed the face of a woman of around nineteen. She looked afraid.

"What's her name?" he asked.

"I am afraid I cannot tell you that," replied Anastasiya.

"Why not?" asked Don, a little surprised.

He placed the photo back on the table.

"The parents who send their daughters to my school are very wealthy," began Anastasiya. "As one might expect, they value their personal privacy and expect discretion, not only from those they employ, but those who provide a service to them. If I were to lose the confidence of one such family and they were to remove their daughter, it would not take long for other families to follow suit. I'm sure you understand the delicate situation I am in. In any case, she would probably not be using her real name."

Don grunted.

"You realize this is going to make it more difficult to find her?"

He frowned as something had suddenly occurred to him.

"Do her parents even know she's missing?"

He knew he had to ask, even at the risk of insulting a potential client, who, from outward appearances at least, looked capable of paying handsomely for services rendered.

There was a moment's awkward silence. Don could hear the metronomic tick of the clock on the wall behind him. The afternoon sun had sunk low enough to cast the striped shadow of the window blinds across the office interior. The alternating bands of light and dark made Anastasiya appear the more mysterious. Her eyes, caught in a band of light, blazed an eerie red. It reminded him of a feline predator stalking its prey from the shadows.

"Of course they do, Mr Stone," replied Anastasiya. "They are in Europe at this present moment and will be returning as soon as they are able. I am here on their behalf. Besides, this is not the first time their daughter has gone missing. They have become quite familiar with her, how would you say, little adventures."

"So, she's done this type of thing before?"

"Yes," replied Anastasiya tersely.

Don nodded. He picked up the photo again for another look.

"I'll need more information. This photo's not going to be enough," he said finally.

"I have since found out that she had become involved with a

man. Manuel Mendez is his name. I have an address."

Her tone had softened.

"Can I assume that you've already visited this address?"

"Yes, I have," she responded tersely. "On more than one occasion. But I have had little success in locating the girl or this Manuel Mendez."

Don nodded. He'd heard of Manny Mendez. As far as he could recall, Manny was a small-time dealer and pimp. It'd been a while since his days on the force, but he'd kept in touch with a few of the guys down at the precinct. What would a PI be without a few police contacts?

"I'll see what I can do. It's not going to be that easy, especially if you don't want to involve the law," said Don.

He searched the woman's expression for a hint of the value she placed on finding the girl, but could discern nothing.

'Fuck it,' he thought.

"I charge $ 1,500 a day, excluding expenses."

"I accept, Mr Stone. But only on the condition that you locate her within the next five days."

"Any particular reason?" he asked.

"The girl's parents, of course. They will be here then, and I would want to see them reunited. You understand?"

Anastasiya volunteered another friendless smile.

"Of course." Don could not help raising his eyebrows.

The woman was obviously lying.

'Mommy and Daddy don't even know their daughter is missing,' he thought.

"Right, Ms Strajinksi, I'll just finish with your contact details and then get on the case right away."

◊ ◊ ◊

With the paperwork done, Don had seen the headmistress to the door a short while later. He returned to his desk, sat down and lit a cigarette. He took a long draw and exhaled, the acrid smoke mingling with the scent of the woman's perfume which still lingered in the air. Don studied the photo.

'Taken from a security camera,' he thought.

What he could not figure was why he'd been given this one? The headmistress must've had other photos. So why this one? The broad was hiding something. She had to be.

"What trouble are you in, I wonder?" Don asked the girl in the photo.

'If you've hooked up with Manny Mendez then you certainly got more than you bargained for,' he thought.

The girl stared back at him from the photo. Alone. Afraid. Don took another long drag from his cigarette. He sat looking at the photo a while before placing it carefully back on the desk. Don took out his cell phone and hit the quick-dial.

"Hi, Stacey. Yeah, it's me, Dad. So, how've you been?"

Don's grizzled features softened along with the tone of his voice. If there was anyone he still felt something for in this fucked-up world, it was his daughter.

"I know it's been a while, Jellybean. I'm sorry. I've been really busy lately, but I promise I'll come by real soon. What's that? Yeah, of course I do, you know that don't you?"

The conversation proceeded along familiar lines—he the absentee father, desperately attempting to establish some kind of relevance in his thirteen-year-old daughter's life, and she the betrayed child, responding with a moody petulance born from the broken trust.

"Your mom wants to speak to me?"

Don's face hardened.

"Sure, put her on. Bye, Jellybean, love you."

Don waited a moment for his ex-wife to take the phone.

"Hi, Anne." he began, and was cut short as his ex-wife launched into a well-rehearsed tirade. Don waited for her to finish. He had little choice, really.

"Look," he said finally. "I'll have your alimony payment by the end of the week. Can you give me till then, at least?"

More terse responses followed before Don hung up. He stubbed out what was left of his cigarette in the ashtray on his desk and reached for another cigarette.

'Jesus Christ! Divorced three fucking years and she still hadn't stopped squeezing.'

He reached for the bottom-right-hand drawer of his desk and pulled it open. The bottle of bourbon rested innocuously alongside a sheaf of paper. The bottle's cap had never been cracked. Don stared at it a moment. Three fucking years.

'Don't be even more of a cliché, Don. You're better than that. Better than she'll ever give you credit for, at any rate.'

He slammed the drawer shut. The drink was a demon best left alone. It was time to earn some money.

Mendez had an extensive rap-sheet. One phone call to his contact and he should get a lead on Manny's last known address. This was as good a place to start as any.

8

The cops had it under control. The female cop with the perfect ass and expensive wardrobe turned to her partner, himself oh-so-perfectly groomed.

She: "The bullet the lab extracted from the body is the same as that taken from Gaines."

He: "A thirty-ought-six?"

Forensic Geek: "Exactly." The geek moved to access a battery of computer screens from which a dazzling array of data and graphics covering every conceivable aspect of bullet trajectory, ballistics, specifications, history, and what-have-you could be seen.

"Judging by the bullet, you'd think it'd been fired from a Springfield. But Gaines was hit from at least 1300 yards. The Springfield's effective range is 1000 yards. That got me thinking."

The geek tapped away at the keyboard and another dazzling visual display followed.

"The range and trajectory are consistent with only one other commercially available rifle. The Dragunov SVD."

This was the cue for a grim look of determination as the hero-cop with the chiselled jaw leaned over the geek for a closer look at the screens.

"Looks like we've got our man, Jenna."

Faith watched the TV with little interest. Her mind had more important things to occupy itself with than the mindless drivel on the flickering screen. She stole a look at John seated at the other end of the couch.

'Either he's really enjoying this shit, or he's good at pretending,' she thought.

Faith looked over to where Matt lounged in the armchair, his long legs stretched out to rest on the coffee table. One of his toes poked out from a holed sock. He hadn't cut his toenails in a while, she noted. A picture of an evil troll from a children's fantasy popped into her head. She suppressed a giggle. His expression hadn't changed the entire evening. Faith couldn't decide if she was wary of him because he was so sullenly quiet, or because he so obviously disliked her. Whatever the case, it looked like they had decided she was going to stay.

At least that's what she'd assumed the moment the boys had bought her some clothes and a few personal items soon after leaving the church. She looked at John again. He was different from Matt. He cared. What she hadn't quite decided yet was whether it was because he was attracted to her or because he felt sorry for her. Whatever the case, and even though she knew the men to be killers, the fact was, in a weird way, she felt safe.

Her thoughts were interrupted by a knock at the front door. John reached for the remote and turned down the volume as Matthew moved cautiously to the front window, his hand resting on the pistol tucked into the back waistband of his pants. He moved the curtain a fraction then relaxed visibly.

"It's Father O'Connor," he said.

He reached for the door handle and let the priest in.

Faith eyed the man who appeared in the doorway.

'So, this is who they've been waiting for,' she thought.

The priest was a tall man with a sallow complexion which appeared even more washed-out against the prerequisite black suit which hung on his bony frame. He shook the men's hands in turn and turned to Faith, offering a brief smile.

"Good evening. I am Father O'Connor," he said.

He extended his hand in greeting. Faith shook the proffered hand.

"Hello," she said. "It's, ah, nice to meet you."

There was a moment's awkward silence as Faith and O'Connor continued to shake hands, both drawing out the moment as they searched each other's eyes.

"Should we go into the kitchen? There's more room in there," interrupted John.

"Of course," answered the priest.

He relinquished the girl's hand.

They all filed into the kitchen and sat at a small, square table covered with faded red vinyl.

"Would anyone care for some coffee?" enquired John.

He was obviously attempting to break the tension in the air.

Father O'Connor shook his head irritably.

"No, thank you, John."

Faith and Matthew also shook their heads. No one wanted coffee.

"You did not give me your name," said O'Connor, peering at the girl enquiringly.

"Faith."

O'Connor raised an involuntary eyebrow.

"Faith," he repeated.

The irony was not lost upon him.

"Where are you from, Faith?" he asked.

"A small town in the Midwest," volunteered the girl, poker-faced.

Father O'Connor understood why the girl was deliberately being vague, but he would have been happier had she been a little more forthcoming. Realizing that further questions concerning her personal details would only make her more evasive, he decided to change tack.

"Manny, the man you were with. He did not treat you well, did he?"

His voice had taken on a softer, more fatherly tone.

"No," replied Faith quietly.

"You understand that he was guilty of many crimes? He sold drugs. He forced women, young women, into prostitution. I knew him to be guilty of at least one murder."

Faith nodded.

"Then you understand why I had to send Matthew and John to him?"

"Yes."

"I have been a priest nearly forty years, Faith. Most of that time was spent right here in the community I still serve. I have shared their joy and I have shared their grief. They have come to me with their hopes and their fears. They have revealed their deepest secrets.to me. I have earned that trust, and that is no small thing. I tell you this not as a point of pride—no man of the cloth would—but so that you may better understand what I am about to say."

O'Connor placed his hands palms-down on the table and pursed his lips, as though carefully weighing his next words.

"You understand?"

"I think I do," Faith offered.

She hoped it was the correct answer.

The priest nodded.

"A number of years ago, one of my parishioners came to me. He was a devout man. A hardworking, honest man. In fact, he was one of the most honest men I ever knew. This man needed my help. He was worried about his daughter. She had been abused by her husband, you see. So, he'd done what most any father would do. He'd confronted the man and threatened him with violence, should he ever lay another finger on her. For a time, things improved. But only for a time. When things turned bad again, he'd gone to confront the man, but to his surprise, his daughter had defended her husband. That is unfortunately the way with many women who suffer these circumstances. They continue hoping the man they fell in love with will change for the better. He had then pleaded with his daughter to leave her husband, but she would not. She was a devout Catholic herself, you understand—she believed in the sanctity of marriage. She believed her husband would change. That is why this man had come to me. He asked if I might speak to her instead. He hoped that I might convince her to leave her abusive husband. He begged that I might go so far as to insist she leave him. For her own good."

"And did you?"

Faith could not help asking, despite having already guessed the answer. Had she reflected upon it she would have admitted that her words were more accusation than question.

The priest looked at her a moment. The question had cut deeper than he would have cared to admit.

"Of course not. My responsibilities as priest include upholding the sanctity of marriage. I explained to him that I could not advise her to leave her husband, but I promised I would visit her and strongly encourage her and her husband to attend counselling. I think he was disappointed, but he agreed with me nonetheless."

"You went to see her?" Faith pressed.

"Yes, I went to see her," replied O'Connor. "We talked. She was scared. I see that now, but all I offered then were words. Looking back, I think she was waiting for me to give her permission to leave him, that perhaps she was hoping I would tell her leaving her abusive husband was not a sin or a failure on her part. That I would say it was the right thing to do under the circumstances. But I did not say these things, and that was my failing."

An uncomfortable silence followed. The steady hum of the refrigerator in the corner of the kitchen seemed to grow louder. The priest cleared his throat.

"A few weeks later, she was dead," he said. "Her husband had been high on crystal meth. He beat her to death."

"I can understand how that would have upset you," said Faith quietly.

"No, I don't think you can," replied O'Connor.

The priest suddenly appeared very old, and his shoulders seemed to slump as though under a great weight.

"I had seen her grow up," he continued. "I was the one who had christened her. I was the one who had been present at her confirmation, and the one who had presided over her marriage. I was the one who buried her. But I was also her uncle. Her father was my brother and I had failed not just her, but him also. Afterward, my brother Jacob had come to me for an answer. Why would a just and loving God allow this to happen? Had not he been a faithful man? Was she not innocent? But all I could do was offer the same empty bible stories I had offered so many others—the trials of Job. The faith of David, and so on."

Father O'Connor shrugged and shook his head.

"Jacob shot and killed her husband at the man's trial. Of course, the Law threw the book at him. After all, a law-abiding man is supposed to let justice take its course, yes?"

Faith didn't volunteer an answer.

The steady hum from the fridge filled the silence again.

"The years in prison were not easy, on him or my sister-in-law," said O'Connor finally. "She left him, eventually. Understandable, I suppose. He had cut himself off from everyone, you see. He wouldn't even allow her to visit him. Said that he didn't want anyone to see him that way. In there, like an animal, with all those others."

Faith nodded as though she understood.

"Then, last year, he asked that I visit him," continued the priest. "He had not let me see him until then, you understand. I did not know that he'd been diagnosed with lung cancer. Ironic, considering he'd never smoked a day in his life."

The priest shook his head briefly, as though still not quite believing it himself.

"I attempted to hide my shock when I first saw him. But it was difficult. For both of us. He had become a frail, broken man. Like a shadow fading from the world. 'Help me understand'. Those were his first words to me. Help me understand why. Surely, I, a man of God, would have an answer? But the truth of it was, I had no answers. Nothing that made sense, anyway. Nothing that would ease his suffering. As much as I wanted to, I could neither share his grief nor bear his load. He died a month later."

Father O'Connor sat back in the chair, trying to read the girl's expression. He knew his story would evoke in some a sympathetic understanding as to his subsequent actions, while others might judge him. In which camp was she?

The girl's expression was carefully neutral. He noticed the fingers of her one hand were picking nervously at the chipped nails on the other. Faith followed the priest's gaze to her fidgeting hands.

She smiled shyly and stopped.

"Sorry," she said.

"I have told you my story not to elicit your sympathy, nor to justify my actions. I have told you so that you might understand why."

The priest's tone was unapologetic. His grey eyes blazed defiantly, inviting a response.

"I don't know what you want me to say, Father," said Faith. "To be honest, you don't need to justify anything to me. Thing is, if John and Matthew hadn't got me outta Manny's house, I might never have gotten away. I owe them and, in a way, I suppose I owe you. I would've been glad to help where I could, no matter what. Anyway, things got pretty fucked—I mean, messed up—last night with those things attacking John and Matt."

"Things?" enquired the priest.

He suddenly understood she meant the thing John had alluded to that morning. O'Connor felt annoyed—not at the girl, but at himself for having allowed her to become the focus of his attention, the distraction he could not afford.

'Not human.' Those had been John's words. He turned to John.

"Perhaps you should tell me what occurred last night."

John cleared his throat.

"We found out that Manny had gone to this school."

"School?" interrupted the priest.

"Yes, the Whitby Foundation. Some sort of finishing academy for girls. Anyway, we—"

"How did you know he would be there?" interrupted O'Connor.

"It was Faith who told us where he'd be," replied John. "Matt and I had gone to Manny's and that's where we met Faith."

O'Connor turned to Faith. There was a hint of suspicion in his voice.

"So, you knew he'd be at this school?"

"No, actually," replied Faith defiantly. "John and Matt said they wanted to talk to him. All I said was that he might've gone to the address he'd written down after his phone call."

The priest's tone worried her, especially considering Matt's words earlier that morning. What would it take for these men to trust her?

"It was just a lead. For all Faith knew Manny could've been anywhere," volunteered John quickly. "Matt and I decided it was as good a lead as any, so we went there. We found his car parked outside a little way down the street. I told Faith to stay in the car then Matt and I went over the wall to scout the place."

"I hope that was your only intention, John," said O'Connor. "I'm sure neither of you even would even consider eliminating this man in front of some schoolgirls?"

There was a hint of irritation in his voice. He was used to more professionalism from his boys.

"Of course not. It was just a recon," interjected Matthew testily.

He was still annoyed at himself for having let John take the lead the night before. If it'd been up to him, they would've stayed in the car and waited for Manny to come out. Then they'd have taken care of business. At the time, he'd thought John had allowed the fact Manny had beat the girl to cloud his judgement, so he'd decided to let John have his way. Mostly this was because it amused him to see John riled up, and to think John might take pleasure in killing Manny, which was even more amusing because John was the one who took O'Connor's personal crusade seriously. He, on the other hand, enjoyed the killing. He'd developed a taste for it in Afghanistan. Nothing quite beat the high of having that kind of power over someone's life.

"That's right," agreed John. "Just a recon. Anyways, we thought we heard a female cry out. We thought Manny was hurting a girl or maybe even something worse. We kicked in the door and that's when we saw them. These naked girls all over him. They were feeding on him, draining the blood out of him."

O'Connor looked incredulous.

"Are you telling me these girls were vampires?"

"I know it sounds like something out of a movie, but I don't know what else they could've been. These girls, they had fangs. Their mouths were red with Manny's blood. They turned and attacked before Matt and I had time to think," explained John.

"It was them or us," added Matthew. "We just defended ourselves. It took four full clips to drop those bitches."

"It didn't stop one of them jumping Matt, though," said John. "If it hadn't been for Faith with the Tactical, things might've been a lot different."

He flashed Faith a reassuring smile.

The priest looked quizzically at Faith.

"John asked that you stay in the car, yet still you followed, and with a shotgun no less?"

She shrugged.

"I thought I heard shooting. I thought that maybe John and Matt were in some sort of trouble."

The priest was surprised.

"You didn't think that perhaps the boys could take care of themselves? You thought that you, someone with no real experience, could make the difference?"

The whole story seemed too unreal and the girl showing up in the nick of time just made it appear the more implausible to O'Connor. He looked at John and Matthew in turn. What were they hiding?

"Are you sure of what you saw last night? Are you sure that what you shot was not human?"

A newspaper headline screaming the murder of innocent schoolgirls appeared in his mind's eye. It was not comforting.

"Father, Matt and I are certain. Vampires, demons, whatever, those girls were not human," replied John earnestly.

"The bodies," added Matthew. "They withered after a while too. Looked like old parchment. It just didn't seem real, but it happened there right in front of us."

He wanted the priest to believe.

"And Manny? Did you leave him there?" enquired Father O'Connor.

"We did what we were there to do. Anyway, whatever those things did to him, it looked like he was changing into something, some kind of monster. I think their bites must've infected him, but Matt and I weren't gonna wait around to see. We shot him dead and then we left quickly."

"You left the bodies there?"

Father O'Connor was uneasy. The boys had had twelve kills to date. Each perfectly executed. Neat. Tidy. No comebacks. No innocents caught in the crossfire. The way he'd envisaged his crusade against the evil of the drug gangs from the start. Now everything appeared to be unravelling. The boys had involved an outsider, the girl. They called the people they'd killed vampires. Vampires! The stuff of myth and pulp novels. Were they attempting to justify their actions? Had they made some kind of dreadful mistake? He would have to investigate for himself if he was ever to believe them.

John sensed the priest's disappointment.

"I'm sorry, Father," he said. "It seemed the only thing we could do under the circumstances. We didn't know if there were any more of them around. Besides, with all the shots fired, and the screaming, we were using silencers, but the neighbours might've still heard something."

The priest nodded.

"I understand, John. I think, though, that under the circumstances, it would be best for you to remain inactive for a while. This will allow me some time to carry out a little investigating of my own. This is not to say I don't believe what you and Matthew have told me. I would just like to confirm the possible threat we might be facing for myself."

The priest pushed the chair back from the table and stood up.

"I will call again in a few days. Until then, I would prefer you all to remain here."

His tone invited no argument.

"We'll be waiting, Father," replied Matthew. "Besides, I don't reckon whatever or whoever those things were last night will want any cops snooping around."

"Allow me to be the judge of that, Matthew. Consider also that if these creatures exist, any who still remain will no doubt be seeking revenge for what you did," reminded the priest.

"We thought of that," replied John. "But seeing as there's no connection between Manny and us, Matt and I didn't think we need be that concerned."

"That may be the case, John," said O'Connor, "but it'd be wise to remain vigilant."

He looked directly at Faith.

"Now, does anyone have anything else they'd like to say?"

No one answered.

"I will bid you all a good night, then," said O'Connor.

He rose from the table and turned to leave.

"Matthew," he said, "Would you mind accompanying me to the car? I have something for you."

O'Connor left the kitchen, with Matthew following close behind.

◊ ◊ ◊

Matthew stood expectantly alongside Father O'Connor as the priest fumbled in the dark with his car keys. The house had been purposely chosen in an out-of-the-way area with no streetlamps.

"Matthew, I want you to keep an eye on the girl. I do not trust her," he said.

O'Connor grunted with satisfaction as he finally located the keyhole.

"I told John not to bring her," said Matthew defensively. "She's only gonna get in the way."

"That may be the case. It has also occurred to me that she may have some link to that school. How else would Manny have the address?"

Matthew grunted. He hadn't thought of that. But then again, thinking had never been his strength.

"Here, take this," said Father O'Connor, handing Matt an envelope. "Funds for the next project."

Matt took the envelope.

"I thought you said to lay low?" he asked.

"I did," replied O'Connor. "But I needed an excuse to talk to you alone. I'm afraid this girl's predicament might have clouded John's judgement."

"Do you want me to get rid of her?" asked Matt carefully.

"No, Matthew," responded O'Connor brusquely. "I don't think we need to resort to anything that extreme."

It was not the first time O'Connor had noted Matthew's almost-casual approach to murder. The darkness prevented him from seeing Matthew's expression, and in some way the priest felt relieved, perhaps fearing he'd see the face of a monster of his own making.

"Besides, we do not know the extent of her involvement at this stage," he added quickly. "She might be an innocent in all this. There's an old saying, Matthew: Keep your friends close and your enemies closer."

"Which in this case means?"

"Which means you do nothing, Matthew. For the time being, at least. At best, she has no connection to this school and ends up being a useful member of the team. At worst, she is involved, and we have something far greater to concern ourselves with than drug lords. Time will reveal," said O'Connor.

He turned the ignition. The car rumbled into life.

"Good night, Matthew," he said finally.

O'Connor's car pulled away slowly leaving the lone figure of Matthew standing in the dark.

'Do nothing? Are you kidding me?'

Matthew scowled. Things had been going so well until now. Everything, just the way he'd planned. But with the girl showing up, everything had gotten complicated and surreal. Vampires? This kind of thing just didn't happen in the real world. But it had, and now his perfect plan was in danger of unravelling.

With any luck, O'Connor would find that the girl was connected to the vampire women. It would sure make his life so much easier if she were. One word from the priest and bang! Things would be back on track. If it hadn't been for John, he'd already have taken care of it. Which was a pity, because he'd have enjoyed seeing the look on the little bitch's face the moment he pulled the trigger. But now he'd have to let the priest figure it out. Just so long as O'Connor did it soon. Hopefully the priest wouldn't then get it into his head to go on some wild vampire-hunting crusade. Live and let live—that's how he felt on the matter. Who cared if those things were out there, feeding on a few dumb fucks? So long as they didn't get in the way of the plan, then everything would be sweet. Not O'Connor's plan. His. The one where he ended up rich.

"It all boils down to one thing in the end," said Matt to himself. "Get rich, enjoy life and fuck everyone else."

Wasn't that the essence of being alive?

Matthew watched the car's red taillights recede into the blackness. He turned and walked back toward the house whistling an odd little tune.

9

Six Years Ago

Father O'Connor looked at the two young men seated before him. Both had spent much of their young lives in and out of foster care or group homes, though the experience had shaped each in different ways. John was quiet and introspective, and Matthew, in contrast, outspoken and quarrelsome. It was debatable whether John's introspection or his friend's belligerent attitude was the direct result of their experiences or just inherently part of who they were. O'Connor himself had often pondered this, though not only of these two, but of all those others he'd known during his time counselling at the Home. Did nature defeat nurture every time? Could the killer really be guided towards a more benign pursuit? Who was to know for sure?

"You're both decided, then?" he asked.

"Yes, Father," replied Matthew. "Signed up yesterday. Four years active duty, army."

"Signed up? What about the selection process?"

John shifted uncomfortably in his chair.

"We took the exam a few weeks back, Father," he replied quietly.

"John aced his ASVAB," added Matthew quickly. "The recruiting sergeant said he had the potential to do almost anything, but he's joining the infantry with me."

Did O'Connor detect a hint of envy in Matthew's voice? He'd also noted the boy's choice of words: John was 'joining' him, rather than having 'chosen to join' him. Why not encourage his friend with the 'potential to do almost anything' to do exactly that? Isn't that what any true friend would do? He looked at John but saw nothing in his expression to say he felt anything to the contrary.

"And the physical exam?"

"Completed that yesterday," said Matthew. "All we need now is your consent."

O'Connor frowned.

"My consent?"

"Yes, Father," replied Matthew, "I mean, we could just wait a couple more months until we turn eighteen, but we figured why not just go for it now?"

"I'm afraid it's not that easy, Matthew," replied O'Connor patiently.

"What do you mean?"

"I cannot give my consent. That is for the bishop to decide."

"But you will ask him, won't you?" pressed Matthew.

The priest nodded.

"I will raise the matter with him at our next meeting."

Matthew looked puzzled.

"The next meeting, when will that be?"

"In two weeks."

"Two weeks?" exclaimed Matthew. "But that's too long, Father! Can't you get hold of him now?"

The priest allowed a brief pause. He could understand their impulsiveness, and in some way, he envied them. There were days he wished for those simpler times. The invincibility of youth, where this world offered only boundless opportunity. Ah, to be young again! But he was not, and his years as a priest had shown him more than his share of the pitfalls of a rash choice made. It was best to allow the boys a week or two to reflect upon their decision. Especially John.

"Commit thy way unto the Lord; trust also in him; and he shall bring it to pass," intoned O'Connor. Psalm 37:5. "Patience, Matthew, is always the best approach in life. I am a man of my word. I will speak with him about this."

The priest looked carefully at the pair. Matthew's expression betrayed his sullen acceptance, but John's was harder to fathom. Was it disappointment or relief he saw written on the face of this young man? He could not tell.

It was John who broke the awkward silence.

"We will wait, Father," he said.

"Thank you, John," replied O'Connor.

The boys stood up from their chairs, excused themselves, and left the priest to his thoughts.

◊ ◊ ◊

"Do you think the old man would bullshit us?" asked Matthew once they were back in their room.

"What do you mean?"

"That whole thing about having to check with the bishop first. You reckon he's just blowing smoke or he's being legit?"

"Father O'Connor's always been straight with us, Matt," replied John. "I don't see any reason he'd lie to us now."

"What?" snorted Matt. "You think priests don't lie? Gimme a break! Just read the papers about how the church has been covering up all that child abuse for years. Those fuckers lie any time it suits them."

"That's way off point and you know it," objected John.

"Is it?"

"Damn straight it is. How does the church covering up child abuse and O'Connor lying about having to get permission from the bishop even relate?"

"Okay, so maybe they're not in the same ballpark but that still doesn't mean O'Connor won't lie if it suits him," pressed Matthew.

"Has he ever lied to you?"

"No."

"Okay, and have you ever known him to lie to anyone else here?"

"Not that I know of, but that doesn't mean he hasn't."

"Look, Matt, I'm taking him at his word. He said he'd speak to the bishop, and he will, and nothing you say is going to change my mind."

"Maybe he just doesn't want to see his favourite get hurt."

"Christ, that old chestnut!" said John shaking his head. "The onetime he says a few good things about me and suddenly I'm his favourite. The old man doesn't operate that way and you know it."

"Fine, forget I said it," said Matt, holding up his hands in mock surrender. "But don't act all surprised when our request gets knocked back two weeks from now."

"That'll be for the bishop to decide."

"Or maybe O'Connor," quipped Matt.

"Give it a rest, Matt."

"Okay, so maybe he does ask the bishop. But he's the filter, isn't he?"

"Meaning?"

"Well, he could twist the whole thing any which way he wants. He could make the thing we're asking seem unreasonable. Maybe even tell the bishop we wouldn't cope with the military, or something along those lines."

"Father O'Connor would never do anything like that," replied John firmly. "It's not in his nature."

"You're way too trusting, boy," chuckled Matt. "You keep thinking like that and someday you're gonna see your ass."

"Be wise as serpents and innocent as doves," smiled John, "Isn't that what the bible says?"

"Christ, now he's got you quoting the good book!" laughed Matt.

"You can't deny there's some truth to the words though."

"Whatever, man. Look, you say the old man will come through for us and I say he's gonna fuck us over. Fifty bucks says I'm right."

"I'm not gonna take that bet."

"Why not, scared you're gonna lose?"

"If you're asking whether I'm afraid I'll lose a bet on O'Connor doing what he promised, then no, I'll win that bet every time. But that's not the real issue here. It's whether the bishop will consent to our request or not, and that's something I'm not willing to bet on."

"But we're not betting on the bishop, we're betting on O'Connor."

"You're deliberately missing my point, you dick!" snapped John. "What you're saying is if our request gets denied then that means O'Connor didn't speak to the bishop which presupposes the bishop would say yes, no matter what. And there's no way you'd know that for sure."

"That's my point exactly."

"What?"

"There's no way I can know which way the bishop will swing, just like there's no way you can know for sure that O'Connor will speak to him like he promised."

John studied his friend for a moment.

"Fuck you," he laughed.

Matt grinned. "Glad we're finally on the same page."

At that moment he caught sight of one of the Home's ten-year-old boys walking by the room.

"Hey, Chad!" he called out. "Come here, boy."

A small skinny boy with brown hair and large dark eyes turned and entered the room.

"Yeah?"

"Don't yeah me, squirt. Say, yessir," ordered Matt.

The boy eyed him warily.

"Well?"

"Yessir?"

"Good boy. What are you up to?"

"Nuthin."

"Is that so? Well then, you can go downstairs and get me a Coke."

"What, now?"

"No, yesterday, you little twerp! Now get on it before I kick your skinny ass!"

The boy turned and left the room quickly.

"I'm sure gonna miss pushing these little runts around," chuckled Matt as he stretched out on his bed.

John eyed his friend thoughtfully and shook his head.

◊ ◊ ◊

True to his word, O'Connor spoke to the bishop two weeks later and consent was given to allow the boys to join the army. The bishop's exact words had been, "We need more brave young men like this who are willing to fight for the forces of justice and the true way."

O'Connor would often reflect on this and all the other 'what-ifs' which had led to his crusade against the gangs. What if he'd not spoken to the bishop and instead guided the boys to some other career? What if he'd chosen to encourage his niece to leave her abusive husband? What if her husband had not chosen to get himself high on meth that night? What if her husband had not beaten her to death in a drug-induced rage? What if he'd been able to console his brother Jacob better? What if Jacob had not managed to smuggle the gun into court? What if the bailiff on duty that day had been faster? What if Jacob had missed? And, after Jacob's miserable death in prison, what if he'd chosen to believe in God's justice?

'Vengeance is mine; I will repay, saith the Lord.'

Except that never happened in the real world.

It was when he was at his most despondent that Matthew and John had come to see him. They'd only just completed their four-year contract with the army and had been contemplating whether to extend their service when they'd heard of his trouble. It was Matthew who talked John into leaving and Matthew who'd first proposed cleaning up the streets.

'Let us be your sword of justice, Father.'

John's words, but Matthew's idea. Matthew had also proved remarkably resourceful, first at getting the information and then with procuring the weapons they needed. O'Connor's dead brother had left him the house in the will and he'd used the money earned from the sale to recruit the boys into his war on street drugs. This was not a war of vengeance; this was a war to save the vulnerable from being exploited by the worst of society.

At least that was what he continually had to convince himself he and the boys were doing.

10

The large four-poster bed dominated the centre of the room. Delicate carvings of gods and goddesses formed an elaborate pattern of entwined bodies that spiralled up the length of each post with thin gold tendrils snaking about their limbs, connecting each with the other in an intricate web that extended along the bedframe to coalesce into the flowing hair adorning the carved features of the Countess Anastasiya, which dominated the centre of the headboard. The bed's ostentatious design was equalled by the elaborate baroque furnishings of the rest of the room, which, to all appearances so out-of-step with the 21st Century, was not where Anastasiya slept. It was where she dined upon her victims.

A young man lay spread-eagled on the bed—his body, drained of its life's blood, appeared unnaturally pale against the red satin sheets. Sightless eyes stared from his ashen face. Anastasiya lay naked beside him, her leg draped across his groin to feel the last vestiges of warmth seep from his corpse.

She looked across at Eden, who lay opposite her. The girl had stretched out, a look of self-satisfaction upon her sated features. It was she who had enticed the young man back from the nightclub.

The seduction of prey was the part Eden enjoyed most. Anastasiya allowed her this pleasure, deriving her own in turn from watching Eden copulate with the victim. Writhing bodies joined in frantic union, each consumed by a different need—for him, a lust driven by the animal need to procreate; for her, a desperate hunger driven by the virus's need to feed on human blood. Anastasiya never tired of watching Eden's athletic form being fucked. Once aroused, she would enter the bedroom. Invariably, she would find the man more than willing to accommodate an additional nubile body on the bed.

Later, he would be less willing to part with his blood, of course, but by then it would be too late.

Anastasiya looked at the dead man's features once more. He appeared to be in his early twenties, well-groomed, and educated. She imagined he had a family somewhere. A girlfriend, perhaps? A wife? It was certain someone would miss him. How long would they mourn him? A year? Two years? Her lip curled into a smile of self-reflection. How long since she'd lost the need to empathize with humans? Each passing year, she'd found it more difficult to see them as anything more than walking vessels of sustenance. Yet she herself had once been human, vulnerable to all the frailties of that species. Until the coming of the plague.

She cast her mind back to a time long ago. Back to when the comet had appeared—a bright knife-slash rending the fabric of the night sky, spreading fear amongst a superstitious people. When the plague had followed soon after, many felt justified in claiming the comet had been God's mark of punishment upon them. Indiscriminate to man, woman, child, peasant, noble, priest. No one had been safe, nor could anyone tell who would succumb to the plague and who would not.

Anastasiya and her sisters and mother had fallen ill, but her father had remained untouched. He had been inconsolable, for he knew as well as any that infection meant certain death. From the appearance of the first pustules to the last gasping breath from blood-filled lungs, none had managed to survive the disease's inexorable passage. Yet

Anastasiya had survived, and her father, though grief stricken at the loss of his wife and daughters, had taken comfort in this small blessing. The true price, however, had become apparent within days of her miraculous recovery. She remembered well the horrified look on her father's face at finding her crouched over a servant girl's body, her face and nightgown smeared with blood. That he had chosen to see the loving daughter trapped within the diabolical creature before him was testament to a father's love, no matter the cost. So had begun the endless cycle of stalking, of killing, and of feeding.

Anastasiya frowned, annoyed for having allowed herself to brood on the past. There was no profit in it.

'Nil profici respiciens.'

Besides, there were issues of far more pressing concern. Her acolytes had been murdered, and worse, the killers were out there somewhere, free to strike whenever they wished. She had already set Lotho to work upgrading their security system and she'd hired the PI to track down the killers. Yet despite this, she felt unease; if she'd been truthful, the loss of her acolytes had upset her more than she was willing to admit. The fact was that without them, she felt naked and vulnerable. She'd been alone in the beginning, the only one of her kind. The hunter, yet also the hunted.

In those early years, her survival had been all that mattered. It was then that she'd finally understood what she was. The first human she changed with her bite seemed to confirm what she'd already begun to believe: She was a god. From then on, and for as long as she cared to remember, she'd always maintained a small group of followers. A god needs to be adored. A god needs to be worshipped. But one attack had eliminated most of her followers and she, their omnipotent god, had not been there to save them. What kind of god was she, then?

She leaned over to the nightstand and pressed a concealed buzzer. Moments later, the bedroom swung open and the large manservant appeared.

"Lotho, I need this attended to," said Anastasiya.

She gestured to the dead body and got up from the bed, apparently unconcerned that she was naked. Lotho lifted the corpse, deftly slinging it over his shoulder as though the body were an empty husk. It would be a while before the change commenced and the corpse was reanimated as a mindless, shuffling creature. A monster driven by the virus to feed on any living thing within reach. A monster whose bite would infect its victims. Experience had taught Lotho that he had enough time to destroy and dispose of the corpse before then. Anastasiya watched him leave the room before she pulled on her silk robe.

"Eden," she said.

Eden opened her eyes, then yawned and stretched her lithe body languorously.

"It is time to get up," said Anastasiya. "Come, we have much to do."

◊ ◊ ◊

It was early afternoon when Don jumped the fence at the back of the house his contact had given as Mendez's address. He'd been watching the place for a few hours, so he was certain no one was in. The backdoor stood slightly ajar. He frowned. Not quite what he'd expected from someone with something to hide. Was he already too late?

Don moved systematically through the house, checking each drawer, cupboard or likely hiding place for a lead on where Manny Mendez was or could be. Though sparsely furnished, the rooms still managed to have an unkempt, dingy look about them. Even for a small-time pimp and pusher, Manny didn't seem to have much to show for his efforts.

'Probably used as much as he dealt,' he thought to himself.

Don stood looking around the main bedroom. The unmade bed looked like it hadn't been used in days. He went through the bedside drawers, but found nothing except a little more of the same drug paraphernalia he'd noted in the lounge room. He opened the wardrobe. Save for the few summer dresses hanging forlornly to one side, most of the clothes appeared to be Manny's. He cast a critical eye over the designer labels. Manny sure had expensive taste.

He turned his attention to the woman's dresses. They looked cheap. He pulled the first dress off its hanger. Size 6. 'Probably the girl's,' he reasoned to himself. The next dress proved to be the same. He tossed the dress casually onto the bed and turned his attention to the nearby set of drawers. The first two revealed more of Manny's clothing. The last drawer contained some of the girl's clothing: panties, bras, T-shirts. Whoever the girl had been, she'd left in a hurry. What struck Don was that, besides a few clothes, there were no other personal items related to the girl, or any girl, for that matter. For a man who apparently pimped girls from time to time, this struck Don as decidedly odd.

He looked around the room. There had to be a hiding place somewhere. Or a lock-up? He hoped for the former, all-too-aware of the delay hunting for a lock-up would have to his five-day deadline. He slid his hand along the underside of each drawer, determined to find some clue. There was nothing.

Don went back to the bed and got down on his hands and knees to peer under the frame. Again, he found nothing.

'Too obvious anyway,' he thought.

He was about to stand up when he noticed the scoring along the timber floorboards at the base of the set of drawers. The drawers had been moved, probably more than once. He got to his feet and went back over to the drawers. Being a big man, he had no problem pushing the heavy piece of furniture away from the wall. Set into the drywall was a sliding panel, which he pushed back to reveal a hidden compartment within the wall. He reached in and retrieved the plastic-wrapped packages, placing each on top of the set of drawers, then unwrapped each package in turn. The first revealed small nuggets of crystal meth. The next, marijuana. The last contained cash and a small 9mm pistol.

'Nothing out of the ordinary,' he thought.

Don counted the money. Almost a thousand dollars. He pocketed the cash. He was still not satisfied, so he crouched down again and pushed his hand and forearm all the way back through the opening for a final feel around. His fingers felt something just within reach. He gave a satisfied grunt. Was this the lead he'd been hoping for? He pulled it out. It was a small, flat tin box with a colourfully printed lid. He pried open the lid and inside was a stack of polaroids.

He thumbed through the photos. He blinked. Jesus Christ!

"Who the fuck are you?" a voice growled from behind him.

He spun around with the photos still clutched in his hands. Standing in the doorway were two heavily tattooed Hispanic men of medium build. Both were armed.

'Typical gangbangers,' he thought. 'Last complication I need now.'

"I came to see Manny. He always gives me good shit," answered Don.

He hoped the lie would hold long enough so he could better position himself.

"What the fuck you take us for, ese? No way Manny deals with you!" snorted one.

The other one waved his pistol with casual menace.

"You a cop or something?" he enquired.

"Do I look like a cop?" retorted Don.

"What you got there?"

The meaner-looking gangster moved forward and snatched the photos from Don's hands. He flicked through the stack and whistled.

"This some fucked-up shit you got here, man!"

He handed them back over his shoulder to the man behind.

"Check it out, homes," he sneered. "Looks like we got a collector here, man."

He moved in close and patted Don down, searching for a concealed weapon.

"He's clean," he said and stepped back.

"If you say so," muttered the other man, who was now more focused on the contents of the photos than Don. "You check for an ankle holster?"

"Nope."

He reached down towards the PI's ankles.

Don struck then, grabbing the gangster by the ears and pulling his head forward as he brought up his right knee in one fluid motion. Blood sprayed from the man's shattered face as Don shoved his unconscious form back into the second gangster. He moved in quickly before the startled man could regain his balance, his left hand grabbing the gangster's gun-hand at the wrist whilst striking with his right to snap the man's arm at the elbow. The man's scream was cut short as Don completed the combination with a hard-right elbow to the solar-plexus. He delivered the coup de grace with a fist to the man's temple dropping him unconscious to the floor.

Don unholstered the .38 from his ankle with a practised movement and turned to train his weapon on the first gangster. There was no need—the man remained where he had fallen. Don reholstered his weapon, reached down, and picked up the photos that lay strewn on the floor. He left the room without looking back.

Don made his way back to his car along the same back-alley he'd used to access the house. He opened the car door and slumped back into the seat, his adrenalin rush slowly subsiding, and looked down at the photos clutched in his hands. Don knew he should look at them now so he could make sense of what he'd seen the first time. He also knew it was more important that he place distance between himself and the gangsters back at Manny's house.

'Jesus Christ,' he thought, 'what the fuck did this girl get herself into?'

Don turned the ignition, gunned the accelerator, and pulled away sharply from the kerb.

11

For Meredith Young, it was a night much like any other. She'd surfaced from her drug-induced slumber at around four that afternoon. It'd taken time to get the energy to pull her aching body from the urine-stained sheets, but she had, motivated more by the knowledge that she'd need to feed her habit soon than by anything else.

There had been no milk in the filthy apartment, so she'd settled on a bowl of dry cereal and a mug of black coffee. None of the other working girls she shared the place with had been there when Jimmy dropped by. Jimmy was her supplier and her pimp. He'd been annoyed at finding her home rather than earning her keep so had decided to motivate her by putting a cigarette out on her arm.

'Where the fuck you think you gonna get another hit if you don't earn, bitch?'

She could still smell his alcohol-laced breath as he'd spat the words out, his acne-riddled face inches from hers.

So there she stood, a tall, skinny nineteen-year-old shivering in the cool night air, waiting for her next trick. One bad choice after another had got her to this point and there seemed to be no way of going back.

It'd been a slow night. She looked up and down the street, her demeanour revealing an agitated mood. The desperation she felt was fuelled by a mix of her drug craving and the fear of Jimmy's displeasure if she were to go back empty-handed. The other two hookers who shared this section of the street with her had been picked up by customers a short while earlier, and usually this would be the cue for her to step back from the kerb. She felt more secure with the other girls around when she got into a john's car. But not tonight. Tonight, she needed to earn.

A red pickup cruised into view and slowed as it neared Meredith. The driver appeared to be in his fifties—a blue-collar type with slicked-back hair and wiry arms covered in tattoos. He pulled up next to her and lent over the passenger's seat.

"Hey, girl, what's on the menu?" he leered.

Meredith offered a forced smile.

"Whatever takes your fancy, hon," she said.

There was a knot in her stomach. This was probably going to hurt.

"Well, then, maybe you should hop in so's we can go somewhere more convenient," he said.

He pushed open the passenger door and motioned for her to get inside.

Meredith hesitated. A set of headlights appeared at the end of street. She stepped back onto the kerb away from the pickup and a look of fury flashed across the man's face. He was about to say something, then noticed the headlights in his rearview mirror. He pulled the door shut.

"Fucking bitch!" he snapped.

The pickup's thick tyres squealed briefly as he punched the vehicle into gear and pulled away.

Meredith could not help but feel relieved. She turned to watch the approaching headlights that soon took the form of a long black limousine that slowed to a stop alongside her. The neon light from the nearby shopfronts reflected off its highly polished surface, giving the vehicle an eerie, otherworldly look. A black chariot from the underworld. The tinted windows hid the occupants from view, reflecting instead the outside world back at itself. Meredith looked at her distorted reflection staring back at her in bemusement.

'Maybe they were lost,' she thought.

The girl's reflection disappeared as the window descended silently.

"Good evening," said the Countess Anastasiya.

"Uh, hi," offered Meredith.

"I was wondering what you would be doing alone on the street at this hour?"

"Working," answered the girl shortly.

'Is this woman for real? What the fuck does the bitch think I'd be doing standing here this late? Reporting the news? The last thing I need is some rich chick wannabe bible-pusher preaching to me about how I could do so much better with my life,' thought Meredith irritably.

"Good. Perhaps then you would like to join me for the evening?" Anastasiya smiled.

Meredith blinked. She hadn't expected this response. Then again, she'd only been on the game a few months, so she couldn't speak from much experience.

"Uh, sure, why not?" she said.

Meredith walked round to the far passenger door. The uneasy gnawing in the pit of her stomach returned. She opened the door and gave the deserted street a final look.

'If I went missing now, no one would ever know.' The dark thought crossed her mind.

Then again, what did she have to lose? Meredith swung her skinny frame into the backseat and closed the door. The limousine pulled away smoothly from the kerb and proceeded along at a leisurely speed.

Meredith stared at the Countess seated alongside her. The woman was undeniably beautiful. In both dress and bearing, she was elegance personified. Meredith suddenly felt more inadequate than she usually did. What could this woman possibly want with her? She suddenly realized that the woman was staring back at her, studying her with open interest.

"Where are we going?" asked the girl, a little uneasily.

"Back to my home. We will find it more comfortable there," offered the Countess with a smile.

Meredith felt her body pulled back into the black leather seat as the limousine accelerated onto the motorway. She smiled weakly at the elegant woman.

There was no going back now, she realised.

◊ ◊ ◊

Meredith sat on the edge of the large four-poster bed. She had just taken a hot bath and the short silk robe felt refreshingly cool against her skin. It had not been the first time a client had requested her to bathe, but it had been a first when the client had proceeded to scrub her down.

'Probably part of the foreplay,' she supposed.

She looked around, noting the bedroom's baroque décor and ornately decorated bed. Bach's "Cello Suite No. 1" floated through the air. The deep mournful sound had a strangely calming effect on Meredith, although to her untrained ear, it sounded much like any other classical music. She looked around but could not quite determine where the sound was coming from.

The door opened and the Countess entered, naked but for a long red silk robe tied loosely at the waist. Another young woman followed closely behind, wearing a shorter red robe. Meredith frowned.

"This is going to cost extra," she said using a businesslike tone.

"Of course."

Anastasiya smiled and moved sensuously toward the girl.

The other woman moved round to the end of the bed and removed her robe, revealing a well-toned figure with large, firm breasts.

"I'm Eden," she said.

The nubile woman slid lithely onto the bed.

Meredith smiled uncertainly at the woman, then turned back to find that the Countess had disrobed and now stood naked before her.

"Shall we?"

The Countess motioned for her to remove her robe.

Meredith obliged and sat down on the bed. She lied back, closed her eyes, and relinquished her body to the lust of the two women, letting her mind drift to another place as her body responded mechanically to their caresses. The Countess traced a languorous pattern around each of Meredith's pink nipples with her tongue before moving up to nuzzle the girl's neck. She could hear the girl's heart beating rhythmically within her chest, each thump offering to deliver the blood she craved. She looked down to where Eden licked the inside of the girl's thigh, tracing the line of the femoral artery. Eden looked up expectantly, her eyes filled with bloodlust. Anastasiya smiled, her canines extending as she did. Eden followed suit, a low hiss issuing from her lips.

Meredith's eyes flickered open. Cold terror washed over her as she felt vice-like hands pin her to the bed. Anastasiya and Eden sank their fangs deep, gulping down the red blood that pumped freely from the girl's arteries.

Meredith screamed, a desperate high-pitched cry that soon dwindled to a forlorn moan as she felt the life flow out of her. The women continued to feed until almost every drop was drained.

◊ ◊ ◊

Don lay propped up against the pillows, smoking a postcoital cigarette. He looked over at the nubile well-tanned form of the woman sleeping alongside him and allowed himself a wry smile. Tammy Sloane was one hot piece of ass. A few months back, he'd contrived to run into her at the local gym. The wife of a rich real-estate tycoon, Tammy did little else other than spend her absentee husband's money and enjoy regular extramarital affairs. The husband had grown suspicious and hired Don to investigate her. It had not taken Don long to discover her affairs, but instead of reporting this fact to her husband, he'd decided to have a taste himself. George Sloane had the reputation of being an obnoxious prick who didn't care who got hurt in his business dealings, so Don felt no guilt at all.

Tammy had been waiting for him when he'd arrived at his apartment. He'd found her on his bed wearing nothing but a seductive smile. George was away on business, so she had decided to take advantage of the situation. She'd been as horny as hell, and who was he to disappoint? Don smiled wryly. He took another draw on the cigarette then suddenly remembered the photos.

'Fuck!'

He was immediately annoyed at having allowed the lure of easy sex divert him from the case at hand.

'Should never have given her a key,' he thought.

He exhaled slowly and watched the cigarette smoke drift away. The girls he'd seen in the photos seemed to form in the smoky haze. Dead girls? Live girls? He hadn't had the time to study the photos at Manny's place to be certain. Then Tammy's sex ambush had derailed any thought of them once he'd gotten back to the apartment. He looked over to where she lay—the woman was in the deep sleep of the wickedly content.

Don swung his legs over the side of the bed, picked his boxers off the floor and pulled them on, and walked over to where he'd tossed his jacket over the lone armchair in the corner of the room. He retrieved the photos from the jacket pocket and was about to leave the room when he remembered his cell phone on the bedside table. He walked quietly back over to the bed, picked up the errant phone, and left Tammy to her slumber.

Don sat in the apartment's small lounge. The photos were spread out on the coffee table before him, each of a girl in their late teens or early twenties. Don picked one up.

'Polaroid,' he thought. 'Didn't think they still made them.'

He flipped it over. A name had been printed on the back in Manny's spidery scrawl.

'Jackie', it read.

He turned back to the picture-side. A redhead in her late teens stared back at him with a bemused smile. The photo had been taken close-up with the flash, which gave her features a washed-out, sallow look. He thought he recognised her from one of the other photos and started sifting through the pile until he located it. In this photo, Jackie was not smiling—she was dead. The photo showed her lying naked on a bed. She'd been strangled with a length of nylon rope.

A grim thought occurred to him then. He placed the two photos of Jackie next to each other then picked up another photo of a living girl.

'Monique.'

Moments later, he paired it up with another photo of the same girl. In this one, she'd been strangled, her naked body arranged in much the same way Jackie's had been.

What then followed was a grisly game of matchup as Don paired photos of living girls with their dead selves. Finally, fourteen matched pairs lay before him. There was one spare. He looked at the photo. It was the girl he was looking for. He looked at the back and read the name.

'Faith.'

He flipped it over again and studied the photo. It had been taken in Manny's bedroom. The girl sat in the middle of the un-made bed with her legs pulled up under her chin. A black tee-shirt appeared to be all that she had on. A partially smoked cigarette protruded from between the fingers of one of the hands clasped around her ankles. Her eyes stared blankly into the camera with a look of self-loathing. How long had she been with Manny when he took the photo? How long had she been missing from the school? Was she still alive? The fact that there wasn't another photo of her meant she probably was.

For now, at least.

Don faced a dilemma. If he went to the cops with the evidence he had against Manny, it would mean losing this job and potentially getting involved in something a whole lot messier. Besides, as he knew only too well, getting the law involved would almost certainly over-complicate things. Complications meant delays, and delays meant the girl could end up dead.

Not to mention he'd been given the shaft by the force before, he reminded himself bitterly. He'd been a cop in a previous life. A twice-decorated detective with more than twenty years' service. Hard working, hard drinking, and hard gambling. He was a walking, talking movie cliché. Don never did anything by half-measure. It had only a been a matter of time before the gambling debts had started to stack up. Inevitably, he'd resorted to taking bribes to help pay off the debt. Internal Affairs had eventually caught him in a sting operation, and despite his flawless record, he'd seen his career and pension go down the toilet.

'You'd be a real hero if you solve this case,' said the voice inside his head.

His cell phone buzzed on the table. Don reached over and looked at the number. It was his contact at the local precinct.

"Jack, you got something for me?" he answered with his voice low.

He didn't need an interruption from Tammy now.

"Just the stuff you asked for. Manny Mendez's arrest sheet," said the voice on the line. "Not much to go on, I'm afraid. He's been arrested a few times. Mostly drug-related, but all minor stuff. Spent a few years in Juvie but nothing after that. He's suspected of being linked to the disappearance of two teenage prostitutes, but we haven't been able to get any real leads. These girls drift in all the time from who-the-hell-knows-where. Most times, if they get arrested, they give false names. You know how it is. We've pulled him in for questioning a few times, but he always has an alibi."

'If you're going to say something, say it now,' said the voice in Don's head.

There was a long pause as he struggled with his conscience.

"Don? You there?" asked Jack.

"Yep, I'm listening," said Don. "Has Mendez got any associates?"

The moment had passed. Would there be consequences to his

decision? Only time would tell.

"Yes, one. Name of Joe da Silva. But I don't think questioning him is gonna help you much."

"Why is that?"

"He was found shot dead in an alleyway a few days ago."

"Dead?"

"Yep. We're still reviewing footage from store security cameras in the area. If we're lucky we might have our suspects on film."

"Gang related?"

"Probably. Joe has an older brother, Carlos da Silva. He's the current gang leader of Los Malditos. There's talk of another gang muscling in on their turf. Anyway, words out that Carlos is looking for anyone connected to his brother's murder. He's out for blood. You may want to stay clear of Mendez for a while."

"I'll keep that in mind," answered Don.

A mental picture of two hoods out cold on Manny's bedroom floor surfaced briefly.

"Thanks for the help, Jack. We should catch up some time."

"That we should, Don. It's been way too long."

"We'll talk again."

Don hung up.

He looked down at the photos. If Mendez had murdered these girls, then like most serial killers, he'd have wanted to keep his souvenirs. Yet he'd disappeared without them. In fact, it appeared he'd left his entire stash behind. Had he taken the girl?

He considered the grainy photo of Faith given to him earlier by the school headmistress. When and where had that photo been taken? The headmistress obviously knew, so why had she not been more forthcoming? What was she hiding? What did she hope to gain by jerking him around?

'Enough of this bullshit,' thought Don irritably. 'She'll have to come up with some real answers if she wants my help.'

He looked at his watch. Eleven-thirty. Too late to call now.

'First thing in the morning,' he promised himself.

He gathered up the paired photos of the girls. He'd never needed to hide anything in his apartment before, but couldn't risk Tammy, or anyone else for that matter, stumbling across these. The last thing he needed now was being suspected of being a serial killer.

Don walked over to the kitchen counter and retrieved a sharp knife from the rack. He moved back to the settee, got down on his hands and knees, and proceeded to cut some of the stitching away at its base. Don pushed the pack of photos into the slit he'd created. Tammy stirred in the bedroom. He stood up quickly, scooped up the lone photo of Faith, and padded softly toward the bedroom, placing the knife back in the rack on his way out.

◊ ◊ ◊

Meredith's eyes flickered open. She stared vacantly up at the ceiling as her mind struggled to make sense of what had happened.

Had it even been real? No, it didn't seem possible. A nightmare then, surely?

She lay there awhile. Her body felt weightless, as though she were floating in a dark womb of comforting silence. She was safe here, safe from her nightmare. Safe from the hell of her life.

'I want to stay here. Floating in the tranquil dark, away from the world and its evil. Nothing can touch me here.'

The sound of a clock penetrated the murkiness, each metronomic tick louder than the one before, each pulling her inexorably from her torpor. Finally, reluctantly, she surfaced. Meredith sat up slowly and looked around her. A rush of cold terror washed over her with the realization that the nightmare was real. She clamped a hand to her mouth and stifled an involuntary scream. Panic welled up within her, threatening to overwhelm her brittle psyche. She grabbed the robe beside her and pulled it on, clutching it to her. Covering her nakedness somehow made her feel less vulnerable.

She slid off the bed and ran over to the door. It was locked. Meredith stood holding the door handle, reluctant to give up the hope of escape, and looked around the room for another way out. There were no windows. There were no other doors. She was trapped. The panic rose within her again.

"Let me out!" she screamed.

She hammered at the door.

There was no answer.

"Let me out, you fucking bitch!"

The solid door remained silent and implacable. Meredith kept hammering at the door for the next half-hour, her frustrated screaming eventually dwindling to desperate pleas. Eventually she sank sobbing to the floor. There was to be no escape. With that realization, Meredith picked herself up and returned to the bed, resigned to whatever fate awaited her.

◊ ◊ ◊

It was another hour before the agony began. At first, Meredith felt a tingling in her fingers and toes, very much like pins and needles. The sensation spread, moving up her limbs to her torso and then to her head. She opened her eyes wide in a desperate attempt to rid them of the unwelcome sensation. It did not help. The pain suddenly intensified, and she screamed and fell back on the bed. Her body shuddered with involuntary spasms as Meredith felt the liquid fire course through every vein. It was as though her very being was being consumed. Her breath disintegrated into desperate gasps snatched between the surging waves of agony.

It was then that she became vaguely aware that someone was standing next to her. It was the Countess. Meredith tried desperately to move but found her body unresponsive.

Anastasiya leaned over Meredith and looked at her intently.

"So, I am correct," she said with grim satisfaction. "You are of the chosen."

'Help me!' cried Meredith.

Except that no words spilled from her paralysed lips.

"Now you will take my blood," said Anastasiya. "It is the antidote and the door to another life!"

She extended her pale forearm over the girl.

In her other hand, she drew an ornate silver knife across the flesh of her forearm. The skin opened behind the knife's trail, dark blood welling up in the cut. Anastasiya dropped the blade and placed her thumb and forefinger on either side of Meredith's jaw, forcing the girl's mouth open. She tilted her arm, allowing the rivulets of blood to flow into the open mouth.

The girl gagged momentarily, then swallowed the cold liquid. The effect was immediate—a thousand points of light exploded behind Meredith's eyes and exhilarating warmth radiated through her body, replacing the intense pain of moments before. The feeling was unlike any drug she had ever experienced, and she wanted more. Meredith suddenly grabbed the proffered arm, sucking hungrily at the gaping wound.

"Enough!" snapped Anastasiya.

She pushed the girl back.

Meredith growled like an animal separated from its food and lunged at the Countess. Anastasiya parried the girl's clumsy attack and pinned her to the bed, one hand gripping her throat.

"You will soon learn to listen to my command," she hissed venomously, tightening her grip on Meredith's neck.

The girl gasped for air and grabbed ineffectually at the hand at her throat, but could not loosen the Countess's vicelike grip. Anastasiya relaxed her hand slightly so that the girl might breathe.

Meredith coughed fitfully.

"What have you done to me?" she demanded.

Anastasiya smiled.

"I have given you life," she said. "A new beginning."

"Please, let me go," whimpered the girl.

Anastasiya frowned.

"Why would I allow you to crawl back to the wreckage of your past life? Why? So that you can be a slave to your drugs? A plaything for men to abuse? Something to amuse them?"

"No, I won't do that anymore. I promise," answered Meredith.

She almost believed the lie herself.

"As if the choice were yours to make," sneered Anastasiya.

She released her grip on the girl's throat.

Meredith was not sure what the Countess meant, but rather than risk the woman's displeasure, she decided to resist the urge to bolt for the door beyond. She lay still and allowed her body to relax. Meredith had, after all, become quite adept at feigning acquiescence to whatever a client demanded.

"What is your name?" enquired Anastasiya.

She leaned forward and brushed the hair away from the girl's face. The gesture did not stem from any natural concern, but rather an attempt to allay the girl's fear.

The girl responded with an uncertain smile.

"Meredith," she said quietly.

"Meredith," repeated Anastasiya.

She turned slightly to address the third person in the room.

"Eden, meet my new acolyte. You will instruct her in our ways. Ensure she understands what it is I expect."

Anastasiya stood up from the bed. She looked down at Meredith.

"Do not disappoint me," she said.

She turned and strode purposely from the room.

Meredith watched the Countess leave. She looked back at Eden. Who was not to disappoint? Had the words been directed at her or had they been directed at Eden, who now stood looking at her with frank disdain?

"She meant you," offered Eden. "And she also meant me. I'm responsible for you."

Eden sat down on the edge of the bed, folding one long leg beneath her.

"Come on, sit up," she instructed. "Let us talk."

Meredith sat up, drawing her knees up under her chin. She pulled the robe in about her legs and looked sullenly over at the blonde girl seated before her. Sooner or later, she reasoned, she'd be left alone and there'd be a chance to make a getaway. She'd play along for now and seize the opportunity when it came.

Eden flashed a patient smile. She tilted her head to one side as she studied her new pupil.

"You still don't realize, do you?" she said.

"Realize what?" asked Meredith.

"You can't leave," replied Eden. "Not now, not ever. For you, for all of us, leaving means death."

Her words held no hint of regret.

"What do you mean 'us'?" responded Meredith. "You mean you're stuck here also? How long have you been in here?"

The pitch of her voice betrayed her panic.

Eden shook her head.

"That's not how it works," she said. "I am here because I want to be. In time, you will feel the same. I promise you."

Tears welled in Meredith's eyes.

"I don't believe you," she sobbed.

"That will change," said Eden. "You will change. In fact, the change is already happening as we speak. Your physiology is changing. You are becoming one of us."

"One of you?" snapped Meredith. "Are you trying to tell me you're some kind of vampire? That's bullshit! I know there's no such thing! Look, I've met my share of weirdos, but what you and that bitch did to me tonight is really fucked up."

"What we did was drain you of your human self," hissed Eden angrily. "We took your blood and in return gifted you the virus of true life."

She smiled, her lips pulling back to reveal long pointed canines.

Meredith shook her head vigorously.

"No," she said. "This can't be happening. It can't be real!"

She shrank back from Eden then, pushing herself back against the unyielding headboard of the bed. The pain suddenly returned, a liquid fire coursing through every artery, causing her to cry out as her body spasmed again.

"You should feel honoured, Meredith," intoned Eden soothingly. "A goddess has placed her mark upon you."

'You're mad,' Meredith wanted to scream, but all that issued from her contorted lips was a low keening.

"Even before tonight, you were special," said Eden. "I'm sure you've felt it. Deep down inside. All those times you've looked at others and felt that somehow you were different. Unique. Earlier tonight, you became host to something transmitted through our bite. Usually this would mean death. To all males and to most females, at least."

Eden moved to straddle the now-prostrate girl and leaned forward until her face was inches from Meredith's.

"I've seen the effects of this disease on those humans, Meredith," she drawled. "It changes them. It changes them into mindless, shuffling creatures thirsting for blood. Any blood. The infection needs blood to survive. Problem is, those humans don't have the gene sequence this viral infection can modify. Without that sequence, your body cannot metabolise the blood. So the infection feeds on what it has, slowly consuming its host cell-by-cell, while all the while that host attacks and feeds, desperate to satisfy a hunger that can never be satisfied. It takes the infection a few days to eat its way through its human host. Then the host dies and the virus dies. I'll bet you are wondering right now, 'Is that happening to me?' Well, the answer is no. There are two reasons for this. One: You're in luck, and something in your genetics has provided the right building blocks for the virus. Two: The blood gifted by our Lady is the catalyst."

Eden kissed Meredith softly on the lips.

"The virus is changing you, Meredith," she said. "You're becoming something better. You will be stronger, faster, and tougher. A demigod amongst human cattle."

Eden smiled briefly, then in one fluid motion rolled off the girl and stood alongside the bed.

"Of course, there is a small price to pay. There always is. That is the way of this world. We'll talk again once the change is complete."

She watched as the prone figure of the girl spasmed again.

"This will take a while longer yet, but I promise you will feel better in the end."

Eden turned and walked from the room, leaving Meredith to her torment.

12

The early morning light kissed the glass panels of the conservatory, bathing the interior in a warm radiance that dappled the tropical foliage and sparkled in every water droplet. Orchids, both rare and common, added their exotic colour to the uniform green of broad-leaf philodendrons, swordlike bromeliads and thick fronded ferns that lined the perimeter of the large pond.

There were three fountains situated at one end of the pond, each in the shape of a female head just breaking the liquid surface. A jet of water issued from each mouth, rising confidently before hesitating in midair to disintegrate into hundreds of droplets, which fell and broke the mirrored surface of the pond with a tranquil tinkle. Anastasiya, clothed in the red robe of the previous night, stood at the edge of the pond. Her long blonde hair hung in loose curls over her shoulders. The robe was tied loosely at the waist exposing the pale flesh and curve of her breasts. Her skin betrayed no hint of perspiration in the thick, moist air of the conservatory.

She stepped onto the water of the pond and walked between the numerous lily pads toward the far side, her footsteps unerringly tracing the path of steppingstones placed just beneath the water's surface. She stepped off the final stone and disappeared amongst the thick foliage, a dissipating set of concentric ripples the only hint of her passing.

Anastasiya was now in her favourite part of the conservatory, the home of her collection of the genus Nepenthes. Hanging from tendrils that had twisted about the carefully arranged trelliswork, the plants presented their pitchers in an orgiastic splash of colour. The lustrous purples and reds of the thickened labia that fringed the top of each pitcher beckoned enticingly, inviting every insect to taste of the nectar that lay stored in its distended lower half. To taste, of course, meant death. Yet the allure of the sweet liquid always proved too powerful to resist.

Anastasiya reached up and pulled a pitcher gently toward her. Floating in the nectar were the partially digested remains of what appeared to be some flies and a moth. Did the insect suspect, Anastasiya wondered, that once inside, there was no way back? Perhaps, she reflected, the insect went willingly to its death, content that it had served a purpose in the world. It had sacrificed its life so that the plant could live. She smiled at the analogy. The eyes of the countless dead stared silently back; if she sought an answer from them, they would give none.

Her reverie was interrupted by the ring of her cell phone. She frowned irritably and looked at the number. Don Stone, the private investigator.

"Good morning, Mr Stone. I trust you are having success at locating my errant pupil?" she enquired in a businesslike tone.

"Good morning, Ms Strajinski," returned the PI carefully. "I'm pleased to say I've uncovered a promising lead."

"This is good news."

"There is a problem, however."

"And what is this problem, Mr Stone?"

There was a hint of irritation in her voice.

The tone of Don's voice was measured when he replied.

"Manny Mendez. It appears he had a thing for killing the girls he hooked up with," he said.

Anastasiya was not convinced.

"This is unfortunate news," she said. "You have evidence of this?"

"I have, yes," replied Don. "So, you can appreciate that this puts me in a predicament of sorts, ma'am. Either I go to the police and tell them what I know, or the girl ends up dead. That's hoping she isn't already."

There was a pause as he waited for her response.

"She is not dead, Mr Stone. Of that I can assure you," countered Anastasiya testily.

"You know that for certain?"

"Yes."

"That photo you gave to me," said Don. "It's from one of your security cameras, isn't it?"

Anastasiya allowed herself a brief smile.

"Yes, Mr Stone, it is," she said. She was not disappointed.

"When was it taken?"

"Four days ago," she replied.

She was quite aware of what the PI would ask next.

"Anything else I should know?" pressed Don. "Like, was she with anyone, perhaps?"

"Yes," said Anastasiya. "But then you suspected that, did you not, Mr Stone?"

Her long fingers traced the thick pink fringe of a plant.

"Ms Strajinksi, you came to me for help in finding this girl. Keeping this type of information from me isn't making my job any easier, you understand? Worst case is, you could get this girl killed."

It was Don's turn to sound irritated.

"I am aware of that, Mr Stone. But, as you must appreciate, I also need to keep the reputation of this institution in mind. Still, I assure you the girl's wellbeing is very important to me."

The meaningless words issued mechanically from Anastasiya.

"Good," said Don. "Now we've got that straight, did you get photos of the person she was with?"

"People, Mr Stone," responded Anastasiya. "There were two young men, and yes, I have security camera footage."

There was a moment's silence before Don answered.

"You say two young men?"

"Yes, there were two. Is there something I should know, Mr Stone?" she enquired.

She turned from her plants to focus her attention on his next response.

"Nope. Not right now," replied Don carefully. "I'll be needing those photos, of course. Could you email them to me as soon as possible? I'm sure you're aware that every minute counts."

"Of course, Mr Stone. You will be sure to keep me well informed of your progress, won't you?"

"I'll do that," responded Don.

He hung up.

The man was hiding something. Of that, Anastasiya was sure. It would not, of course, take much to convince him to tell her what that was. Though this would mean losing his services, she reminded herself.

No. It was best to let everything run its course.

Patience was always the best approach. In any event, she needed time to acquire more acolytes, and time to train them. Anastasiya started back the way she had come.

Lotho hovered over the new orchid blooms. His powerful frame and scarred face seemed strangely at odds with his delicate handling of the plants. He was a combat veteran who'd once revelled in war—countless images of the horrors he'd committed in his country's name were stamped indelibly on his psyche. War's parting gift was the physical injury which had left him a mute. It was in the tending of these plants that he'd found his peace, and in the serving of his mistress that he had rediscovered a purpose to his life.

"Lotho!"

Anastasiya's voice cracked like a whip.

The big man spun around. A goddess walked toward him over

the mirrored surface of the pond. He bowed, averting his eyes, lest the goddess sense his desire.

"The young man I acquired last evening. Bring him to the initiation room now," snapped the goddess coolly as she passed him on her way out.

Lotho bowed again, carefully set down the small implement he had been using and followed in Anastasiya's wake.

◇ ◇ ◇

Don drained the last of his coffee and grimaced at the bitter dregs. He looked over to the waitress at the counter and raised his mug in an obvious gesture for another. He sat back and looked out the window of the diner. The morning crush hurried by the diner, thousands of people set in clockwork motion by their alarms, heading off to the start of another monotonous workday. Don allowed himself a brief smile. One good thing about being kicked off the force, he supposed.

"Too much coffee will kill ya, ya know," said the waitress.

She reached over to fill his cup and he grinned.

"That's what you keep telling me, Lorraine," he said.

"You want anything else?"

Her tone offered more than what was on the menu.

Don gave a sly wink and smiled.

"No, thanks, Lorraine. Coffee's fine," he said.

"Suit yourself, honey."

She laughed and walked back over to the counter.

Don watched her with an appreciative eye. He liked Lorraine. Liked the way her tight uniform fit in all the right places. But that wasn't the only reason the diner had enjoyed his patronage the past fifteen years. He liked the place. He liked that it hadn't changed in all that time. Probably hadn't changed since it'd first opened thirty-odd years ago. No spotty minimum-wage teenager with a plastic smile and a plastic meal here. Nope. He preferred to pay a little extra for the real thing. Besides, why put more money in the back pocket of some cunt of a CEO? So far as he was concerned, the big corporations could go fuck themselves. Them and their shareholders.

The bell above the door of the diner jingled as another customer entered. It was Detective Holland, Don's police contact. He looked around briefly before spotting Don. He walked over and slid into the chair opposite.

"Don't know why you insist on this place. Half the force comes in here. But you know that, anyway."

His tone betrayed his annoyance.

Don smiled.

"Precisely why this is the best place," he said. "Here we're just two old work buddies catching up. Someplace more out of the way and anyone who just happens to see us could get the right idea. Besides, you called to meet."

"That's hilarious," retorted Jack.

He produced an envelope from his jacket pocket and laid it on the table.

"That for me?" asked Don.

"Could be," said Jack.

He pushed the envelope across the table.

Don opened the envelope. Inside was a photo which looked like a still from an in-store security camera. It showed two men aged in their mid-twenties walking by the store front.

"I'm guessing these are the two you think did the da Silva hit?" he enquired.

He was careful to maintain a tone of mild interest.

"Could be," said Jack. "They were in the area about the time we think da Silva was shot. But besides the 9mm slugs in the body and the shell casings, we have little else. The lab's running tests on these now."

He paused and looked at Don suspiciously.

"To tell you the truth I was surprised you wanted information on Mendez and his known associates the other night, especially when one of them gets hit two days before. Is there something you're maybe not telling me?"

"Nope, I just thought Mendez might be tied to the case I'm working," responded Don smoothly. "You know how it is. You gotta eliminate each lead."

He kept his expression neutral and glanced casually at his cell phone lying on the table. With any luck, the Strajinski broad had come through with the photos she'd promised. There was no way he could access his emails now, though. Not without giving the game away. He'd just have to sit it out for a while.

"You want coffee?" he asked, and without waiting for a reply, called out, "Lorraine, cup of coffee for my good friend here?"

Don pushed the photo back into the envelope and placed it casually to one side.

"Case must be interesting if a scumbag like Mendez is involved," noted Jack.

Don shrugged.

"Missing daughter. Divorced parents," he replied. "You know, the usual family feud shit."

"So why Mendez?" pressed the detective. He still sounded suspicious.

"Let's just say some rich girls like to slum it every now and then."

Jack raised his eyebrows.

"That's one dangerous habit to have, especially if she gets mixed up with a character like Mendez," he said. "You could give me her details. Who knows? I might be able to help."

Jack was obviously still fishing. He suspected Don was hiding something but couldn't be sure.

Don waved his hand dismissively.

"Thanks, but I think this lead is a dead end," he said. "Besides, the father said she hadn't been involved with Manny for months. This was just me hoping to get some traction on the case."

He paused as Lorraine approached the table. She placed a cup in front of the detective and proceeded to fill it with coffee.

"You wanna see the menu?" she asked.

Jack didn't bother to look up.

"No thanks, I already ate," he replied.

Lorraine raised her eyebrows.

"Tough crowd," she muttered and left the men to their conversation.

Jack leaned forward.

"I don't think I need to point this out," he began. "But if Mendez is mixed up with the da Silva hit, anyone in the way could get themselves killed."

He searched Don's expression.

"I appreciate the concern, but I really don't think this case is gonna get me on anyone's hitlist." replied Don evenly. "Besides, I can handle myself. You know that."

Jack nodded.

"And the photo?" he asked. "I suppose you won't be needing it now, seeing as there's no connection to your case."

The detective was still suspicious. Don couldn't help feeling a little irritated, but knew he'd have done much the same if he'd been in his friend's shoes.

"Wish it did, Jack. Looks like it could've been a big help to the both of us," said Don.

He pushed the envelope back across the table.

"You sure?" pressed Jack.

Don smiled.

"One hundred percent," he replied.

The men eyed each other for a moment and Jack laughed suddenly. The tension evaporated. He took the envelope and slipped it back in his jacket pocket.

"So, how's Jackie and the kids?" asked Don.

Jack picked up his coffee cup and leaned back against his chair.

"Ah, you know, same old same old," he replied. "Did I tell you she quit her job?"

"No, you didn't," responded Don amiably.

He knew he'd have to play this one out. Any move to look at his phone would serve only to raise his detective friend's suspicions again. Nope. He'd have to appear interested and suppress the urge to look at the email and the potential lead it promised. As much as he liked his friend, a long half-hour or more lay ahead of him.

◊ ◊ ◊

Meredith woke with a start and found she was still on the bed. It took her a few moments to realise that someone else was in the room with her.

She sat up. A man in his early twenties sat in a chair near the bed. He wore baggy jeans, a T-shirt, and sneakers typical of a college student.

He smiled nervously.

"You're finally awake. They must've drugged you. I'm Sam by the way," he said.

Meredith didn't respond.

"I've tried the door," Sam continued. "It's locked, and I can't find any other way out. Maybe you and I can figure this out together."

Meredith sat quite still. She stared at the young man with a frank interest which unsettled him. He couldn't understand why she wasn't as scared as he was. Perhaps, he reasoned, she was just too shocked to respond.

He leaned forward on the chair.

"Look, I'm a friend," he said, attempting to put her at ease. "They put me in this room just like you. We're in this together. Maybe we can figure a way out."

Meredith swung her legs over the side of the bed and got up. She smiled with a hiss, her pointed canines now clearly visible.

"What the fuck?" stammered the shocked young man.

The chair toppled over as Sam fell backwards. The girl laughed and advanced toward him with feline grace. He scrambled quickly to his feet and snatched up the chair, holding it before him like a makeshift shield. Sam backed slowly towards the door, keeping the chair between him and the vampire girl.

The vampire came on, a beast of prey moving in for the kill. Sam continued his backward shuffle until he found himself pressed back against the unyielding timber door.

"Let me out," he yelled desperately.

Meredith moved closer and the man attempted to push her back, jabbing the chair into her chest. She responded with surprising speed, grabbing the chair by one of its legs and wrenching it easily from his grasp. Meredith flung it against the far wall and darted forward, easily sidestepping the desperate swing of his fist to grab him by the throat. She lifted the shocked man off his feet back up against the wall. A strangled gurgle issued from Sam's lips as he frantically tried to prise the steel fingers from his throat. He kicked impotently at the girl until finally he passed out.

Meredith released her grip then and his limp body slid to the floor. She straddled the prostrate man, grabbed him by the hair, and pulled his head to one side to expose his neck. Meredith hesitated, savouring the moment before her first kill. She looked down at her victim, her focus on the hypnotic pulse of his carotid artery, the sound of his heartbeat echoing loudly in her head. The rhythmic beat and its promise of life-giving blood finally destroyed the last vestige of humanity remaining within her.

She fell on him then, sinking her teeth deep to drink the precious liquid her being craved. The pain forced Sam back from unconsciousness. He screamed and tried to move but found it impossible with Meredith's legs pinning his arms to either side of his torso. He screamed again and twisted his head as he attempted to get her teeth out of his neck. She tightened her grip on his hair and sank her fangs deeper, gorging herself on his blood. His struggles weakened, then finally ceased as the last of his blood flowed from his body. Sam's eyes glazed over. With a final sigh, his life was gone.

Meredith sat up. She had drunk without a pause and now found herself out of breath. She wiped the blood dribble from her chin and waited a moment for her breathing to return to normal. She stood up and looked down at the lifeless husk that had been a man. Somewhere deep within, she knew she should feel regret but found that she could not.

A hint of a smile touched her lips. She felt more alive now than she had ever before. What had Eden said? Stronger. Faster. Tougher. Yet even more than that, she could feel the power of it all. Meredith stepped over the body and went back to wait on the bed.

An hour passed before the door opened. It was Eden accompanied by a large, well-built man. She walked over to where the corpse lay and studied it briefly.

She turned to the big man.

"The change has started," she said. "You do not have long, Lotho."

The big man merely nodded. He walked over to the body, lifted it off the floor, casually draped it over his muscled shoulder, and strode from the room without looking back.

Eden approached the bed. She smiled.

"A demigod amongst human cattle," she said.

"Or a monster," Meredith countered warily.

An introspective mood had followed in the wake of the adrenalin rush of the kill.

"Only to those without understanding," said Eden patiently.

She sat down on the edge of the bed.

"Understanding? How can you expect anyone to understand?" asked Meredith. "I have become death. Do you think people would bow down and worship me knowing that? I don't think so. They'd hunt me down like an animal. You tell me I'm wrong. Go on."

Meredith looked pleadingly at Eden, who placed a reassuring hand on Meredith's thigh.

"Only if you allow it," she said. "I have been with the Countess Anastasiya for nearly fifty years. We have lived in many different places. Never in all this time have people discovered our true nature."

Meredith frowned.

"Fifty years?" she asked. "But you don't look that old."

Eden laughed.

"One of the perks of being what we are."

Meredith's interest was aroused.

"You mean I'm immortal?"

Eden laughed, but it was meant without malice.

"Not quite," she replied. "You will age, just very slowly. Before you ask, no, you will not burn in sunlight, you will not shrink from a holy cross, and holy water will not burn you nor garlic, nor most anything else, for that matter."

"I thought you were a vampire. That you'd changed me into one, too," said Meredith.

"Vampires are the stuff of fiction, the product of mankind's nightmares," replied Eden. "We are something much more real. The similarities with fiction are just coincidence. The virus within you does make you stronger, faster, and tougher than any human. You will also never suffer illness, and your body will regenerate itself if injured."

She waited for the full meaning of her words to sink in.

Meredith looked down at her hands clasped in her lap. She felt overwhelmed by so many questions, each clamouring to be first. Time passed in silence as Eden waited patiently for the inevitable question. Meredith finally looked up at Eden.

"When you left me before, you said there was a price," she said. "What is that price?"

"You must serve the Countess," replied Eden.

"And if I choose not to? If I choose to leave here instead? What will you do?"

She had always been proud of being independent and, in her opinion at least, that she'd never relied upon anyone else in her life.

The fact that her own choices had placed her in the position she was currently in did not occur to her, even now. Deep-down, Meredith despised the thought of having to answer to anyone.

"Then you will die," said Eden simply.

"You mean you will kill me?" asked Meredith.

She searched Eden's expression for an answer.

"I won't need to. The virus will do that."

"But you said I was different from most other people, and that the Countess's blood helped change me," countered Meredith.

She sat upright and pulled her legs underneath her, an unconscious attempt to place distance between herself and Eden.

"You are different, Meredith," reassured Eden firmly. "The blood has helped initiate the change. But it cannot sustain it. To survive, you need blood from the Countess. Without her gift, you will die. The virus will destroy you cell-by-cell. You will become one of those mindless creatures. Alive-yet-dead."

She allowed a moment's pause before continuing.

"Of course, you have the freewill to choose. You will always have that."

Meredith suppressed the string of obscenities perched on the tip of her tongue. Then something occurred to her—how could she have been so stupid for not having realised it sooner?

"You need her blood, too," she said smugly. "You need it just as much as I do."

"Yes," replied Eden simply.

"Then you're trapped, just like me."

Eden smiled.

"I choose not to think of it like that. Besides, serving the Countess is its own reward."

"Are you for real?" snapped Meredith indignantly. "Serving is its own reward? Give me a break! You might as well be her slave. That's what we are, you know, her slaves. She can make us do anything she wants. We're like her puppets."

"And yet, she does not," replied Eden patiently. "The Countess found me in much the same circumstances as you, Meredith. Working the streets to feed a habit. How much longer do you think you would have survived had she not come for you?"

Meredith pouted.

"I was doing okay," she retorted. "Besides, it wasn't as if I was gonna be on the game forever. I had a plan to get out."

She was not about to concede that her circumstances were anything but of her own choosing.

"That's bullshit and you know it!" challenged Eden.

She leaned forward.

"A year from now you would've been dead. If not from drugs, then by the hand of some psycho john or your pimp. So many ways to die, Meredith, and you know what? No one would care. To them, you'd be just another dead junkie whore."

"We all have to die sometime," responded Meredith petulantly.

Eden could detect the lack of conviction in the young woman's words.

"That may be so, but wouldn't you prefer it to be on your own terms?"

Meredith did not respond, but her expression revealed that she agreed with Eden.

Eden smiled and stood up from the bed. She extended her hands to Meredith.

"Come with me. Let these be your first steps on your path to true life."

13

January 1863

A solitary rider steered his horse through the silent host of fir trees, their pendulous branches heavy in the dank air. The early morning mist eddied about them as they went, adding to the menace that seemed to permeate this most ancient forest. Count Szolayski peered through the gloom.

It shouldn't be much farther now, he thought.

His trusted advisor, Wojciech, had negotiated the deal. All that was left was for him to collect the girl. The dull thud of an axe carried on the still air. Somewhere ahead someone was chopping wood. He spurred his horse to a gentle trot.

It was better to get it over with, before he changed his mind.

Szolayski found the small timber cottage in the middle of a clearing a few minutes later. Smoke rose lazily from its functional stone chimney. A man, bent by old age, stood to one side, a long-handled axe in his hands. The old man placed a small log on the chopping block and swung the axe down, splitting it with a satisfying 'thunk'. He reached down laboriously for another log then, and sensing someone was watching, he turned. A tall handsome man sat astride a fine-looking white stallion. The man carried himself with a natural bearing that hinted at his nobility.

The old man placed the axe against the chopping block and doffed his cap, lowering his eyes as he did. Deep lines carved into his leathery face betrayed a life of suffering.

"Good morning, my lord."

"Good morning," said Szolayski. "You know who I am?"

"No, sir," replied the old man. "It's just that the man told me someone important would come, so naturally I assumed you..."

Szolayski nodded.

"The girl? She is here?"

"Yes, my lord," said the old man. "She is in the house."

"Bring her to me."

The old man shuffled forward, clutching his cap tightly to his chest. A look of anguish filled his eyes.

"She is my only granddaughter, my lord," he said sadly. "Her mother and her father, they died of the plague. So, too, my wife and the animals. I cannot..."

He offered a despairing shrug.

"She will be well taken care of," reassured the Count gruffly.

"My lord, if I may ask, where will you be taking her?"

"The city," replied Szolasyki and waved his hand vaguely toward the west. "She will work for a wealthy family there."

The old man nodded.

"The other man, he said I am not to visit."

He searched the Count's eyes for reassurance.

"It is better this way," responded the Count. "There will be much to learn. She will need to focus on her duties. Perhaps in a few years, she will visit."

The old man nodded apathetically.

"In a few years, perhaps," he repeated without conviction.

"Here," said Szolasyki. "The money which was promised."

He reached down and handed the old man a small leather pouch filled with coin.

"It is getting late," prompted the Count. "We have a long

way to travel."

The old man nodded. He turned, his head bowed, and walked back slowly toward the cabin. Szolayski watched as the old man opened the rickety timber door and disappeared inside.

Moments later, he emerged, a slender, timid-looking girl clutching his hand.

"This is Ewa," said the old man.

The Count swung down from his horse and stood before the pair, a broken old man and his frightened granddaughter.

"How old are you, child?" he asked.

The girl looked uncertainly at her grandfather.

"She is ten," replied the old man.

"Ten," repeated Szolayski.

Tears rolled down the girl's cheeks and she quickly wiped them away. Grandfather had said she should be brave. There was an uncomfortable moment of silence.

"Do not worry yourself so, girl," said the Count. "Your grandfather has been well taken care of, and you will be better off away from here."

"Go now, Ewa," said the old man. "You will be safe, I promise."

Szolayzki took the girl's hand and led her to his horse. He lifted her up onto the saddle and swung himself up to sit behind her. The old man's head remained bowed—he could not bring himself to look at his granddaughter. Szolayski turned his horse away and gently dug his heels into its flanks, urging it into a trot. He needed to get away from this place—away from a broken, hopeless old man watching what remained of his life disappear.

Szolayski and the girl travelled all day, stopping only once to eat a light meal in the early afternoon. Perhaps wanting to remain indifferent to the girl's fate, the Count stayed silent throughout their journey. The girl, too, was quiet, staring stoically ahead as though having resigned herself to whatever lay before her. They reached his estate at night, just as he'd planned. Constructed in the 13th century, the old stone castle had been extensively remodelled in the years since. A man holding an oil lamp stood at a side-entrance. It was Jakub, the Count's most trusted manservant. Szolayski reigned in his horse.

"Good evening, my lord," greeted Jakub.

His voice was hushed as though not wanting to disturb the evening quiet.

"Good evening, Jakub," said Szolayski.

He looked about.

"The rest of the servants," he began, "They have been dismissed for the night?"

Jakub nodded.

"It is as you ordered, my lord."

Szolyaski got down from the horse. He stretched with a groan. It had been a long day. He turned and looked up at the girl.

"Come, girl," he said. "It is time."

He lifted Ewa gently from the saddle and placed her on the ground. Jakob handed him a second lamp which he'd lit and then led the horse away toward the stables. Szolayski took the girl's hand in his and together they walked toward the silent and imposing main residence.

A single light, high-up in one of the building's few remaining towers, was the only hint that the place was occupied. They did not use the main entrance, the Count instead choosing to lead the girl around the building to a small side-door, which they entered. The girl stared in wonder as they walked, rich gilt tapestries and luxurious furnishings alternately appearing and disappearing just as suddenly in the flickering light of the oil lamp. High vaulted ceilings seemed to vanish into the dark above them. It was unlike anything she'd imagined.

They ascended a narrow winding staircase, the lamp's light reflecting dimly off the stone walls of the old tower. Up they went until at last, they reached a solid timber door. The Count reached inside his coat and retrieved an iron key. He unlocked the door and pushed it open.

A young woman squealed with delight.

"Father! I knew you would come."

Ewa stared at the young woman dancing about the room. She was tall and slender, with flowing flaxen hair and porcelain skin. She looked like an angel. The young woman stopped in front of the girl and leant forward so that her face was close to Ewa's. Her eyes were ice-blue. The young girl felt a chill of fear; she somehow sensed yet did not understand the feral hunger which lurked there.

"What is your name, little one?" enquired the angel.

"Ewa," replied the girl softly.

"Ewa," repeated the angel. "Do you like dolls, Ewa?"

The girl nodded her head.

"I have dolls, Ewa. All the dolls you could ever wish for. Come, let me show you."

The angel took the girl's hand in hers and led her around the large bed. Strewn about the floor was a bewildering array of dolls—large porcelain dolls with pert ruby lips, rag dolls with straw-like hair and button eyes, small wooden dolls with delicately carved features, and every other type of doll between. Still more had been heaped against the room's stone wall.

"Why don't you play with these, Ewa, whilst I speak with my father?"

The little girl looked up at the angel uncertainly.

The angel reached down, scooped up a large rag doll from the floor and offered it to the little girl.

"Her name is Sophia. Why don't you play with her?"

Ewa took the rag doll and held it tightly to her chest.

"Come," said the angel. "Why not sit over here?"

She led the girl to the dolls piled against the wall. The girl knelt in front of the dolls and studied their faces. The dolls stared back blankly. She reached for an especially pretty-looking one, then another. The angel smiled. She turned. Szolayski remained standing at the door.

"Father, I'm so pleased to see you," said the angel. "Come, please sit with me awhile."

The Count hesitated.

"Anastasiya, I—"

"Please, father," said Anastasiya. "I have missed you. It is lonely here."

"I'm sorry, Anastasiya. I have been so busy of late," said Szolayski. "But I promise to visit you more often from now on."

He locked the door and then walked over to the bed and sat down next to his daughter.

"Mother, Oliwia, and Elzbieta," began Anastasiya, "Do you visit them every day?"

The Count nodded sadly.

"Yes, I visit your mother and sisters every day," he said. "I tend their graves myself. I tell them how much we miss them. And I tell them about you."

"What do you tell them, father?"

"I say that you are as beautiful as ever, how proud I am of you, how proud I am that you have managed to stay strong despite all that has happened. And I promise them that I will find a way. I will find a cure, no matter the cost."

Anastasiya hugged her father.

"Thank you, father," she said. "For everything."

The Count responded stiffly, stroking Anastasiya's hair as she lay against him. She had always been his favourite. Even now he found it difficult to reconcile the spirited young girl she'd once been with the monster she'd become. In his mind's eye he could still see the creature crouched over the bloodied corpse of the servant girl. A monster, dripping with blood, glaring at him, its wild eyes red with rage. A monster who wore the face of his beautiful girl.

Yet he loved her. How could he not? She was all that he had left. The only remaining connection to his beloved wife. Szolayski gently pried his daughter away.

"Come," he said. "Let us talk. I'm sure you have much to ask me."

They talked for nearly an hour, mostly of things inconsequential, the Count carefully avoiding the troubling news that the Tzar's armies had now mobilized against the Polish rebellion. He'd promised to join his Polish brother officers a week ago yet found he could not bring himself to leave her. Whilst they spoke, he noticed how Anastasiya looked over to where the young girl played every so often. And each time she turned to look back at him, for a brief moment, he thought he saw in her eyes the hunger which lurked there. How could he know who this person truly was? A monster only pretending to be his daughter, or his cherished Anastasiya, the baby girl he'd once cradled in his arms.

"I really must go," he said finally. "It will be dawn in a few hours."

He rose to leave and Anastasiya grasped his hand.

"Father," she said tearfully, "I'm sorry."

He looked into her eyes and then he saw her, his Anastasiya, trapped within the monster she'd become. The Count squeezed his daughter's hand gently, then turned away to unlock the door. He did not look back as he pulled the door closed behind him. Nor did he pause when he heard the little girl's strangled whimper. Szolayski locked the door, then turned, his head bowed in sorrow, and descended the stone stairs.

14

"Faith appears to be fitting in," said Father O'Connor.

He looked out the kitchen window to where John stood speaking with the girl. Faith sat in an old tyre-swing, her slim legs dangling so that her feet just touched the ground. She was rocking herself gently back and forth on the balls of her feet and talking to John, who leant against the tree. The priest noted the relaxed and intimate body language of the two with some concern. Perhaps allowing the girl to stay had not been the best idea, especially if she and John became romantically involved. Would it cloud the boy's judgement? If the vampires were in fact real, and it turned out she was in league with them, would John find eliminating her difficult? He would have to keep an eye on the two, he decided. Especially if he wanted to prevent unnecessary complications later.

O'Connor realized Matthew had ignored his remark. He looked over his shoulder to where the young man sat, methodically cleaning the stripped sections of the pistol that lay on the bench in front of him.

O'Connor cleared his throat and spoke a little louder.

"I said, Faith appears to be fitting in."

"What? Oh, yeah, suppose so," responded Matt brusquely.

"John's taken a shine to her, that's for sure."

O'Connor noted Matthew hadn't even bothered to look up from his cleaning. He looked back through the window at the intimate scene.

"It appears so," he said. "That doesn't bother you, does it?"

"Nope," responded Matthew.

His tone betrayed otherwise.

"Just so long as it doesn't interfere with our work, I don't care what those two get up to."

"I'm sure John wouldn't allow that," said O'Connor.

He hoped his tone sounded more convincing to Matt than it did to him. O'Connor rubbed his temples in a futile attempt to relieve the stress that had been building the past few days, suddenly feeling tired and very old. Just as God had failed him, so, too, had he failed his brother and his niece. But it was God who'd proved impotent. This war was his way of atoning for that failure. God had failed, but he would not.

John and Matthew were his swords of justice. Without them, his crusade would founder, and he would have failed his brother and niece a second time. He could not allow that. He needed to trust his boys. He needed for his work to continue. His crusade was the only way he could right the wrongs committed against the innocent.

His attempts at confirming some truth to the boys' wild story had so far proved unsuccessful. The school existed, that much he could confirm. The number was right there in the phone book. Yet despite the countless calls he'd made to speak with someone he'd only been greeted by an answering machine. The recorded voice informed him in a cordial monotone that the school was in fact full; however, further enquiries could be made by sending a stamped self-addressed envelope to them requesting details of the school, the curriculum, and so on. But why, he wondered, with all the technology available today, had they given no email address? Why did the school have no presence on social media? It appeared almost as though the school did not want to be reached. This alone was suspicious, but still did nothing to confirm Matt and John's fantastic story.

O'Connor shook his head to refocus. If he wanted this resolved, he would have to rethink his approach. He realised this. It would require risking a visit to the school to ascertain firsthand if there was any truth to their story. The most obvious way would be to pose as a prospective parent, driving right up to the gate and requesting a meeting. He would be a bit pushy, even. Demand to meet with the Head Mistress. Yes, that was it. He wondered if he should take Faith with him. It would certainly make the whole thing appear more convincing—they would look like a father and his daughter looking to gain entry to a prestigious school.

No!

He pushed the thought away as quickly as it had occurred to him. He could not trust her. The thought that she may in fact be connected to the school refused to go away. Had John been foolish, inviting the girl to join their enterprise?

'Perhaps,' he thought, 'but you are no less a fool for wanting to enter what could be a den of vampires.

In his mind's eye, he watched them mutilate his drained body and shuddered. Was this truly his only option or was there perhaps some other way? He thought for a moment and nodded to himself, a look of determination replacing the worried frown he'd worn these past few days.

"Matthew," he said, turning to face the young man cleaning the pistol parts, "I am going to pay a visit to that finishing school."

Matt placed the pull-through and barrel back on the table and looked up at Father O'Connor.

"Oh? When?" he asked.

"Tomorrow morning," replied the priest.

"And if something happens?"

"Nothing will happen."

Matthew frowned. "How can you be so sure?"

"These beings, whatever they are, have probably been around for a long time," reasoned O'Connor. "My thought is that it would not be in their interests to kill indiscriminately. That approach would almost certainly have led to their discovery before now."

"So you believe us?"

Matthew searched the priest's expression for confirmation.

"I'll be straight with you, Matthew," responded O'Connor. "You and John have earned that. My answer is that I'm not sure. Although I am, for one thing, relieved I've seen nothing in the newspapers about the incident."

"Meaning?"

"Meaning that what you and John claim you saw could in fact be real."

Father O'Connor picked his words carefully. He'd wanted to say that he'd felt relieved that no innocents had been killed, but knew this would have betrayed the true depth of his misgivings to Matthew.

"Thanks," answered Matthew sullenly.

The priest offered an indulgent smile, much as a parent would a wayward child.

"Of course," said O'Connor. "This does not mean our work can recommence just yet."

Matthew leaned forward in his chair. His eyes narrowed.

"What about the next assignment? I have all the information we need to carry out the work!"

"You will wait. For a few more days, at least," instructed the priest soothingly. "I need to be sure that our work has not been compromised, Matthew. Visiting this school will allow me to do that. This you should understand."

Matthew scowled belligerently.

"But you said we were going to make a difference, Father. You said that together we were going to clean up the streets. How are we gonna do that hiding out here?"

O'Connor noted his expression and wondered, not for the first time, whether Matthew had been his best choice for this work. It wasn't because he wondered whether Matthew enjoyed killing —it was something more troubling. Every so often, Matthew's mask appeared to slip, allowing him a glimpse of something far more sinister within the boy. But was this in fact the case, or was O'Connor allowing his paranoia to affect his judgement?

Trust. He needed to trust his boys, he reminded himself. But just how much trust should anyone dare place in any man?

"Please tell John and the girl I bid them goodbye," said O'Connor finally. "I will call in a day or two. I should have a clearer picture by then. I think perhaps then we will be able to return to the work at hand. All being well, that is."

He walked up to Matthew and placed his hand on the man's shoulder in a gesture of conciliation.

"I'm sure you understand."

"Sorry, Father. I forgot myself," replied Matthew. "You're right, of course. It's best to wait until you feel ready to continue."

"Good man," said the priest. "Until later, then."

He walked quietly from the kitchen.

Matthew resumed cleaning the weapon, the benign expression he'd flashed O'Connor replaced by one of brooding contempt.

◊ ◊ ◊

The old tree stood at the end of the sprawling, untended backyard. Its crooked trunk had been bent by both wind and time. Gnarled branches spread their leafy canopy, a refuge against the heat of the noonday sun. The sun's light pierced the foliage here and there to bathe the area beneath in dappled hues.

A young man and woman talked within its comforting shade. They had been in each other's company a few days now, and though they'd had the opportunity to talk, this had been limited by a natural caution resulting from their unique situation. Now, encouraged by the tranquillity of their surrounds, or perhaps just by some unspoken mutual consent, their casual conversation drifted to something more personal.

"So, why did you get into this?" Faith asked.

She tilted her head to one side with an air of nonchalance as she looked up at John. She was not judging him, he realised. Nor was it out of morbid curiosity. She was genuinely interested.

John laughed and shook his head.

"Three days," he said.

"What?"

"It took you three days to ask," he said, smiling.

"Why? Did the other girls ask you sooner?" Faith shot back in jest.

"Other girls?" he asked, then understood the joke.

Yes, but they weren't around long enough, he wanted to reply in jest.

But he didn't, realising instinctively that a flippant response might easily cause Faith to retreat into herself once more. She felt comfortable enough with him to ask the question and he wanted to tell her.

"Well?" she pressed.

Even though she'd persisted with her question, a hint of uncertainty had crept into her voice. Had she unknowingly hit a nerve? Crossed some unseen line? She stopped moving the swing back and forth and looked at him expectantly.

John looked at her a moment. Her large hazel eyes were framed by long dark hair, which fell over her shoulders in unruly curls. She wore a short summer dress that accentuated her slim figure. The bruising on her legs had disappeared, he noted.

"Nope, no other girls. You're the only one that's ever been here," he said.

He paused as he considered his next words.

"If it's some vengeance kind of thing you think I'm on you're gonna be disappointed."

"Try me."

"My parents were killed in a car crash. Hit and run. It turned out to be a drunk driver," he said. "Pretty ordinary, I suppose. I mean, it happens to plenty of others, but I was nine at the time and, well, it hurt. I was suddenly alone in the world. We had no other family, you know — no grandparents, cousins, nephews, that sort of thing. Losing the people that you love like that, it does something to a person. It makes you realize that maybe being close to anyone just opens you up to all kinds of pain. And that maybe you've really got no control over anything, that no matter what you do you can't stop bad things from happening. So the only way to protect yourself is to be close to no one. That way, you get to feel like you can have some sort of control in this fucked-up world. So, that's what I did. I just cut myself off from everyone. That meant I was pretty much a loner at the last group home."

"Is that where you met Father O'Connor?"

"Uh-huh. He took over when I was fifteen. Before that, things at the place had gotten really bad."

"You mean like..."

Faith's voice trailed off. She found it difficult to even think the words.

John understood what she'd intended to say and shook his head.

"No, nothing like that. No sexual abuse, if that's what you're thinking. Not to me, at least. The priest before Father O'Connor was just too old, that's all. He let things get outta control. There were a bunch of older boys there. Real mean fuckers. They used to beat the shit outta the younger boys—anybody who was weaker than them, for that matter. They took our food, money, anything they felt like, really. Their leader was a boy named Greg Boyd. He took a liking to one of the younger boys. Or maybe it was one of his buddies; I can't recall now. Anyway, they came for the boy one night. I tried to stop them. Got the shit kicked outta me for my trouble and they did what they wanted. The kid was never the same after that."

John's voice trailed off. There was an awkward silence as he wrestled with the memory.

"We found him a few days later," he said finally. "He'd hanged himself."

"I'm sorry," Faith responded automatically.

She realized it probably sounded like something social convention required her to say, but what was the alternative?

John shrugged.

"It was his way of dealing with what had happened."

"And Boyd?" she asked.

"Nothing. The Church went into damage control. Boyd and the others were sent to homes out of state and the old priest was replaced."

"By O'Connor?"

John nodded.

"So things got better?"

He nodded again.

"But you weren't happy?"

John smiled. The girl smiled back. Both knew that she'd stated the obvious, but that the words had needed to be spoken. The fact that she'd said them was an acknowledgment that she understood.

"You ever play Diablo?" asked John, suddenly changing tack.

"No," she replied with a quizzical look.

"It's an old PC game. You play as a character following a quest. Basically, you get to go into different lands and kill all the demons and monsters. In the original, you went into this cathedral that went down sixteen dungeon levels. I got hooked on that game. I loved going into a level and cleaning it of all evil. I wouldn't be happy till I'd killed off every last motherfucking demon or undead ghoul. That's how I like to think of what we're doing now. We're cleaning out a level. We're getting rid of all the Greg Boyds in the world."

John made a sweeping motion with his hand, as if to emphasize his words.

"What about those things from the other night?"

He shook his head.

"I don't know," he said. "I wish I had an answer. I wish I could say that that was the last of them. It would make Father O'Connor very happy, at least."

"You think there's more?"

"Don't you?"

"Honestly? Yes. I do," conceded Faith. "It's just that I'd prefer there not to be. You know what I mean? Things seem complicated enough without them getting in the mix. And what if they decide to come after us?"

John shook his head.

"Nah," he said. "They'd 've come after us by now if they knew who we were."

"I suppose you're right."

"Think about it. They can't exactly come out and say they're looking for a couple of strangers who gunned down some of their friends who just happened to be feeding on a human being at the time. It'd be in their best interest to lie low, or maybe just disappear. Skip town and go someplace else. I mean, for all those vampires know, they could've been the real target."

"Vampires?" Faith raised her eyebrows.

John shrugged.

"Can't think of a better name to call them," he said. "After all, vampire legends have been around for thousands of years. Who's to say some of those myths aren't based on reality?"

Faith nodded.

"I suppose. Okay, for want of a better word, let's call them vampires. I still would be happier if they weren't creeping around feeding on people. That's one reality I can do without."

"If all they do is prey on the likes of Manny Mendez, then why not live and let live? Leave them be and they leave us be," offered John.

Faith was not convinced.

"You really think they'd only prey on scum like Manny?"

"No, but it was a thought," replied John. "It would certainly make our job a whole lot easier."

He sat down with his back against the tree and reached over, pulled a stem from the long grass, and chewed on its end thoughtfully. Faith nodded but said nothing. The pair sat in silence for a moment, each contemplating their own situation.

"The other night. You know, for a moment, it felt just like the game," wondered John out loud.

"Except if they'd killed you, there'd be no hitting the restart button," reminded Faith.

"Good point!"

They both laughed, not only at his understatement but at the absurdity of it all.

Another comfortable silence followed. A light breeze rustled the uncut grass. Bees flitted amongst the scattered wildflowers. A dove nearby cooed softly. Faith could feel the tranquillity of it all seeping into her like a drug—it made a person never want to leave.

She stole a glance at John. How was it she felt as though she'd known him all her life?

"You mind if I ask you something?" asked Faith carefully.

"That depends."

"Depends?"

"On what you want to ask. I mean, I'd rather not go into the specifics of what Matt, and I have done in the past. Wouldn't want to make you an accessory and all."

"No, it's nothing like that," reassured Faith quickly. "But if you don't want to answer, just say."

John smiled.

"Okay," he said. "What do you want to know?"

"Father O'Connor. What he's got you and Matt doing. It just seems so extreme," ventured Faith. "I'm sorry, I mean I'm not judging you or anything. It's just, well, he's a priest, isn't he?"

"There's been plenty of warrior priests throughout history. Men that were driven to action," replied John. "Well, maybe he's just like one of them. That's what I'd like to believe, anyway. But the truth is, I think something inside Father O'Connor broke the moment his brother died. He wasn't the same man I knew as a teenager after that."

"How did he find you again?"

"I kept in contact with him after leaving the home. After school, Matt and I did the whole 'let's join the military' thing and we both joined the Army. We served our time and decided at the end of our enlistment that it was time to move on. Maybe try something else. We hadn't been out long when I paid Father O'Connor a visit. I told Matt what had happened to him, so he went to see O'Connor, too. They got to talking and one thing led to another and well, I think you can figure the rest."

"John? Can I speak with you for a moment?" asked a voice from behind them.

It was Matthew who'd suddenly appeared.

The pair jumped like a pair of teenagers caught necking.

"What's up, Matt?" asked John.

His voice betrayed his annoyance at the intrusion.

"The old man was just here," said Matthew.

John seemed surprised.

"Father O'Connor was here?" he asked. "It's not like him to leave without at least saying hello."

"It was a quick visit. He happened to be in the area," explained Matthew. "He saw you and Faith sitting out here chattering away like two doves and decided not to disturb you both."

"Still no reason not to come out and say hi," responded John testily.

"It's what happened," insisted Matt. "Anyway, we got to talking about the Valdez hit and he sort of agreed we should do it."

"What?"

"Looks like the old man finally came around."

"You sure?" enquired John.

He was mildly suspicious at the priest's sudden change of heart, or at least Matthew's version of his conversation with O'Connor.

"He seemed pretty adamant yesterday."

"Yeah, well things change," replied Matthew. "I pointed out

we had some solid information on where Valdez would be today and that if we didn't do it now, we might not get another chance for some time."

"I'm just surprised he didn't call me in so we could discuss it together, that's all," noted John suspiciously.

Matthew shrugged.

"What do you want me to say? Maybe, he decided to make this the exception. You can call him if you like. Check it out if you don't believe me. I'm sure he wouldn't be too annoyed."

"You know that'd break protocol, Matt," replied John pointedly.

He couldn't decide who he was more annoyed at, Matthew or O'Connor. Both, for different reasons, had apparently chosen to make an important decision without him. Matthew, he could understand but, O'Connor? Why? How would it profit him?

"So are we on?" pressed Matthew.

"Yeah, if that's what the old man wants, then sure, we're on."

"Alright, then, 'cos I've got an idea," said Matthew.

He turned to Faith.

"You said you wanna help out, didn't you?"

"Yes," she replied carefully.

Matthew grinned fiendishly.

"Well, then, girl, this is your chance."

"Hold on, Matt," interrupted John. "Faith's still pretty new to all of this. Don't you think we should leave her out of it for now?"

Matthew turned to Faith.

"What do you say, girl," he pressed, "you think you up to it?"

Faith folded her arms across her chest. Sure, she was scared, but there was no way she was going to let the asshole intimidate her.

"I was up to it the other night, don't you think?" she replied.

"Faith," interrupted John quickly, "you don't need to do this. Matt and I can handle it."

Matthew shook his head.

"She's gotta get her hands dirty sometime, John," he said.

"Especially if she wants to earn her keep around the place."

"It's okay, John," assured Faith. "I wanna help out."

"You sure?" asked John.

His concern for her was obvious.

Faith nodded and smiled. Her stomach was a knot of nerves, but she was determined to go through with whatever Matthew had planned. Besides, the last thing she wanted was to give him the satisfaction of seeing her back down.

'Asshole! I'll show you just what this girl can do!'

Matthew grinned contemptuously.

"Okay, so the girl wants to step up," he said. "That's good. It's about time. Alright, then, let's all go inside so's I can explain my little plan."

John and Faith followed quietly behind Matthew as he swaggered back toward the house. If either one had reservations their expressions revealed nothing.

15

Rafael, or Ralf to his friends, sat perched on the weathered timber balustrade that ran along the raised front porch of the old house. It was a house which, although nondescript in appearance, happened to be the residence of the local drug dealer and a known associate of Carlos da Silva. His lanky physique and tattooed arms made him appear much older than his fifteen years. He took a long drag on his cigarette, filling his lungs with nicotine-sweet smoke then exhaled slowly. Rap music spilled from inside the house, the aggressive beat interspersed by the sound of laughter. Ralf looked backed over his shoulder at the front door and scowled.

'Fuck, man, why I always gotta be lookout?'

He pulled on his cigarette again. Emilio and Esteban were having all the fun.

'Gonna fuck that chick good, while all I get to do is stare at an empty street!'

Of course, he knew somebody had to be on-watch, and being the youngest, he realized, meant this unenviable task usually went to him.

'Can't be too careful with all the shit that's gone down the last few weeks,' he reminded himself. Luis, Miguel, and now Joe. All gunned down. No one seemed to know what the fuck was going on, so the word out was to lie low. Take no chances.

At that moment, a lone figure caught his eye. It was a young woman, moving down the street toward the house. She was slim, with long dark hair that hung in untidy curls over a faded denim jacket and short summer dress. He watched her approach, enjoying the way the light breeze caused her skirt to rise seductively up her long legs every now and then, promising a glimpse of something more. The girl stopped in front of the gate.

She smiled.

"Hi," she said. "Is Emilio here?"

"Who's asking?" he replied in a hostile tone.

"Cindy," she answered, still smiling.

"What you want with Emilio, Cindy?"

Her smile faded.

"Thought maybe he could help me out."

"Help you out with what, bitch?"

The girl stepped forward, her hands gripping the wrought-iron gate of the six-foot steel fence that fronted the property. She looked about furtively.

"You know..." she said suggestively.

"No, I don't know," sneered Ralf. "I do know that maybe you got the wrong house."

"Please," the girl insisted. "I've been here before. Emilio, he hooked me up with some rock."

Ralf feigned surprise.

"Say what?"

"Some rock."

"Fuck off!"

The girl seemed undeterred.

"Please, I need it," she whined. "My regular supplier, he's out of town."

Her knuckles whitened as she tightened her grip on the bars.

"I don't think you heard me right, bitch. I said turn that skinny little white ass round and keep on walking."

"Please, I'll do anything. Please let me see Emilio."

She pushed up against the bars of the gate.

A thought occurred to Ralf then, and for the first time, he was glad that Emilio had been too cheap to install the closed-circuit monitors he'd always insisted were needed.

He grinned lasciviously.

"You say you'll do anything?"

"Anything you want, just let me in," she pleaded.

"Okay, then, I'll let you in. But before you get to see Emilio, you and me gonna have a little fun. We understand each other?"

The girl nodded vigorously. Ralf slid off the banister and swaggered over to the gate. The girl continued to cling to the gate's bars as though releasing them might mean losing the chance to gain her entry. He pushed up against the bars so that he was within inches of her. She looked up at him expectantly, hazel eyes burning with an odd intensity.

"You smell nice," he chuckled.

He pushed his hand between the bars onto the inside of her thigh. His hand slid upward but she countered, moving deftly just out of reach.

"No, first let me in, then you can..."

Her voice trailed off. She looked up coyly, hands fidgeting suggestively at the hem of her short dress. Without a second thought, Ralf punched in the code and pulled the gate open just enough for the girl to slip in.

"On your knees, fuckhead!" snarled the girl.

She pushed a silenced 9mm pistol into the startled boy's face.

Ralf hesitated, momentarily stunned by the sudden turn of events.

"Now!" the girl urged.

The appearance of two heavily armed men added emphasis to her words.

He dropped to his knees with his hands raised in a mute display of surrender.

"The code," the girl demanded.

She pushed the extended barrel hard against his forehead.

"Three, one, one, nine," he stammered.

Faith kept the weapon trained on Ralf as she stepped back to the gate. She looked back briefly to locate the keypad and punched in the code with her free hand. Matthew and John moved in quickly, silenced pistols at the ready.

"Get up," growled Matthew.

He grabbed Ralf by the scruff of his neck, yanked him to his feet, and half-dragged, half-pushed the frightened youth toward the front door. The rap music and laughter from inside the house continued unabated, the occupants blithely unaware that death approached. Faith and John followed close behind.

Matthew pushed Ralf up against the door, grabbed the boy's hair, and yanked his head back, simultaneously pushing the pistol barrel into the small of his back.

"Now, open the door nice and slow," ordered Matthew.

Numb with terror, Ralf fumbled for the door handle. Tears rolled down his cheeks. He opened the door.

Up to that point, Emilio Valdez had been having a pretty good day, made all the better by watching his lieutenant get a blowjob from a very generously proportioned prostitute named Valerie. Esteban reclined on the couch opposite him, his legs apart with the half-naked woman kneeling between them diligently applying herself to the task of fellatio. The woman's ample white rear undulated back and forth in rhythmic accompaniment to the bleach-blonde head moving up and down over the man's crotch. Emilio liked the way the woman's silk thong split her ample cheeks, stretching down to just cover the plump labia of her sex. He'd decided it was time to have a taste of the action and was about to undo his trousers when he heard the door open behind him.

"Ralf, what the fuck I tell you about..."

The rebuke died on his lips as his looked over his shoulder.

John fired one shot. The bullet hit Emilio in the temple and emerged with part of the back of his skull in a spray of blood. The dead man crumpled over onto the blood-spattered couch. Emilio's trusted lieutenant never got to see his boss's end, exiting this world about the same time with two neatly placed rounds to the heart fired from Matthew's weapon. Without a moment's thought, Matthew fired two more into the unwitting prostitute, still on her knees. The unfortunate woman slumped down between the dead man's legs, her face still buried in his crotch. The silenced rounds, though surprisingly loud in the confines of the lounge room, had been effectively masked by the loud music.

Faith turned angrily on Matthew.

"You didn't have to kill her!" she exclaimed. "She had nothing to do with this!"

"What? You think this is a game?" snapped Matthew irritably. "This is how it's done, girl!"

He turned to John and pointed to where Ralf cowered near the front door.

"Let's finish it and get going."

John nodded and raised his pistol. The boy curled himself into a ball, covering his head with his hands—an ineffectual but natural response to his impending death.

Faith moved to stand between John and the prostrate boy.

"No, John, please, don't do it!" she pleaded. "He's just a boy."

John hesitated as he looked into the face of the girl standing between him and the boy he had been about to kill. Her expression was a strange mix of emotions. He could see fear, but he could also see frustration and anger. She was not afraid of him, he suddenly realized. She was afraid for him, and then he understood her frustration and anger. They were not directed at him, they were because she was afraid that if he shot the boy, he might lose the last of his humanity, and she felt powerless to stop that from happening. He knew then that killing this boy would mean losing her and he finally understood he did not want that to happen.

"Please don't, John," she said. "Not everyone in this world is Greg Boyd."

John lowered his pistol.

"He's not much younger than you, girl," growled Matthew with casual menace.

He stepped quickly past her, raised his pistol, and fired two rounds into the prone figure.

"What the fuck has Greg Boyd got to do with this anyway, John?"

"You, fucking asshole!" screamed Faith.

She launched herself at the surprised man, but John grabbed her and pulled her to him.

"No, Faith. Not here. This is not the place," he said soothingly.

He held the struggling girl close.

"I told you she'd only get in the way!" snorted Matthew.

He brushed past the pair, opened the front door a small way, and peered carefully outside.

"It's clear," he said over his shoulder. "Now, unless you want us all to get caught, I suggest we leave, pronto."

◊ ◊ ◊

Across town, a black Mercedes S-series pulled up to the imposing iron gates of the finishing school.

'The Whitby Foundation Finishing Academy for Girls,' the sign set into the large stone wall read.

An intercom mounted to a slender steel pedestal stood a small distance from both wall and gate. Sited above the iron railings was a remote camera. Father O'Connor sat for a moment and composed himself. He wore an expensive grey suit, pressed white shirt, and red tie. The Mercedes was a hire. His hope was that he would appear to be a successful business executive.

He took a deep breath before reaching over and pressing the buzzer on the intercom. There was no response. He pressed the buzzer again. Still no response. He waited. The moments ticked over with the soft purr of the Benz's idling motor. He reached over and pressed the buzzer once more. His eye caught the movement of the remote camera as it swivelled on its mounting, and he pretended to ignore the unblinking eye that now studied him, reached over, and pressed the buzzer again.

"Can I help you?" a female voice enquired.

Her foreign accent was accentuated by the electronic distortion of the intercom.

Father O'Connor cleared his throat and responded as smoothly as his nervousness would allow.

"Ah, yes. Hello," he said. "I'd like to enquire about enrolling my daughter in your school, ma'am."

"You seek enrolment for your daughter? For this year?" enquired the voice incredulously.

"Yes."

"You are aware that the school year has already commenced?" The voice said, sounding slightly amused.

"Yes. I must apologize, but I have a good reason," explained O'Connor. "Also, your school comes highly recommended."

He waited for a reply, the car's idling motor ticking away the seconds.

"Look," he added, "I'm not used to conducting interviews like this. Could we perhaps agree on a time to meet convenient to both of us?"

The silence grew uncomfortable.

He reached over and pressed the buzzer again.

"Hello?"

"I would prefer if we held the interview now," said the voice suddenly.

The large wrought-iron gates swung silently inward as if by command. The priest hesitated. He felt uneasy. Was this due to the boys' wild story or was it his own survival instinct alerting him? He could not tell. The gates stood open, an invitation for him to enter.

"God have mercy upon my soul," he said.

He depressed the accelerator and the car rolled smoothly up the winding driveway toward the waiting mansion.

◊ ◊ ◊

"Please wait in here," said the girl. "The headmistress will be with you shortly."

She showed O'Connor into a large, ornately furnished room.

The priest turned to thank the girl but found that she had already disappeared. There had been nothing about her to suggest anything but that she was a student at an exclusive school—well-groomed, dressed in a navy-blue blazer with badge embroidered on the pocket, white shirt with bowtie, plaid skirt, long white socks, and simple low-heeled black shoes. Besides, he reminded himself, vampires hardly went about their business in the daylight. If the myths were to be believed, that is. The large silent butler who had first opened the front door had admittedly been disconcerting, but the girl had soon appeared, introduced herself courteously, and led him to this room. 'Eden,' she'd called herself, if he remembered correctly. He had never been good with names.

O'Connor stood just within the doorway and surveyed the room's interior: a typical response for anyone in unfamiliar surroundings but magnified in this case by his underlying fear. The furnishings had a stately baroque feel to them; slender, ceiling-high windows set into the far wall bathed the interior of the room with warm daylight. Along the length of another wall was a bookcase, stretching from ceiling to floor and filled with leatherbound books.

The painting which dominated the wall to his left caught his eye. It too stretched from ceiling to floor and took up half the wall's length. Intrigued, he ventured into the room and stood before the painting. His eyes were first drawn to the naked figures which floated up along the left side of the canvas, their pale flesh contrasting starkly with the dark swirl of greens and yellows. To him, they appeared as ethereal figures drifting aimlessly along in a dreamlike trance, apparently unable or unwilling to change their state of being. His gaze drifted down along the line of figures to the foot of the painting, where a female face emerged from the darkness, her enigmatic gaze penetrating, all-knowing. To the right, rising out of the sea of colour, a face. In fact, he thought to himself, there appeared to be the hint of another face, larger than the first, within the flowing lines. He bent forward, his eyes tracing the deft brushstrokes.

"Do you doubt its authenticity?" enquired a voice coldly from behind him. "Or perhaps you speculate as to its worth?"

Startled, O'Connor spun around.

"Excuse me?" he said.

Before him was a woman of striking beauty. He felt transfixed by her gaze and for a moment felt unable to respond more eloquently.

"I could not help notice how closely you were studying the painting, that is all," replied Anastasiya. "My comments were not intended to offend."

Her tone suggested otherwise.

She walked over to stand alongside O'Connor and gazed at the painting, as though admiring it for the first time.

"Klimt. An inspired artist," she said. "A founding member of the Secession, as I recall. Vienna was an interesting place then."

Anastasiya extended an elegant hand and ran her fingertips lightly along its surface, tracing the swirling lines of paint.

"To gaze upon this work, to truly appreciate the inspiration, the emotion and intention behind each brushstroke—that is a gift of but a few," she said. "Most humans would not even care to stop and look, caught up as they are in the self-importance of their brief part in the drama of life. There are those who might stop a moment and attempt to comprehend the painting's meaning, but they too succumb to the siren call of life's play and move on without understanding. Perhaps it is the curse of the modern world."

Anastasiya turned and looked searchingly at O'Connor. He shrugged.

"All the world's a stage and all the men and women merely players," he responded finally.

O'Connor hoped the Shakespearean reference sounded more sophisticated to her than it did to him.

Anastasiya's eyebrow arched slightly. She offered a chilly smile.

"You have read a little, I see."

The priest smiled ruefully.

"Only in my youth," he conceded. "I don't have much time for it these days, caught up in the drama of my life in this modern world, as it were."

O'Connor mentally admonished himself for his flippant response. Nothing would be gained in antagonising the woman.

"If that is what you say," she replied.

An uncomfortable silence followed. O'Connor and the woman studied each other, her cold blue eyes seeming to penetrate his very being, and he felt himself wanting desperately to look away, but realized it would make him appear duplicitous.

It was Anastasiya who finally broke the silence.

"You have requested an interview, Mister...?"

"Oh, I do apologize. Mister Jameson. Colin Jameson," responded O'Connor politely. He extended his hand in greeting.

"I am Ms Strajinski," replied Anastasiya. Her hand was icy cool to the touch.

"How do you do," said O'Connor. "As I mentioned before, I'd like to enquire about enrolling my daughter in your school."

"Why this school in particular?"

"As I might have said, it comes highly recommended."

"Highly recommended? I am pleased to hear that," said Anastasiya. "Might I ask who recommended this school?"

"Friends of mine. Acquaintances, really. Jack and Jenny St Clair."

He noted Anastasiya's growing suspicion.

"Oh, they don't have a daughter here," he added hastily. "Friends of theirs do. Or so they say. Perhaps it was friends of their friends. I really don't seem to recall."

"Ah, friends of friends," she said in mock-surprise. "Of course, who else? I would have liked to thank them for their recommendation, but then, I don't suppose you remember their names?"

"Regretfully no," shrugged O'Connor with feigned nonchalance.

"Regretful, yes."

Anastasiya allowed another moment of uncomfortable silence.

"Your daughter," she said suddenly. "Where is she at the present moment?"

"She's with her mother. New York," replied O'Connor. "We're separated. It's been almost a year now."

The well-rehearsed lies rolled off his tongue.

"How old is your daughter, Mister Jameson?"

"She's seventeen."

O'Connor realized this sounded odd, considering the obvious disparity in age.

"She's from my third marriage," he added by way of explanation.

Anastasiya smiled politely.

"I understand. What is her name?"

"Faith," responded O'Connor. There was no need to lie about this, he decided.

"Faith. What a delightful name." She offered another icy smile.

"There is a certain protocol to follow, you understand, Mr Jameson?"

"Yes."

"I would of course require a formal interview with her."

"Yes, of course."

"You mentioned before that you had good reason?"

"Good reason?"

"Yes, when you talked over the intercom. You said you had a good reason for wanting to enrol your daughter at my school at this time."

"Ah, yes. My ex-wife. She and her new beau intend holidaying around Europe for a few months. I thought it best for Faith to be closer to me. Geographically, that is. In truth, we've grown quite apart these last few years. I have a demanding schedule, you understand," explained O'Connor.

He feigned an appropriate look of regret.

"Not so busy that you found the time to come here today," noted Anastasiya coolly.

"That is true," responded the priest quickly.

Another awkward silence followed. O'Connor attempted to remain nonchalant under the penetrating gaze of his hostess. Did she suspect he was lying?

"What is Faith doing now, Mr Jameson?"

"Not much, I'm afraid. She wanted a year off before finally deciding on what she intends on doing with her life," answered O'Connor.

He was attempting to keep the details as vague as possible.

"I see," she said. "And is she aware that you intend to enrol her at this school?"

"Yes, I have mentioned it to her in passing."

"Mr Jameson, this school was established to prepare young women for wealthy society. During their year with us, they learn French, Italian, art appreciation, and social etiquette. My staff and I educate a class of no more than twenty pupils each year. Though I admit schools such as mine are not as fashionable as they once were, I still have a more-than-adequate number of enrolments each year. You can appreciate, then, the need for each pupil to want to attend my school," said Anastasiya.

She knew the man before her was lying but was not entirely sure why. It was for this reason that she had opted for the standard speech reserved for those few occasions she'd needed to explain what it was the school offered. The murder of her acolytes and this man showing up at her gate had to be more than mere coincidence. But until she understood the extent of the threat she might be facing, she would need to keep up the pretence.

"Actually, I'd rather expected to see some of the pupils or teachers about the place," noted O'Connor idly.

The question was more an attempt to deflect attention away from the so-called relationship with his pretend daughter than anything else.

Anastasiya flashed a patient smile.

"They are on an art appreciation field trip, Mr Jameson. The Guggenheim. You know, in New York."

O'Connor merely nodded and offered a weak smile. Silence settled on the room once more.

There was a discreet knock at the door.

"You may enter," commanded Anastasiya.

It was the same young woman who had previously escorted O'Connor to the room. She walked over to her headmistress, a picture of studied grace.

"I apologize for interrupting your interview, Ms Strajinski, but you requested that I remind you of your prior engagement," said Eden.

"Thank you, Eden."

Anastasiya turned to O'Connor.

"Unfortunately, we will have to end our little chat here. I had intended on showing you around the school but that will have to wait for another time. The formal interview, perhaps?"

"Yes, of course," answered O'Connor.

In truth, he felt relieved that their talk had come to an end.

"When had you intended Faith to commence her studies here?"

"When? Oh, soon. I really wanted to see your school for myself. Before I talked more with my daughter, that is."

More lies. For a priest, O'Connor had become rather adept at lying.

"Yes, I see," replied Anastasiya. "There is a waiting list, you understand. I took this interview only because I was intrigued at your rather direct approach. You should speak with your daughter and then contact me at your earliest convenience. We could discuss details then. Now, if you will excuse me."

She extended her hand.

"Goodbye, Mister Jameson, perhaps we will meet again presently."

"Oh, certainly," lied the priest.

He shook her hand in parting.

Anastasiya gave a knowing smile, then turned and strode from the room. O'Connor watched her leave. Had she seen through his lies? He realized then that he couldn't be certain. He turned and looked at the young woman standing in the room with him. There was something odd and decidedly malevolent about the way she was looking at him, he decided.

"Could you please follow me, sir?" requested Eden.

She gestured for O'Connor to follow.

◊ ◊ ◊

A short while later, O'Connor sat safely in his rental car and made his way back to the main gate. He slowed to a stop as he approached the wrought iron gates, and for a heart-stopping moment, thought they might not open. Then the gates swung open silently and O'Connor was through, turning right into the quiet street and accelerating away from the mansion. He kept looking in his review mirror. He was not being followed.

He turned the radio on. Animated voices from one of the local station's shows filled the car. The human voices were oddly comforting. His mind ticked over with the enormity of the problem he potentially faced.

Vampires!

Inhuman creatures hunting people, feeding upon their blood. Committing indiscriminate murder. Would that include the innocent? He had no doubt that it would. What was he to do? Turn from the path he had chosen and have his boys hunt these creatures down? But how many were there? How difficult would they be to kill? He realised he had little to go on and no way of acquiring the information he needed.

Getting the information on gangsters had been relatively simple. He had Matthew to thank for that—the young man had been remarkably resourceful, gathering the information and even suggesting potential targets, though quite how he'd managed to attain this information, O'Connor had never ventured to ask. Perhaps it was because he didn't want to know the answer.

More concerning was the thought of losing his boys to one of these creatures. This was a very real possibility, especially if they were to attempt an attack on the mansion again. Should he then just ignore the creatures? Let them be and continue with the work at hand? He had sacrificed so much already in choosing this way—the way to put things back in order. God—the god he had worshiped for so many years—had failed to do just that. So he had taken up the sword, and by doing so, had given up his faith and his soul. Now he faced a choice: turn from his goal and risk everything to rid the world of these creatures or allow them to exist while he continued with his personal crusade?

At least, he reflected, he could trust in his boys again. At least he could have them recommence the settling of accounts and this, for now at least, would be of some meagre consolation.

Anastasiya had watched the car leave in her monitors. By then, of course, she'd known O'Connor was not who he had claimed to be. Lotho had broken into the visitor's black Mercedes while she and the so-called Mr Jameson had talked. He had discovered the car-hire slip in the glove compartment. She smiled to herself.

'Such an amateur!'

Lotho had informed her the moment she had left her visitor and, she supposed, she could have chosen the more direct approach then and there: torture. Lotho was most proficient at dealing with those unwilling to part with information. There was also Eden—not as subtle, yes, but no less effective. She picked up her cell phone and dialled a number.

"Hello, Ms Strajinski, what can I do for you?"

It was Don Stone.

"Mr Stone, you are progressing well with your investigation, I hope?"

"I've got one or two leads," replied Don carefully.

"I have another job for you."

"This have anything to do with the girl?"

"Not exactly, Mr Stone."

"I see. What do you have for me, then?"

"A vehicle registration for a hire car. The car belongs to Sable Car Hire. I am interested in the person who hired the vehicle today."

"Okay, I'll get on it."

"This is most important, Mr Stone. Please give it priority," said Anastasiya.

She followed up with the registration number before hanging up with a succinct "Goodbye, Mr Stone."

16

1887

Excited passengers thronged the decks of the steamship Servia as it moved silently up the Hudson River. Purser George Smythe stood on the upper deck with his coat collar turned up against the cool of the crisp morning air. Ordinarily, he preferred to remain in his quarters and concern himself with the business of the ship's finances, but not on this morning. He stepped forward to the balustrade and looked down at the passengers on the lower deck. Many stood at the ship's rail to stare at the most recent addition to New York, the Statue of Liberty. Most appeared to agree that it was an impressive sight—the crowned visage gazing impassively, the gilt torch held aloft—a symbol of hope to all who arrived in this land of promise.

The ship sailed on toward its berth, the statue passing by its port side, but Smythe had already turned to a more pressing concern. His eyes scanned the sea of faces below for one person. Someone he knew to be responsible for the disappearance of three young men lost on this voyage.

Why, then, had he not exposed this person? The reason was quite simple: Revealing what he knew would expose his own secret. George enjoyed the intimate acquaintance of men. In fact, seducing impressionable young men on these voyages had always given him an illicit thrill, even more so because it happened to be a punishable crime in most countries. The excitement of seducing his next conquest had also alleviated the unbearable tedium of his otherwise mundane job on board ship. But this had changed two weeks into the voyage, when his lust had turned to horror.

George gave an involuntary shudder as he recalled that night. He'd gone to meet Jonathan, his latest beau, at the spot he always used for his romantic liaisons. Upon approaching, he'd been alerted by the sound of a struggle in the dark. Rather than rush in, he'd crept forward and been confronted with a sight he'd never forget. It was his lover pinned effortlessly to the deck by a young woman. He'd watched transfixed in terror as she'd gorged on her victim's blood until finally his struggles had weakened and then ceased. Her hunger sated, the young woman had lifted the dead man with an ease that belied her slender frame and tossed him overboard. She'd then turned and looked directly to where George hid in the shadows yet had made no move toward him. For what felt like an eternity, she'd stood silently until finally she'd turned, and with a disdainful laugh, walked off into the night.

He had seen the stuff of nightmares—a monster walking amongst them, preying upon whomever she wanted. And what could he say without sounding like a madman, or worse, have his secret life revealed? No. It was better that he remained silent. And better yet to watch her leave the ship to be swallowed up in the mass of humanity that was America. Anywhere but here, he thought.

George froze. A young woman looked back at him, her ice-blue eyes regarding him with an open malevolence. She was strikingly attractive, blonde hair styled to complement her elegant dress—the very latest in European fashion. It was her—the same, yet so different from that night. He found himself unable to look away from her penetrating glare.

Then, as suddenly, she turned away and he was free. He stepped back from the balustrade and breathed out.

Would his erstwhile lover or the other two men ever be missed? He thought not. The fact that the men had been from steerage rather than first class meant the Company would probably be able to keep the whole affair quiet.

'They'll probably just put it down to falling overboard due to drunkenness,' he thought bitterly.

In any event, it didn't matter. He'd already decided this would be his final voyage.

17

Tammy Sloane walked out of Dan's Fitness Centre on an exercise high, yet despite this, she still felt unsatisfied.

She'd just spent the best part of two hours on her daily workout. Today it had been high-intensity circuit training followed by forty-five minutes of yoga. She was proud of the fact that she never missed a workout. That and watching what she ate meant that at thirty-three, Tammy had a body any twentysomething swimsuit model would envy.

In the parking lot, two middle-aged housewives passed her on their way to the next exercise class. She opened the door of her red sports car and looked back, casting a critical eye over the comfortably overweight women. She'd never get like that, she promised herself. No, she enjoyed looking the way she did, and she enjoyed the way men looked at her. True, her D-cup breasts were courtesy of Dr Alan Jackson of Beverly Hills, but the rest was all her own hard work.

She slid behind the steering wheel and closed the car door. A turn of the ignition filled the car interior with Beyoncé and a blast of cool air from the A/C. She sat for a moment, enjoying the crisp air caressing her flushed skin. Ordinarily she would have taken a shower at the gym rather than leave wearing her perspiration-soaked spandex, but she was horny. All the way through 'downward facing dog' and 'cobra,' she had thought of nothing else than getting into the shower with Don. Now she could almost feel the warm water cascading over their entwined bodies as they fucked.

Tammy smiled. She'd had her share of lovers, but Don was something else. She put the sports car into gear and pulled out of the parking spot.

A few minutes later found her negotiating the midtown traffic. She punched Don's private number into the cell mounted on her dash. The phone rang a few times before Don answered with a casual: "Hello?"

"Hi, lover," purred Tammy. "I'm just leaving the gym, all hot, sweaty, and horny. I thought about getting a shower at your place. Care to join me?"

There was a pause.

"Now's not a good time."

Tammy frowned.

Now's not a good time? What the fuck did he mean, not a good time?

"Oh, I think now is the perfect time, Don. And I'll make it more than worth your while."

"Look, Tammy, I'm on an important case, so now's not a good time."

"Are you fucking someone else?"

There was a dangerous edge to her voice.

"Why would you say that?"

"You don't want to fuck me, so you must be fucking someone else."

"I'm not fucking anyone else," said Don. "I've got a deadline to meet, that's all."

"A deadline? You've never had one of those before. She a redhead?" persisted Tammy.

"Jesus, woman!" snapped Don. "When I say I'm on something important I mean just that. Just give me a few days!"

He put down the receiver without waiting for her reply.

"You fucking sonofabitch!" screamed Tammy at the mute cell on her dash, her face twisted with indignant anger. She reached over to press the redial then stopped herself.

'You sonofabitch. That's fine,' she decided.

If he had something more important, then fuck him. She'd have him crawling on his hands and knees begging for it the next time, she promised herself.

"That's the way it's gonna be, lover. Gonna make you crawl, baby," Tammy sang over the beat pumping from the car stereo before running out of made-up lyrics and settling for humming the tune instead.

The next song was slower, a love song. Tammy's mood became more reflective. What was he up to? Was he hiding something? She was under no illusions about Don Stone. It'd taken a few dates before he'd come clean about what he did for a living, but by then, she'd already found out for herself, having had another PI investigate him. Don hadn't, of course, mentioned that he was working for her husband, but then she was not so naïve as to believe otherwise.

It was in her interest to keep this man close, and if she got to enjoy fucking him and watching him fuck her husband out of his money at the same time, then so much the better. She'd come a long way from being Mary Ann Jones. That girl had been dirt-poor. White trash trapped in a small town with no prospects. That was a girl with blood on her hands. Revealing that secret would ruin her. Despite his assurances, had Don still been investigating her? Dig into anyone's past deep enough and you were sure to find some dirt. Had he discovered her secret? Did he know?

She needed to know. She'd have to see him tonight, she decided. That or spend a sleepless night wondering what he knew. One thing was for sure: She'd be damned if she'd let Don or anyone else threaten everything she'd worked so hard for. Tammy accelerated toward home with Don Stone set firmly in her sights.

◊ ◊ ◊

Anastasiya sat in front of a row of flickering monitors. One screen held her interest—it showed her acolytes training. She watched as Eden put Lilith and Meredith through a series of combat moves. It was important for her acolytes to explore the physical feats their new selves were capable of, and to understand their limitations. She knew how intoxicating the virus's gift could be. The apparent superhuman strength, increased agility, and heightened senses, all coupled with an almost limitless energy—a heady mix for any human to digest. The fact the virus had changed them to satisfy its own need for human blood might not occur to them.

At least, not at first. That realization would only occur to them later. When it did, they would either learn to accept or begin to resent their new lives. But Anastasiya would not, could not, allow resentment to fester within her progeny. Resentment led to anger, and from that, to a nihilistic desire to destroy all life.

Killing people indiscriminately could only lead to their existence being discovered, and death the only outcome she or her kind could expect. Anastasiya had always dealt with any of her acolytes she suspected of this anger swiftly. This usually meant simply killing them. Why, then, had she not eliminated Bethany? She was not certain. Perhaps she had seen something of herself in the stubborn girl. Or perhaps it was because at first Bethany had accepted, embraced even, her new self. Besides Eden, Bethany had been with her longer than any other, and so she had counted her amongst her most trusted. Only recently had she noted Bethany's change in mood. Had she been influenced by one of the newer converts? Or had the endless cycle of hunting and feeding finally eroded her conviction? Anastasiya had no way of knowing the answer to that question—Bethany had ceased to exist. What she was certain of however, was the result of Bethany's indiscretion—the loss of her precious acolytes and the potential danger that the killers would expose her to the world.

Her cell phone rang. She looked at the number. It was Donald Stone.

"Good evening, Mr Stone."

"Hello, Ms Strajinski," answered the PI. "I have the information you requested."

Anastasiya smiled.

"You do not disappoint, Mr Stone," she said.

"Thank you," said Don. "I'll admit, though, that I'm a little baffled as to what this has to do with the girl."

"This is not related to that case," replied Anastasiya testily. "It is a favour for a friend, that is all. Do you have a name, Mr Stone?"

There was a slight pause before Don answered.

"The vehicle was hired by Father Samuel O'Connor. He's the priest at St Augustine's church out at—"

"I know where it is."

"Okay, then, if there's nothing more, I'll say goodbye," responded Don cooly.

"Before you go, Mr Stone, the photos of the two men I emailed you earlier today," began Anastasiya. "Have they provided you with a potential lead? Some information which might get you closer to finding the girl?"

"Not yet," replied Don. "But I'm confident I'm on the right track. Now if you'll excuse me, there is the matter of a deadline I have to meet."

"I'm glad you have not forgotten your commitment to me," said Anastasiya. "Because I certainly have not. Goodbye, Mr Stone."

She hung up. Don placed his cell phone on the coffee table in front of him.

'That Strajinski broad is one cold bitch,' he thought to himself.

He sat back on the settee and stared blankly at the flickering images on the TV promoting the latest must-have item. Infomercials. These were the modern-day pimps who fed society's greed.

He reflected on what he had on the girl thus far. It wasn't much. He knew her name. He knew she was linked to Mendez, and that Mendez had killed at least fourteen girls. The two suspects linked to the da Silva hit just happened to be the same two men in the cropped security photos Strajinski had emailed him. He knew the girl had to be linked to these two men. Confused rich kid or not, she certainly appeared to enjoy some dangerous company. Or at least have a penchant for getting mixed up with the wrong type of people.

He'd drawn a blank on Mendez's whereabouts. The man had simply dropped off the radar. It was as if he'd ceased to exist. Had he been killed by the two men? Considering what had happened to Joe da Silva, it was a very real possibility. So if they had killed him, how had that happened?

Don pondered the possibilities.

Let's suppose the girl had figured out Manny was planning to murder her, he thought. Suppose she'd managed to get away from him. Where would she go? Back to the school? It was the most logical conclusion. Suppose, then, that Manny had come after her, only to run into the two killers waiting for him. How had they known he'd be there? The Strajinski broad? No. He discounted that immediately. Why even involve him if she'd hired two hit men? Obvious, really, but an idea which had to be discounted.

This left the girl, Faith. Had she organized a hit on Mendez? If that were the case, where did she know the two men from? More to the point, who in the hell were they? For some reason, he got the impression they were ex-military. Problem was, he had no way of confirming this. He could hardly go back to Jack now and ask him to get the information, especially considering he'd already informed him that these men had played no part in his case.

So Mendez, a blank, probably dead. The two men, nothing to go on. The girl, a name—Faith, but other than her probable connection to all the men, nothing. Then there was the headmistress, Strajinski. She was the only link between the other four. A thought occurred to him then: The priest? Could he also be involved in this mess? The fifth person in this growing web of deceit. Suppose he was involved. How had the headmistress gotten a lead on him? There were a lot of unknowns, but Don was certain of one thing. Ms Strajinski knew more than she was letting on. He'd been in the game long enough to know when someone was hiding something. What was she up to? What was her angle? Given the time, he'd have done some digging into who this headmistress really was. But at this moment, he didn't have the luxury of time. Two days left to find the girl and no solid leads.

'Except for O'Connor, that is,' he reminded himself.

The priest had to be involved—every fibre of his instinct felt it.

'Well," thought Don to himself. "There's no time like the present. I think I'll take a drive down to see O'Connor now.'

He picked up his cell phone and stood up from the settee. At that moment, the door to his apartment opened. Don turned quickly, going to one knee to reach for the revolver in his ankle holster then stopped. It was Tammy.

"Jesus, Tammy, don't you ever knock?" growled Don.

He holstered the small revolver and stood up.

Tammy pouted seductively.

"Now is that the way to treat your favourite girl?" she purred. "Especially when she's gone to all this trouble?"

She let the overcoat she'd been wearing slip down off her shoulders. Apart from the thigh-length nylon stockings and garter belt, she was naked. Don noticed that she'd shaved almost all her pubic hair and had trimmed the remainder into the shape of a heart poised enticingly above the cleft of her sex. Pure porn star. He'd have to follow up on the priest in the morning, he promised himself.

◇ ◇ ◇

Faith lay in the dark and stared distractedly up at the ceiling. It was late. The experiences of the day had left her feeling physically and emotionally drained, yet the comfort of sleep eluded her. Shooting the vampire who had tried to kill Matt had felt right. John killing Manny had felt justified. She'd joined John and Matt because with them, she no longer felt helpless and afraid. The idea of going after drug dealers and pimps had been appealing—payback for the hell she'd gone through these past few months. She'd felt empowered by the thought of setting things to right. But watching Matt gun down the prostitute and the boy had destroyed that feeling. The idea of setting things right and the reality of following through on that idea had turned out to be so very different.

She wondered if O'Connor would have a change of heart if he were to see his boys in action. Not that it mattered. The priest could keep his private war; she wanted no part in it. The real question was, would O'Connor let her walk away? How far-gone was he? Would he, *could* he, as a man of God, give the order to have her eliminated? She knew Matthew would not hesitate once instructed to.

But not John. She felt sure of that. Not because he was attracted to her—she could see that he was—but because it was not in his nature. Faith realised that not knowing how O'Connor would react left her with only one choice: run. Therein lay her predicament. Where could she run to? Back home? No. Go back on the street? Fuck no!

So, she was stuck—for the moment, at least. There was, of course, the option of convincing John to come with her. Play on his affection for her. But this presented its own problem. She liked him. She liked him a lot. At least, she felt as though she did. Having realized her predicament of late, she'd begun to question her feelings for John. Had she become attracted to him because deep-down, she'd realized he might be her only means of escape?

'You bitches are all the same. You use that pussy to control men. That's how you get what you want. I've had to work for everything in life, and you just shake that ass, and it all falls in your lap,' the spiteful leering face of her Uncle Pete growled inside her head.

Faith sat up, goosebumps on her skin. She shivered. A person could run all they wanted, but no one ever escaped their past. Our minds made sure of that, dredging up unwanted memories in cold technicolour flash-back. She hated herself then. Hated herself for doubting. Faith shook her head. Either you let your inner- demons beat you or you beat them.

She swung her legs over the side of the bed and got up. She would go to him now. Not for sex—that would just compound her own doubt—but for comfort. She wanted to feel the warmth that only human contact could give. She wanted comfort, and if she hated herself for needing that, right now she didn't give a fuck.

Faith opened the door to John's room as quietly as she could. She slipped inside and closed the door carefully behind her.

"John, are you awake?" she whispered.

"Yeah, I'm awake," replied John quietly. "I couldn't sleep."

"Can we talk?"

Faith didn't wait for a reply and walked quietly over to the side of the bed.

"Sure," he said.

She sat on the edge of the bed. She could almost make out his features in the darkness.

"Today, Matthew shooting the boy like that," she began. "It kinda freaked me out."

"I'm not surprised," said John. "To tell you the truth, it's got me thinking, too."

"Oh?"

"What? You think I always go around killing just anyone?"

John sounded annoyed.

"No, it's not that. I mean, I don't," replied Faith carefully. "I just thought you'd be used to it by now."

"I did, too. Fact is, every other time, it's just been us and a bunch of bad guys with guns."

"You mean drug dealers?"

"Yeah, mostly. I suppose I've been a fool to believe something like this wouldn't ever happen."

"You mean that someone innocent might get killed?"

There was a moment's silence.

"Yes."

"What now?" asked Faith.

John shrugged in the dark.

"I'm not sure," he said. "You know, today, I almost shot that kid. You stopped me. That's when I realised."

"Realised?"

"That somehow I'd lost something of myself," replied John. "You know, it's not easy to just up and kill a person. To do it, you have to find some way of justifying your actions. Even then, even when you've justified the reason to yourself, actually pulling the trigger is a whole other matter. It helped me to see them as something less than human. You know, to put them in the same category as, say, murderers or paedophiles. I mean, what those people do to others causes so much pain and suffering. It destroys so many lives. Ridding the planet of them seems reasonable, especially when you've convinced yourself. So you kill one, then you kill two. Each time it gets that much easier to just point the gun and pull the trigger. Then one day, you're standing in front of a frightened kid, and he seems no different from the last person you killed."

"I'm sorry," said Faith quietly.

"Don't be," said John. "I'd be fool to think that going after the dealers the way we have has made me any better than them. I started out thinking I was going to make a difference. Maybe, in some small way, I have. But the fact is, I can't see it. Not now. All I can see is a man aiming a gun at a kid begging for his life."

"You mind if I join you?" she asked carefully.

"Uh, okay..."

His voice failed to hide his surprise.

Faith slipped into the bed alongside him.

"Just so we're clear—this isn't going to lead to sex. I just needed to be near you, and I figured maybe you needed to be near someone too," said Faith.

She placed her head on his chest.

They lay there in the dark, she listening to the steady beat of his heart, and he content to feel her warm body near to him.

◊ ◊ ◊

The house had a distinct modernist architectural style—steel and concrete components combined to form a functional building with sharp aesthetic lines. Set in the hills of the upmarket suburb, it appeared no different from any of its equally pretentious neighbours. Had any of the suburb's wealthy inhabitants chosen to look beyond their gilded cages, they might have noted at least two things that set the owner of this house apart from them: First, the high number of security cameras sited at various locations around the property; second, the two large well-dressed men that lurked menacingly near the remote-controlled main gate. The rear of the building extended out to overlook the lower terraced garden dominated by a long rectangular pool. A window, spanning ceiling to floor, ran the length of this part of the house to give an unrestricted view of both the pool area and the valley beyond.

Dragan Millovic stood at the window and watched two nubile blondes frolic in the well-lit pool below. Their play had that faux-sexy, performative self-awareness which revealed they knew he was watching. He looked beyond the girls to where the myriad of twinkling lights revealed the extents of the city that lay sprawled over the valley. One day, it would all be his.

Dragan smiled. One day.

Matthew stared at the back of the gang boss's head. Millovic had ignored him for the better part of five minutes now. This and the fact that he also chose not to face Matt were intentional. It certainly had nothing to do with any mutual trust. The armed bodyguard that lurked in the corner of the room attested to the true extent of their relationship. No. This was Dragan's way of telling Matthew he was not considered an equal. Matthew chose to ignore the obvious slight and cleared his throat.

"We carried out the hit as you ordered today," he said carefully.

"The information I gave you was good, yes?" responded Dragan over his shoulder.

"Yes, the information was good."

"You want more, yes?"

Matthew gritted his teeth.

"I want more, yes."

"When this is finished, you will be very rich man," noted Dragan casually.

"That depends. You've only paid me half the agreed amount so far," replied Matthew pointedly.

Dragan turned to face Matt now. He looked annoyed.

"That is what we agree, yes?" growled Dragan. "Half up-front, half when job is finished."

"Oh, I'm not complaining," replied Matthew. "Just pointing out a fact. I always keep my end of a bargain and I'm sure you'll do the same. After all, it was me who came to you with this proposal in the first place."

"Yes. You kill da Silva's people. Make it look like the Mortagua brothers. They start war. When all is over, I move in. You forget one thing."

"What's that?"

"War has not started," Dragan said, scowling.

Matthew smiled.

"Oh, it will," he assured. "You just need to give it more time. Let it build to a critical mass. A couple more kills should push da

Silva over the edge. He won't have a choice. It's either that or lose the confidence of his men."

Dragan stroked his chin in contemplation.

"Yes, time," he said. "We will wait, we will see. But soon, I hope."

He walked casually over to the low Luigi Zani-designed coffee table—image was everything—and picked up a large brown envelope.

"Your next target," said Dragan.

He handed the envelope to Matthew.

Matt opened the envelope and briefly scanned the contents. These included a few pages detailing the target address, a list of gang members known to frequent the house, times, dates, and so on. Accompanying the documents were photos of the targeted gang members.

"I'll see it gets done," said Matt.

He pushed the contents back into the envelope.

"Good," said Dragan.

"It's time I headed back," said Matt, turning to leave.

"So, when all is finished, you get what you want, and I get what I want," said Dragan.

Matt turned back to face the gangster.

"Yes," he answered simply.

"What about your partner? What about your priest?"

"I'll take care of them," said Matt.

"Of course," Dragan said, smiling knowingly.

He motioned to the bodyguard.

"Let him out."

He watched Matthew walk from the room, his cold black eyes never leaving his prey.

'Yes, you go now. Soon we talk again, but then it will not be so pleasant for you,' thought Dragan grimly.

He went back to the window and looked down at the two bikini models in the pool. Beautiful women, fast cars, designer suits, fancy houses. This is what America was to him. This is what he'd promised himself years before, fighting in the war-torn streets of Mostar. Accused of war crimes, he'd escaped to the U.S. America, a land where men could be anything they wanted, where anything was possible—at the right price.

The door opened behind him. It was the bodyguard.

"The tracking device. It is installed on his car?" enquired Dragan.

The bodyguard nodded.

Dragan smiled.

"Good," he said.

He'd never intended on honouring his agreement with Matthew in the first place. After all, how could one honour any deal with a person willing to betray their own side? How could anyone trust a traitor? His plan had always been to eliminate Matthew and John once the war between da Silva and the Mortagua brothers was raging.

But then da Silva had approached him a few weeks back with a proposition: Join with him, and together they would eliminate the Mortagua brothers. The deal was that once the Mortaguas were eliminated, they'd split the gang's territory equally. He didn't trust da Silva any more than he trusted Matthew and was sure da Silva would turn on him given half the chance. But he knew da Silva was under pressure and needed the extra firepower, so he and his men were in little danger for the present.

Besides, the agreement with da Silva had allowed him to get close to the man. This made it all the easier to destroy him when the opportunity presented itself later. The fact was, he'd never liked the idea of betting on the unpredictable outcome of war between the rival gangs in the first place. He preferred to rely on something far more certain: his own ability. His new deal with da Silva also meant he could get rid of his real liability sooner than planned.

'Yes, Matthew, we will have a talk soon, and before I'm finished you will be begging to give my money back. Then, when it pleases me, I will cut out your heart slowly.'

He chuckled at the thought of the look on Matthew's face when the blade pierced his chest.

18

Srebrenica 1995

Korporaal Heymans wrinkled his nose. The stench was inde-scribable.

It was understandable, he supposed, considering the tens of thousands of people crammed into this place. Access to the out-side world had been cut off by the Serbian offensive more than a year ago. In the months following, the Serbs had tightened the noose slowly, taking the small outlying villages one-by-one, forcing more and more terrified civilians to flee to the already-overcrowd-ed town. Enemy artillery routinely shelled the battered settlement. There was no electricity, little running water, and not nearly enough places for all the people to fit.

Even though conditions had deteriorated quickly, it had not prevented ARBiH troops from stubbornly holding on to the town and its surrounds. Inevitably, it was the civilians cowering in their bombed-out homes or makeshift tents who suffered most. What little food and medical supplies made it through went straight to the fighters. The UN security council had declared the town one of its safe areas, and even despatched troops from UNPROFOR, the United Nations Protection Force, to maintain some semblance of order. But this had done little to remedy the situation, and the town had slid inexorably into a vision of hell.

People, emaciated from months of starvation, slunk between the ruins like wretched animals scratching for anything edible. Young women sold themselves for cans of stewed tomatoes, and those with the means gave up every possession for what scraps remained on the black market. The dead lay forgotten in the streets, their bodies slowly decomposing along with the last remnant of everyone's hope.

Heymans looked back at the other men in his four-man squad. They looked demoralized and exhausted, and he suddenly realised they must see the same in him. The Serb attack launched days earlier had easily driven back the weakened Bosniak forces. Outposts of the Dutch UN troops assigned to protect the enclave had also fallen one-by-one, the soldiers either captured or now retreating, as he and his men were, to the Dutch compound. Panic-stricken people streamed past the soldiers, their faces wild with terror. Every now and then, the harsh crack of automatic gunfire rent the air. Somewhere close by, people were being murdered. The sound spurred the stampede on.

A young girl became separated from her mother in the crush and was pushed to the ground. Her mother screamed as she tried desperately to fight her way back to where her daughter lay, but she was powerless against the tide of panicked people, and to Heymans it appeared as though she were moving away from rather than toward her helpless daughter. He threw himself into the mob, shoving this way and that in a determined effort to get to the girl before she was trampled underfoot. Heymans scooped her up and turned his back to shield the terrified child from the mob. The press of peopled seemed to suddenly dissipate and Heymans found himself standing in an almost-deserted street with the young girl in his arms. Her mother stood in front of him.

"Hlava ti," she said simply.

Heymans placed the girl in her arms. Clutching the girl tightly to her chest, the mother turned and walked away down the street. What struck Heymans immediately afterward was the accusatory look the mother had given him as he'd handed her the child.

'You should be protecting us,' she seemed to say. 'Why are you not protecting us?'

Another woman's scream cut through the air. A different scream this time, one of pain mixed with terror. One of his men turned and ran toward the sound.

"Soldaat Mulder!" yelled Heymans. "Halt!"

Mulder ignored him and turned down a side-street. Heymans motioned to the remaining men in his squad and they followed as he led the way after the errant soldier.

The woman screamed again, and Heymans watched as Mulder ducked down another side-street. A shot rang out.

Heymans and his men quickened their pace. They turned into the side-street to find Mulder propped against a wall, clutching his bloody shoulder. He was not alone—a group of heavily armed men stood to one side.

Heymans signalled his squad to halt and looked at the battle-hardened men facing them. They were VRS, the army of the republic of Srpska. He looked to where Mulder lay, then back to the group of enemy soldiers. Besides being festooned with pistols, knives, and grenades, each man carried an assault rifle and at least two were armed with light machine guns. He weighed his options. They were not encouraging. He lowered his assault rifle and raised his hand in a gesture of truce. One of the enemy soldiers stepped forward and signalled him to come to them.

Heymans turned to his men.

"Mannen, wacht hier," he ordered.

Then he walked toward the enemy soldiers stopping as he drew level with Mulder.

"Mulder, ben je oke?" he asked.

Mulder grunted in the affirmative.

Heymans nodded, then recommenced his walk. The enemy soldier who appeared to be in charge signalled him to stop. The man took a step forward. He was short and thickset, with dark crewcut hair and a neatly trimmed beard. His eyes were black as coal.

"You speak English?" the man enquired.

"Yes, I can speak English," replied Heymans carefully.

A woman's terrified wailing escaped from the building immediately adjacent the group of enemy soldiers. Heymans could hear men laughing and he suddenly understood that the woman was being brutally raped.

"The woman, she is a civilian, she—" he began.

"The woman is not your concern," the Serb cut him off.

"But, your men, they cannot—"

"Cannot what? Have a little fun?" challenged the Serb coldly. "Do not worry, corporal, she will be allowed to go after she has finished entertaining my men."

He smiled and nodded to where one of his men stood guard over two civilian men on their knees. The men faced the wall with their hands placed on top of their heads. Heymans saw from their bloodied clothes that they had been beaten.

"Her brothers, however," said the Serb. "Maybe they will not be so lucky today."

"This is not right," countered Heymans. "This is not war."

"Then you have no idea what true war is, corporal," sneered the Serb. "The Ottomans did much, much worse when they ruled this country."

"That was more than a century ago!"

"But for us it is like yesterday."

"That still does not make this right!" snapped Heymans. "You are allowing your men to commit war crimes."

"War crime?" sneered the Serb. "This is not a war crime, this is restitution."

"You are wrong!" protested Heymans. "This, what you are doing, it is wrong!"

The Serb barked a command, and his men quickly brought their weapons to the ready. Heymans heard his men respond in turn, but he knew they were hopelessly outgunned.

"I think our talk is over, Corporal," said the Serb.

He turned and signalled one of his men to join them. This man had a lithe, athletic build, but his eyes were the same jet-black. The Serb turned back to Heymans.

"You and your men can leave your weapons here. You will not be needing them any longer."

"You know we cannot do that!" protested Heymans.

The Serb shrugged.

"Then you will die, corporal. You and your men," he said coldly. "Now, what is it to be?"

A minute ticked by, then another. Heymans could hear the woman moaning and he could hear the men grunting as they took turns. He looked into the eyes of the devil, and he knew he was beaten. The Serb smiled as Heymans placed his weapon on the ground. He looked at Heymans' nametag.

"Corporal Heymans," he read. "I am Dragan Millovic and this is my brother, Goran. Remember us, corporal Heymans, because we are going to remember you."

Florian Heymans quit the Dutch Army a few months after his return from Bosnia. In 2005 he testified against Dragan and Goran at their war crime trial. Both men had disappeared without a trace after the war and were sentenced in absentia. Heymans was found dead in his small apartment a year later. His throat had been slit.

19

Tammy lay in the dark listening to Don's steady breathing. She supposed she could've chosen the more expedient way of getting him to sleep by slipping a few sleeping pills into his dinner, but she hadn't wanted to arouse any suspicion in Don. Besides, fucking him to the point of exhaustion had been so much more fun. Though, had Tammy cared to acknowledge the fact, it wasn't the sex, but the power she felt having the man at his most vulnerable. Her on top, riding him, dictating the pace. Pushing him to the brink only to pull back, hold him there, feel him plateau, then start the teasing once more. An ever-increasing cycle until she chose the moment of release. She, always the one in control.

Tammy had been lying awake the past hour, waiting until she felt certain he was sound asleep. Finally, when she thought it safe, she slipped silently from beneath the covers, stood up, and looked at Don. There was no movement.

Tammy crept over to the small desk in the corner of the bedroom. She knew Don often worked from his apartment and hoped his current case files were there. His laptop lay open on the desk, the screen dimmed in standby mode. She reached over and activated the laptop, light from its screen spilling over the desk to pierce the darkened room beyond. Tammy looked back at the sleeping form dimly illuminated in the wan light. There was still no movement. Good. She looked back at the screen and frowned. She would require password access.

'Shit!'

Tammy hadn't counted on that. She thought for a moment then typed in S-T-A-C-E-Y. Access denied. So, it wasn't his daughter's name. What then? Favourite football team? First car? First pet? The list was endless.

'Fuck it,' she decided.

She turned her attention to the folders that lay to one side of the laptop. Tammy opened the topmost and started flicking through its meagre contents. Arrest sheet, some half-scribbled notes in Don's handwriting, composites, and a few photos. She froze.

Staring back at her from one of the photos was a face from her past. Could it be? She picked up the photo and held it closer to the laptop screen's light. Yes! Her stomach turned. The floor felt as though it were shifting beneath her, threatening to give way. How had he found out? What else did he know? Tammy gripped the side of the desk and steadied herself. Resisting the urge to take the photo, she replaced the folder's contents and pushed it to one side.

Don stirred in the shadows. She froze. Should she risk being caught? No. Not now. Not here. She needed time to think. Don moved again. Tammy crept back across the room and slid beneath the covers.

"You leaving?" mumbled Don sleepily.

"No, lover. Just needed to use the bathroom," answered Tammy soothingly.

She moved closer to snuggle up to him.

Don mumbled something unintelligible and drifted back to sleep.

Tammy lay beside him, her stomach a knot of fear. Except she wasn't Tammy Sloane, she was Mary Ann Jones, dirt-poor and desperate to escape an abusive marriage. Desperate to get out, no matter the cost.

And she had escaped. Or at least, that's what she'd always believed. Until now. What she couldn't figure out was just how her past had caught up with her. How much did Don know? What did he intend doing with the information? He obviously hadn't told her husband, of that much she was certain. So what, then? Blackmail her?

Mary Ann Jones lay in the dark thinking about Don Stone and contemplating what she would need to do if she wanted to remain Tammy, wife to the wealthy and ever-indulgent George Sloane.

Across town stood a goddess upon a raised dais, a dark-red robe draped about her naked body. Her arms were outstretched, pale flesh contrasting starkly with the rich colour of the robe. She held a small ornamental knife in her right. A silver bowl lay before her on a raised, ornately carved stand. The outer surface of the bowl was decorated in an elaborate pattern of intertwined female forms. Anastasiya looked down at the expectant faces of her acolytes. They knelt before the bowl, a sign of their obedience and subservience.

"This is my blood, given so that you may share in the gift of eternal life. When you drink, let it be a reminder of the lasting bond that unites us, and of the trust that I have placed in each of you," intoned Anastasiya.

With a practised movement, she extended her left arm over the bowl and cut across the forearm with the knife. Dark blood flowed freely from the wound into the bowl beneath. The deep cut began to heal, the body's mutated cells working diligently to protect its precious source of life.

Anastasiya lifted the full bowl with both hands and offered it to the first of her chosen. Eden accepted the bowl reverently and lifted it to her lips, drinking deep but careful to leave enough for the remaining two. Anastasiya watched intently as each of the young women drank in turn.

Without her blood, they would die. This ritual, performed every seven days, was a reminder of that truth. She could have chosen to offer her blood without ceremony and allow the act of it to become commonplace. But that would have reduced it to nothing more than a tedious necessity.

Besides, Anastasiya understood the importance of the ritual. It reinforced the bond between each of them and their allegiance to her in turn. Each communion served as a subtle indoctrination of her acolytes into her ideals. Her thoughts would be their thoughts. Their actions merely an extension of her will.

The bowl, now empty, was handed back to Anastasiya who placed it carefully onto the stand. She looked at the three women kneeling before her, each momentarily lost in a trance-like state as the virus within them responded to her blood—an intoxicating high to none but the chosen.

'Now so few,' she thought.

Faces of past acolytes surfaced within her mind's eye, a reminder not only of her past failings but the tenuous nature of all life, even her own. Anastasiya brushed the thought aside irritably. There was no profit to be had in dwelling on the negative. Besides, she had faced worse in times past. Faced worse and survived. This time would be no different. She watched as the kneeling women surfaced from their trances.

"Rise up, my chosen. Come," intoned Anastasiya.

She motioned for the young women to join her.

They followed her through a short passage which led into a room they were all familiar with. A young man lay spread-eagled and naked on the bed, his arms and legs bound to the bedposts. He struggled impotently against the restraints, his desperate cries muffled by a red silk gag. The naked women moved toward the bed with a hypnotic feline grace. They stopped at the foot of the bed, their eyes betraying their bloodlust, and waited for Anastasiya to give her command. The most recent convert, Meredith, was unfamiliar with the ceremony, and so took her lead from the other girls.

"You have satisfied the hunger within your souls, now satisfy the hunger within your bodies," said Anastasiya solemnly.

She turned to look down at the man tied to the bed. She smiled at him.

"I commend your sacrifice."

She turned back to her waiting acolytes and nodded.

The three females fell upon their helpless victim, sinking their fangs into his struggling body and drinking with unrestrained relish. Ordinarily, Anastasiya would have joined them, but the events of recent days had left her with little appetite. Besides discovering the identity of the priest, Don Stone had yet to locate the girl and her accomplices. True, she had allowed Stone five days to find the girl, but his apparent lack of progress was frustrating. She had decided against paying the priest a visit for the present; there was no need to tip their hand to the enemy just yet, especially as she was unsure how or even if the priest was connected to the other three.

Anastasiya watched the girls feed as she deliberated. The tone of Stone's voice during their last conversation had betrayed a hint of unease. Did the man know more than he was letting on? And if so, what did he know?

She turned and walked from the room. It was decided: If she heard nothing from the man by the close of business tomorrow, she would pay him a visit. One look into his eyes and she would know. One look would be enough to decide his fate.

20

I t was morning. Faith lay against John. They were both naked, 'no sex' having turned into 'sex' sometime during the night. She listened to his steady breathing and smiled to herself. The sex had been nice, she decided. No earth-shattering orgasm, no gymnastic Kama Sutra—just two lost people reaching out to each other, finding comfort through the act of physical intimacy. Nervous hands touching, tentatively exploring—like two awkward teenagers doing it for the first time.

She wondered how this would complicate things and decided she didn't care. Right now, at this moment, she felt content. Did John feel the same way? She wanted to turn over and look at him but was afraid to, afraid that their skin breaking contact would somehow undo everything. Faith heard Matthew get up in the next room, then felt John stir.

"You awake?" he asked quietly.

Faith hesitated a moment then replied without turning to him. "Yes."

John put his free arm around her and pulled her closer. He buried his face in her long dark hair, breathing in her scent.

"Don't worry about Matthew. I can handle him," he said.

"It's not him I'm worried about," said Faith softly.

"You mean Father O'Connor?"

His voice betrayed his own uncertainty regarding the priest.

Faith moved then, turning round to face John.

"Yes."

"I'll have to figure that out when the time comes, I suppose."

"Look, last night," she said quickly. "It wasn't planned or anything. I mean, I don't want to come between you and the others. We can pretend like this never happened if that's what you want. You know, go back to just being friends."

Faith searched his expression.

"Well, that would certainly make things less complicated," agreed John.

He saw the look of disappointment on her face.

"But then I never liked doing things the easy way," he added quickly. "Besides, you've got a nicer ass than Matt."

"Asshole."

She hit his arm playfully.

He grinned.

"Hey! Careful. I bruise easy," he said.

The mood was broken at the sound of the toilet flushing at the end of the hall. They heard Matthew walk past the door and into the kitchen.

"Suppose we'd better get going," said John.

He kissed Faith tenderly on the forehead, then rolled over and got up. Faith sat up, pulling the sheet around her. She suddenly felt self-conscious about being naked. John, on the other hand, appeared unconcerned by his nakedness, stretching with a contented yawn before strolling over to the chair where he'd discarded his jeans the night before. Faith watched as he pulled on his jeans (noting with no surprise that he didn't bother with underwear), then his T-shirt. He looked back, perplexed that she hadn't moved from the bed. It then occurred to him that despite the intimacy of the previous night, Faith still wanted her privacy.

He smiled apologetically.

"Um, I'll go see how Matt's getting on with the coffee," he smiled.

Faith waited for John to leave before reaching over the side of the bed to where her T-shirt lay. Moments later, she was back in her own room, thankful that she hadn't bumped into Matt on the way. She realised that he probably knew that she and John had spent the night together but wanted some time to compose herself before having to look at the contempt on his face. In another life she'd been forced to endure that same look from men just like Matthew—men ready to use her to satisfy their carnal appetites without any regard for her as a person, who treated her like a living blowup sex doll. Never again.

Faith regarded herself in the mirror. A young woman of quiet confidence stared back. She had not let the cruel twists and turns of her life destroy her. She was a survivor, and she'd be damned if she'd let a prick like Matthew get her down.

The car's air conditioning struggled valiantly to cool the steamy interior against the uncompromising glare of the mid-morning sun. Don Stone shifted uncomfortably in his seat. It was more an attempt to alleviate the numbed sensation in his backside than rid himself of the equally irritating feeling of sweat-soaked boxers glued to his ass. He'd always hated this part of the job.

He looked over to where Father O'Connor's modest vehicle stood parked against the opposite kerbside. His eyes drifted beyond the car, over the well-tended grounds and prerequisite fountain to the imposing structure that was St Jerome's hospital. Still no sign of the priest. He took a sip from his takeaway coffee and grimaced.

Didn't anyone know how to make a good coffee anymore?

Don's cellular started ringing in the passenger seat. The ringtone was Marvin Gaye's "I Heard It Through The Grapevine," and to Don that meant information from one of his contacts. Was the ringtone inference too clichéd? Almost certainly, but then Don didn't give a fuck what people thought—he saw the humour in it, and that's what counted. He reached over and picked up the cell.

"Brad, my man," he said casually. "What have you got for me?"

His eyes didn't stray from O'Connor's car.

"You didn't give me much time, Don," said Brad. "So probably not as much as you'd like."

"Never mind," said Don. "Just give me what you've got."

"Anastasiya Strajinski," began Brad. "No social security number. No driver's licence. Makes it kind of difficult to get a lead on where she's from."

"What about immigration?" asked Don.

"Checked that out too. No record of her ever coming to this country," replied Brad. "Are you sure she's foreign?"

"Accent's pretty strong but then I suppose she could be faking it, along with her name."

"Well, if her name's fake, she's been using it for a while now. The property was left to her forty-odd years ago as part of a trust fund. She established the finishing academy soon after that."

Don blinked. Forty-odd years ago? Anastasiya Strajinski didn't look a day over thirty. Either that or she had one hell of a plastic surgeon.

"Are you sure about the date?" he asked.

"Yep," replied Brad confidently. "The fund is administered by a law firm out of New York. Name of Whitcomb, Newton, and Moore. Established 1867."

Don frowned.

"Is that it?"

"Afraid so," said Brad. "I can keep digging if you want."

"Oh, I want. Find out what you can about this trust fund. When was it established and by who? Check the property too. I want to know its history. I want to know who owned it before."

"No problem," said Brad. "Might take me some time, though. Could get a little costly."

His voice betrayed his concern about Don's ability to pay.

"I got the money, Brad," replied Don testily. "Just don't fuck around too long, you got that?"

He hung up. His instinct had been right. There was something off about the whole stinking affair.

'Headmistress, my ass,' thought Don.

Who the fuck was this woman, really? And more importantly, what the hell was her angle? At that moment, he caught sight of Father O'Connor returning to his car. Don pushed the speculation to one side and started his car. He waited till O'Connor had pulled away from the kerb before moving out into the traffic. A well-timed U-turn had him following the priest, carefully keeping at least one other car between him and O'Connor.

'Well, let's see where you go now,' thought Don.

◊ ◊ ◊

The morning had passed uneventfully enough. Matthew, as it turned out, had either not noticed Faith's and John's night together, or had simply preferred not to comment.

Whichever the case, Faith had been relieved. She'd helped John clear away the breakfast dishes before leaving them to the business of stripping and cleaning the weapons, and had retreated to the relative privacy of an old swing chair on the back porch. Here she'd curled up with one of the few books she'd discovered in the house. Judging by the title, Pride and Prejudice, the book had to have belonged to a previous occupant. The name Jane Austen meant little to her, but she'd seen the movie, and so had picked it as the best from the limited choice available. Besides, the other books—Dead Souls and Metamorphosis—looked like heavy reading.

As it turned out, the book wasn't that easy of a read, and she found her mind wandering to more immediate concerns. It didn't help, she supposed, that she could hear John and Matt talking in the kitchen, though their words were frustratingly indistinct. Were they discussing her? Was John attempting to find out how Matt would feel about him quitting?

She put aside the book and let her gaze drift over the backyard's long grass and neglected flowerbeds to where the old tree stood. The previous morning spent talking with John under its shade seemed a lifetime away now. In the time since, she'd been witness to the murder of four people and become romantically involved with a killer. Not that any of the events preceding that had been any less surreal; she'd left her small-town life in search of, as the song went, 'something more'. This certainly wasn't what she'd bargained for.

Then again, what could anyone really bargain for in life? She suddenly realised that she could hear another voice in the kitchen. The voice sounded angry. It was the priest, O'Connor. How long had he been there? Faith hesitated. Should she go into the kitchen? Another raised voice joined in—Matt's this time.

'Fuck it,' she thought. 'Better go face the music.'

Father O'Connor stood at the end of the kitchen table, his hands gripping the backrest of the nearest chair. He looked down at the two young men. Matt wore an unrepentant expression and John was visibly confused.

"My instruction was clear. Nothing was to proceed until further notice. Why did you choose to ignore my simple instruction?" demanded O'Connor angrily.

"I'm sorry, Father," replied John. "What instruction?"

He turned and looked at Matt quizzically.

Matt shrugged unapologetically.

"The opportunity was slipping away," he said. "So I made the call, and then we made the hit."

"The call was not yours to make, Matthew," stressed O'Connor.

Matt leaned forward in his chair and glared defiantly at the priest.

"Whose, then? Yours?" he snapped.

O'Connor's knuckles whitened as he tightened his grip on the chair's backrest.

"Yes! Mine!" he thundered. "That has been our agreement from the very beginning. This is my battle, my crusade to cut out the cancer I see in this community. You chose to join me, Matthew. You and John. You are my instruments of justice. I think I need not remind you that it is my funding that allows our work to continue. *My* funding!"

"Yes, you're funding us," growled Matt. "But it's still our necks on the line every time we go out! You say we are your instruments? We are flesh and blood, not mindless pawns. Don't you forget that."

It was Matt's last comment which made O'Connor pause. This and the fact he'd noticed Faith hovering near the kitchen doorway. He motioned for the girl to join them.

"Please, come in and sit," said the priest.

There was a pause as Faith entered the kitchen and took a seat at the table. She offered a weak smile.

"Did I miss anything important?"

She hoped her understatement might help defuse the tension.

John glared angrily at Matthew.

"Important? That depends," he replied testily. "If you mean, is someone here playing by a different set of rules, then yes, I think you missed something important. What do you think, Matt?"

Matt leaned forward.

"Last time I checked, this wasn't a game, John. It's not a game and there are no rules, it's just life or death. I'm the one, John. I'm the one risking my neck to get the information we need. You think that's easy? I get the wrong information and then what? Our next job ends up being our last. You think about that," he said stressing each point with a tap of his index finger on the table between them.

John pushed himself back from the table.

"You still should've discussed it with me Matt," he said reasonably.

"Would you have agreed to the hit if I had?"

"Maybe."

Matt laughed derisively.

"That's bullshit and you know it."

"Fuck you," retorted John.

"That is enough!" snapped O'Connor.

The priest allowed the silence which followed to linger a moment before continuing.

"Fighting amongst ourselves will get us nowhere," he said. "What happened the other night has obviously unsettled all of us."

"What happened the other night was real!" interrupted Matt.

He pointed to the others and then to himself.

"John, her, and me, we all saw them. You said you were going to go to that school. Well? What did you find?"

John looked surprised.

"Father," he queried. "You went there?"

Faith could see John felt betrayed. This was not surprising, considering neither O'Connor nor Matt had seen fit to take him into their confidence.

"Yes," replied O'Connor. "I went there. I needed to see for myself. I needed to meet whoever was in charge. I thought that if I looked them in the eye, I would know for sure."

"Know what for sure?" pressed Matt. He knew what O'Connor meant but wanted to hear him admit to it.

O'Connor offered Matt a look of paternal tolerance.

"I wanted to know if what you and John had seen were real," he said quietly. "I wanted to know that I could trust in your judgement once more and, most importantly, judge for myself what it is we might be facing."

"You mean vampires," said Faith.

O'Connor gave a reluctant shrug.

"For want of a better word," he said. "Yes."

A silence descended on the kitchen as they contemplated the priest's words.

"It just doesn't seem real," said John finally. "I mean the other night, I know what I—what we saw, but I still can't get my head around it. It feels like something straight out of the movies."

The priest shrugged again.

"There are more things in heaven and earth than are dreamt of in our philosophy," he said.

"And what does that mean?"

"It means," said Faith. "That there are things in this world beyond human comprehension. It's taken from Hamlet."

She noted everyone's surprise.

"Miss Stevenson's class—about the only thing I looked forward to in school," she explained.

Matt raised his eyebrows in mock-surprise.

"Well, aren't you full of surprises," he sneered.

He turned to O'Connor.

"So, now you understand they're real. What are we gonna do about them?"

"Nothing. At least for the present," replied O'Connor, raising his hand to quiet Matt before continuing. "We need time to prepare, Matthew. We need time to fully understand what it is we are facing."

"I shouldn't think it could be that difficult," said Matthew. "We killed five the last time and that was no problem."

"You say no problem?" objected John irritably. "If I recall correctly, you needed a lot of help."

Matt shot him a venomous look but held his tongue. The priest chose to ignore the exchange between the two men and continued with his reasoning.

"We would probably require a few weeks, perhaps a month at most," he said. "Given this time, we should be able to acquire the relevant information we need—things like how many of them there are, the layout of the house and grounds, the appropriate weapons, and anything else which may aid us in destroying them."

"You think we have that long? Every day we do nothing is one more day for them to get stronger. They could be out there right now, making more of their kind. We need to act sooner," urged Matthew.

"We don't even know that they can make more of their kind, Matt," countered John. "This isn't like the movies. The other night, we didn't need silver bullets or anything. Sure, it took a lot to take them down, but they didn't get up in the end."

"Your point?"

"My point is they may not work the way we think. They may not be able to turn us into one of them by simply draining our blood," reasoned John. "Think about it. If it were that easy, they'd be everywhere."

"You saw what was happening to Mendez!" countered Matt. "What about that? Something sure was happening to him. He was changing."

John shrugged. He was not about to concede the point.

"Maybe," he said. "Or maybe he was just dying. We'll never know for sure. I know one thing, though—if they had the power, they would already be the masters of this world and we little better than their food. That's nature for you—the dominant species will always subjugate the weaker."

"Is that so?" sneered Matt. "Well, this is one human who ain't gonna wait around for that to happen."

"Be patient, Matthew," said O'Connor calmly. "Everything will happen in due course."

"Do we really need to go back there?" interjected Faith.

It was a not a question motivated by fear.

The men turned to her.

"What do you mean, 'do we need to go back'?" snorted Matt. "How else you think we're gonna do this? Knock on the door and politely ask them to snack on the local wildlife instead?"

Faith shrugged.

"I dunno," she said. "Maybe get them to come to us? You know, to a place we get to choose."

She appeared surprised none of the others had thought of what, at least to her, appeared obvious.

John laughed out loud.

"You can't deny, she's got a point," he said.

O'Connor eyed the young woman with a newfound respect.

"Yes, indeed," he said. "Given the right motivation, these creatures might just be tempted to do just that. The question is, what would that motivation be?"

"And we'd have to think about where to lay the trap," added John. He winked at Faith.

"Weapons," said Matt. "We'll need better weapons for sure."

The fact he'd chosen not to argue or comment negatively was a tacit agreement with Faith. Something he'd never readily admit to openly.

"You have been resourceful in this regard before, Matthew," said O'Connor. "I'm sure you will not fail to deliver this time. I will ensure you have the necessary funds in a few days."

The priest looked about the table and was encouraged to see the look of quiet determination on the faces of his protégés and the girl. Perhaps, he thought, this had all been pre-ordained. This was a challenge, sent to forge his team into a weapon even more deadly than before. Did this include the girl? Perhaps it did, but only time would tell.

"It is time I took my leave. I will be in contact in a day or two. Until then, please remain vigilant," concluded O'Connor.

"Thank you, Father," said John. "I think I can speak for all of us by saying that it's good to have a clear goal again."

He stood up to follow O'Connor from the room, with Faith close behind. Matt chose to remain seated, but his demeanour revealed that he felt as relieved as John, although for an entirely different reason. Their vampire problem had threatened to derail his carefully laid plans—the sooner these creatures were out of the way, the sooner he'd get to finalising the deal with Millovic, and the closer to becoming very rich indeed.

Faith stood on the porch and watched John walk with O'Connor to the front gate. The pair exchanged a few words before the priest walked to his car and got in. John remained at the gate to watch O'Connor drive away then turned and walked back to the girl waiting on the porch. He saw the half-expectant look on her face and answered with an apologetic shrug.

"I wanted to," he said. "But I just couldn't. Not now. Not when he's got so much on his mind."

"I understand. I mean, part of me still wanted you to say something even though I knew..." her voice trailed off.

"Yeah, I kinda thought you might want me to," said John. "Look, sneaking around is probably not the best way to handle this, either. I reckon maybe we just put it out there and let them deal with it. Besides, it's not like we need their permission."

Faith smiled.

"I have no problem with that," she said.

She supposed this was at least a start, but there was so much more she wanted to say to him. 'Let's leave this place now! Forget about trying to fight vampires. Forget about taking on drug gangs. Just go someplace else and start afresh, together.'

Would she ever get to say these things to him? She hoped she would, hoped there would be a time when she'd be able to talk to him about a life beyond this. A life together. She stood on tiptoe to kiss him, placing her arms about his neck as she did.

Don chuckled quietly to himself.

"Well, fuck me!" he muttered.

He watched the young couple from the cover of the trees. The girl he'd been searching for these past days stood there clear as day. He also recognized the man standing next to her. He was one of da Silva's suspected killers. It was also obvious by the way the two interacted that she was no one's captive. The pair went back into the house arm-in-arm.

Don considered his options. Should he just bust in, grab the girl, and take her back to the Strajinski broad, no questions asked? Or should he continue to stake out the place, keep watching and try figure his next play? Doing the former guaranteed easy money, but the latter meant being able to look himself in the mirror.

Don didn't need to think long. He pulled his cell from his pocket and dialled a number.

"Brad," he began. "Yeah, hold on, it's not about that. I didn't expect you to have the information so soon. I need something else from you—can you find out who owns a property? 101 Long Pine Drive."

He waited as Brad accessed Google maps.

"Yeah, that's the place, right out in the sticks. I need the info ASAP, thanks."

Don replaced his cell and looked back at the house. He'd left his car parked along the driveway of one of the few properties scattered along the quiet gravel road but realised sooner or later he'd have to move. That, or risk having some nosey homeowner confront him for trespassing.

He shifted uncomfortably against the tree and cursed himself mentally for being unprepared, again. He thought about what he'd just seen. Had he suspected the priest might somehow be involved? Once he'd got O'Connor's name for the headmistress, that had always been a possibility. But did he expect to find the priest connected to two suspected killers and the girl? Even in this game, this was one for the record books. More importantly, where in the hell did Anastasiya Strajinski fit into all of this? His mind picked through the possibilities.

What if the school was a front for a high-class brothel run by the Strajinski broad? What if the girl, Faith, was working for her? And what if the girl had decided to quit—up and run, without a word? It could be she owed Strajinski a lot of money. Maybe that's all Strajinski wanted: a return on her investment. Or maybe this so-called headmistress answered to someone else. Someone who would not take kindly to having one of their employees quit without notice. Someone who would be expecting an explanation from Strajinski. Someone less-than-forgiving.

Whatever the case, the girl had run, then got mixed up with Mendez before falling in with two suspected killers. But then what of the priest? Where in the hell would he fit into all of this?

Don shook his head as he tried to make sense of everything.

No, there were just too many goddamn unknowns.

He shifted position again and scowled.

Jesus Christ, this was going to be a long, uncomfortable afternoon!

An uneventful hour had passed, and the afternoon sun had started its final decent toward the horizon. Don tried not to look down at his watch—it felt as though time had been reduced to a crawl. His cell buzzed and he pulled it from his pocket and looked at the screen. It was Tammy.

"Hi," he answered, careful to keep his tone neutral.

In truth, he'd started to feel ambivalent about his relationship with Tammy. The sex was incredible, but she'd become way too clingy for his liking.

"Hey, lover," drawled Tammy. "I can't stop thinking about last night. How about a rerun?"

"I'm working," replied Don. "Maybe later."

"I tell you what, I'll come around early and cook dinner. How about it, lover?" pressed Tammy. "Steak, fine red wine, and me for dessert. Me and any way. You. Want. It."

Her voice was husky with illicit promise.

"Oh, I don't know, there's plenty of ways I can think of," drawled Don.

He maintained his visual on the house.

"Well, then, you know where I'll be. Say around seven?"

Don thought for a moment.

'Maybe stick around for an hour or so more, then get home, food, sex, shower, pick up a few things and come back to continue the stakeout.'

Besides, he was pretty sure Brad would confirm what he'd already begun to suspect—that the house belonged to the priest, O'Connor.

"You not getting domestic on me, are you?" he asked.

"No, Don. I just want your cock," purred Tammy. "Seven, sharp and make sure you're on time."

She hung up.

Don shook his head. Who was he to say no to a good fuck?

21

The trio sat and ate their evening meal without speaking. The silence was punctuated now and then by the sound of moths hitting the kitchen window. Faith looked up from her plate of bolognaise and watched with disconnected interest as the insects continued their vain assault on the invisible barrier which prevented them from reaching the light. Did they ever feel frustrated? Battering themselves impotently against that unyielding surface, the source of their desire enticingly always just out of reach. It seemed to her that nature had played a cruel trick on the luckless moth, cursing it with an insatiable need to touch the light, no matter the cost to itself.

'Just like us,' she thought. 'All of us, desperately looking for whatever we think will help fill the void within ourselves. The thing which will make us complete, fix what we think is broken. Only maybe we weren't ever meant to be whole in the first place. Maybe none of us can ever be fixed.'

Maybe that was the whole point. We must accept ourselves for who we are and find peace in that.

"Didn't think my cooking was that bad," remarked John.

Faith turned to John, confused.

"What?"

"It's nothing," he said. "I just noticed you weren't eating, so I thought it might be my cooking."

"No, the food's good."

She shovelled a fork full into her mouth to show she meant it.

"I just got lost in thought," she said. "It's sort of a bad habit of mine. Sorry."

John smiled. He understood.

"Don't apologize. I was just wondering where you'd got to," he said.

Faith smiled at him. She knew then that despite her better judgement, she had fallen in love with him. *Fool of a girl, don't you ever learn?*

"The moths," she said, nodding toward the window.

"It's worse outside with the porch light on," noted John idly.

Matt looked suspiciously at the pair and frowned.

"Does it matter?" he grunted.

"In the bigger scheme of things, probably not," said John. "But we're just making conversation. You, know idle conversation to help the food digest. You should try it."

Matthew chose to ignore John's remark. They continued to eat in silence.

"Actually," began Matt suddenly. "I did want to say something, only I was going to wait till after we'd eaten."

John feigned surprise.

"Oh," he responded deadpan, "So you're finally going to apologize?"

"You're not going to let this go, are you?"

"Should I? You, not filling me in on Father O'Connor's instructions," said John. "But that got me thinking about what else you've been keeping from me."

"Look, you want an apology so badly?" replied Matt. "Then alright, I apologize. It was a one-time thing. The way I saw it, we needed to get the job done, and I didn't see any other way. I was thinking like a professional, which is more than I can say of you these days."

"What do you mean?"

"You really gonna play dumb with me?" said Matt. "You and her."

He jabbed a finger at Faith.

"Both playing house, like nothing else matters. You don't have your mind on the job anymore, John, and that's dangerous."

"That's bullshit and you know it!"

"Guys!" shouted Faith. "Cease fire already!"

She turned to John.

"John, Matt here said it was a one-time thing. Just believe him and let it go."

She turned to Matt.

"Matt, congratulations, you've figured it out. John and I have a thing going. It won't get in the way of anything, so deal with it."

She looked expectantly at the two men.

Matt stared coldly at her. There was a long pause as he considered his options.

"So long as we have an understanding, then I have no problem with it," he said finally.

John sat back in his chair. The tension in the room eased somewhat.

"Fine, apology accepted," he said. "Now, what was it you actually wanted to say?"

"I've got the information on our next target," said Matt.

John leaned forward angrily.

"Christ, Matt," he snapped. "I thought Father O'Connor instructed us to cease fire on the gangs till we settle with the vampires first."

"That he did," Matt said, nodding. "But he also said I should arrange to get better weapons."

"And what has that got to do with making another gang hit?"

"We hit the next drug den and walk away with some top-class equipment," said Matt. "And I'm not talking your run-of-the-mill gangster shit. I'm talking a couple of HK four-one-sixes and maybe even a grenade launcher to boot."

"You forget," noted John grimly. "We go in there and we'll be facing that same firepower. I'm not about to place anyone at unnecessary risk."

He glanced at Faith. Matt shook his head.

"There's no need," he said. "The info I got says that da Silva's called a meet for tomorrow. That means all his captains will have to attend. They'll want to take some of their men along with them. That should mean even fewer people for us to contend with. Besides, there's a back way into this location. There'll be no need to try and bluff our way through the front gate like the last time."

"You really think they'd have that kind of firepower lying around, just waiting for us to go in and pick up?" challenged John.

"Of course. The hardware isn't just lying around," replied Matt. "They'll have it stored somewhere secure. But once we're inside, it shouldn't take much convincing to get one of them to show us where the gear is."

John remained unconvinced.

"If it's so secure, how do you know it'll even be there?"

"Has any of the information I've had so far been wrong?" said Matt. "The stuff will be there, believe me."

"I think we should run this by Father O'Connor," interrupted Faith.

A knot formed in the pit of her stomach. She instinctively distrusted Matt, but realised she had no obvious reason why she should not.

Matt shot Faith a withering look of contempt.

"'We'?'" he responded testily. "I didn't realize you had a say in our plans."

"She was in on the last job," said John. "I reckon that at least gives her the right to question the plan, don't you?"

His tone was uncompromising.

Matt stared flint-eyed at Faith, then turned to John.

"How many missions you and me been on, buddy?" he said. "And I don't just mean for O'Connor, I'm talking back in Afghanistan too."

"Maybe too many," said John. "But that's not the issue here, Matt.

I just think everyone at this table should be able to say their piece."

Matt leaned forward in his chair.

"Look, John," he began, his tone becoming more reasonable. "I just don't think I'd be able to get my hands on that kind of hardware again, that's all I'm saying. You want to take on those vampires with the guns we've got and whatever other shit I manage to get my hands on, then fine, let's do it. I'm up for it, you know that. But once we go in, there'll be no second chances. Let's see how that turns out. One thing is for certain: We won't be able to walk away from the fight so easy, and chances are, one of us will get hurt."

John understood what Matt really meant. Faith was the most inexperienced and the likeliest to get hurt if things turned ugly.

"I'll take my chances," snapped Faith quickly.

She had not missed Matt's inference either and was not about to be used as a bargaining chip by him, of all people.

"No," responded John quickly. "No need for any of us to take unnecessary risks. What information have you got?"

"Father O'Connor said he'd get you the money to buy whatever we needed to fight the vampires," observed Faith. "I don't think he meant for us to do anything like this."

Faith's eyes flashed angrily. She was annoyed at Matt for using John's feelings for her to manipulate him and more annoyed at John's inability to see through the obvious play.

"As I recall, he didn't say not to take out any gang members, either," responded Matt condescendingly. "The fact is, it'd take six months or more for my supplier to locate weapons like these. I don't think we can afford to wait six months, do you?"

"John, we don't have to do this," urged Faith.

"We wait six months, and if we're lucky, we get the firepower we need," said Matt. "Or we hit this place tomorrow and have what we need right now. Then we can go in and take those bloodsucking fuckers out. Sooner rather than later. It's up to you, John, but I know how I'd play it."

"Okay, Matt, I get the point. You win," replied John. "So tell me what you've got."

Faith sat silently and watched as Matt detailed the information on the target house. She felt frustrated at not being able to persuade John to turn down Matt's plan, but realised that anything she said now would only complicate things. And later, when they were alone in bed together? No, she thought to herself, if she truly loved him, she'd not stoop to a postcoital ambush. Besides, doing that would probably play right into Matt's hands, and her relationship with John would suffer.

'Face it, girl, you either stick with your man, or you end up confirming Matt's accusation about you.'

She scowled at Matt.

'You arrogant prick! You think you've got all the answers right now, don't you?'

Faith noted John's businesslike expression as he focused on going through the next day's plan with Matt. It almost seemed as if he were enjoying it. She realised then that getting him to quit this life and go with her was going to be tougher than she'd first thought.

But she also knew she couldn't give up on John. Not just yet. Not until she'd played every card she held. She owed him that much.

◊ ◊ ◊

Don opened the door to his apartment and was greeted with the enticing smell of prime-cut beef on the grill.

"Hi, lover," greeted Tammy cheerily. "I'm almost done. Why don't you go make yourself comfortable?"

She turned back to tending the steaks sizzling on the small portable grill he'd purchased but never gotten around to using.

Don hesitated in the doorway a moment, perplexed. Sure, he'd expected Tammy to be waiting in his apartment, but he hadn't expected her to be cooking, or fully clothed, for that matter. As far as their relationship went, both were firsts.

What the fuck was the broad playing at?

Don closed the front door behind him and walked over to the kitchen counter.

"Everything okay?" he asked.

She looked mildly surprised.

"Of course. Why wouldn't it be?"

"Nothing," he said. "I've just never seen you do anything in the kitchen, that's all."

Tammy picked up a paring knife and waved it playfully in the air.

"Careful, Don, you don't want to upset the chef, especially when she's armed and she's gone to all this effort," she said.

She pointed to the small round dining table in the corner of the lounge.

"Now you go and sit your ass down," she commanded.

Don grinned apologetically.

"Fine," he said. "You win."

He left Tammy to her cooking and sat down on the lounge before picking up the TV remote.

"No, Don. Leave the TV off. I want this to be special. TV's just gonna spoil the mood," said Tammy.

Don looked over at Tammy. He smiled.

"Just so you know, I'm a sure thing," he said. "You don't have to go to all this trouble. Not that I don't appreciate it and all."

"Oh, don't worry, lover," replied Tammy. "I expect you to show your appreciation later. You can count on it."

She turned back to tend to the sizzling steaks.

Don eyed her tight derriere and resigned himself to spending a little more time away from the stakeout than he'd first anticipated. He got up from the couch with a sigh and went and sat down at the small table. Tammy certainly had gone to some effort, he thought, noting that she'd prepared a salad, spicy potato wedges and some sort of rice dish. A small glass jar had been placed in the centre of the table. The burning candle it contained cast a restless shadow against the adjacent wall. Standing to one side was a bottle of red wine and two glasses.

Don frowned. Had she forgotten he was a recovering alcoholic, or had she done this deliberately?

"Tammy, I..." he began.

Tammy walked over to the table with the still sizzling meat on a serving plate.

"Yes?" she asked.

She placed the plate on the table.

What he wanted to tell her was that he'd been sober for going on three years and wanted to keep it that way.

"The wine," he started to explain.

"Oh, I hope you like it," she said. "We are celebrating tonight, aren't we?"

"Celebrating?"

"We've been seeing each other three months now," she said. "Don, I hope you don't see me as just another good lay. Please tell me I mean something more to you than that."

"Seeing each other? In a manner of speaking, I suppose we have," admitted Don carefully. "But if we both want to be realistic, I don't think this is ever going to develop into something more, you know, long-term, Tammy. For one thing, if you leave George, you also leave a very comfortable lifestyle. One that I'm certainly not going to be able to offer you."

He wasn't about to lead Tammy on, even if it meant losing out on good sex. It just wasn't in his nature. Better, he thought, to come to that understanding sooner rather than later especially if she'd somehow got it into her head that this was something more than what it was.

Tammy chuckled.

"Oh, Don, I never expected it would," she said. "But you can't blame a girl for wanting to show a little appreciation, now, can you? I mean, there's so little to appreciate in life as it is, don't you think? George sure as hell doesn't care. All I'm saying is that it's nice to feel wanted. Trust me, a girl needs that every once in a while."

Don relaxed. He smiled appreciatively.

"I can relate to that," he said.

Tammy placed one of the steaks on a dinner plate and followed up with a serving from each dish. She put the dinner plate in front of Don and then did the same for herself. Don sliced into the tender meat. The steak was still pink in the middle, the red juice flowing with each cut. It was just the way he liked it. He chewed each mouthful with relish. Who would've guessed? The woman sure could cook. Tammy uncorked the wine and filled both glasses. She pushed one glass toward him. She smiled.

"Go on, taste it," she said. "Tell me what you think."

"Shouldn't we let it breathe?" he asked.

"Now, Don," purred Tammy huskily, "when a woman opens her legs and invites you in, you don't wait around for a second invitation. I think wine should be taken the same way. So, you gonna disappoint me or what?"

'Fuck it,' thought Don. 'Why not just celebrate having this case in the bag? One glass wouldn't hurt.'

He raised the glass and took a sip.

Tammy pouted with apparent disappointment.

"Is that it?" she enquired.

Don looked at her a moment then slugged the glass back, swallowing its contents.

He raised an eyebrow at Tammy and placed the glass back on the table.

"Happy?" he said.

Tammy laughed.

"Well, you sure don't mess around!"

"Never been known to," he said.

He went back to eating his steak before noticing she hadn't touched her food.

"Aren't you gonna eat anything?" he asked.

Tammy offered a faint smile.

"I just wanted to watch you enjoy your steak before I started with mine," she said.

She cut into her steak, speared a small piece, and popped it daintily into her mouth.

They sat eating in silence. Don regretted drinking the wine and decided he would defer should she offer him more. He finished the steak—he didn't believe in saving the best for last—and then started in on the potato wedges and salad. He looked across at Tammy, noting that she'd barely touched her meal.

"The food's good," he said. "You should try it."

"I'm not that hungry," she replied.

She had a strange, disconnected look on her face.

"You not feeling well?" he asked between mouthfuls.

"I feel fine, Don. I'm just thinking back, that's all."

"Thinking back?"

"To when we first met. I want you to tell me the story again, Don."

"Tell you?"

"The story about when you first saw me. The way I looked and how you knew then that you wanted me like you wanted no other woman before."

Tammy's voice had a needy edge to it, he decided. Was she lying about not wanting more out of their relationship? He hoped not. That was a complication he didn't need right now.

"It was at the gym," he began. "You'd just walked out of the aerobics class. You were wearing those tight little black Lycra shorts and tank top, hair tied back in a ponytail. I remember the perspiration running down your tanned skin. You had the grace of a gazelle. I saw you then and knew George didn't deserve to have you."

Tammy smiled and got up from her chair.

"I'll never get tired of hearing that," she said. "Now, why don't you go sit down on the couch while I take this dress off and slip into something more to your taste? Don't worry about the dishes, I'll clear away later."

Don wasn't about to complain. Doing the dishes was a thing he hated at the best of times. He watched Tammy's ass disappear into the bedroom.

He stood up and the room seemed to spin around him. Don steadied himself against the table, feeling queasy and dizzy at the same time. Tammy hadn't touched her wine, he noted idly. He turned from the table and stumbled over to the couch, slumping down heavily and attempting to locate the TV remote but finding it difficult to focus his vision on anything. Rivulets of sweat trickled down his face. The first wave of nausea hit him hard then, and with it the sickening realization that his drink had been spiked. Tammy!

'But why?'

"Tammy!" he attempted to shout but found he could only manage an incoherent moan.

Tammy appeared in the doorway, still fully clothed. She stood watching him with the same disconnected expression of earlier.

◇ ◇ ◇

She sighed as though regretful.

"I'm sorry it had to end like this, Don," she said.

With supreme effort, Don managed to push himself up from the couch. He lurched forward and fell to the floor, his body contorting in a spasm as the first seizure hit.

Tammy watched him from the doorway.

"It's water hemlock, in case you're wondering," she explained. "Lethal in any significant dose. It was in the wine, as I'm sure you've figured out by now. I also chopped some up and put it in the salad. Of course, I'll be taking the bottle and the glasses. Nobody will think to check for drink—you, being a recovering alcoholic, and there being no booze in the apartment. Besides, they'll have their probable cause of death: a nice salad laced with finely chopped water hemlock. I'll leave no trace that I was even here. All they're gonna find is you, a stupid private dick who got a little too experimental with his salad ingredients."

Don couldn't answer. His jaw had clamped tight, his teeth grinding together with each convulsion. Tammy stepped closer, confident that he was in no state to harm her.

"How did you find her, Don?" she asked. "How did you find my daughter, Faith? Here I was thinking you were on some other case when all along it was me you were still investigating."

She shook her head.

"I won't go to prison, Don. Not for killing that mean fuck. He said he'd show me the world. Instead, he got me pregnant and married at fifteen. That wasn't going to be me, Don. I wasn't ready to live in some trailer park with a deadbeat grease monkey. He caught me cheating on him, so he hit me. That's when I shot him. Shot him dead, took my baby girl and ran. Of course, I knew I couldn't keep her. She was only six months old. So, I left her with my sister. Did she ever tell you about me? Not that it matters now. Never seen the bitch since that night. She probably reckoned I was dead."

Don's eyes rolled back in his head as more violent convulsions signalled the inexorable progress of the poison. There would be no reprieve for Don Stone now, only death. Tammy recognised the signs, having used the poison once before on an ex-husband who'd lived past his use-by date. She'd been planning to use it on George too. The only thing keeping him safe was that he kept putting off changing his will. But his time would come. She would make sure of that. Yes, sir, she would.

"Goodbye, Don," said Tammy. "For what it's worth, it was fun while it lasted."

She gave Don one final look, and if she felt pity, she showed no hint of it. Tammy left Don to suffer his last agonizing moments alone and walked quickly into the bedroom to gather any evidence he might have left at his desk, including his laptop. With that done, she moved methodically through the rest of the apartment, cleaning it of all traces of Tammy Sloane.

◊ ◊ ◊

Anastasiya knocked on Don Stone's apartment door. There was no answer. She knocked again, harder this time. Still no answer. Something was wrong! She resisted the urge to punch through the door, though it was quite within her power.

"Lotho, the door," she commanded.

She stepped aside to allow the big man hovering at her shoulder access. It was an old lock system and didn't take him long to pick. He pushed open the door with a satisfied grunt. Anastasiya stepped inside quickly, followed by her manservant. The smell of death permeated the apartment's interior.

She saw Don's corpse sprawled near the side of the couch.

"A niech go diabli!" she exclaimed bitterly.

She held up her hand to stop Lotho and sniffed the air.

"A woman was here," she observed. "But she has gone. An hour or more ago. Wait here. Touch nothing,"

She ventured further into the apartment's lounge.

Anastasiya looked down at Don's cold body and noted his contorted features. Poisoned! The signs were self-evident. She walked over to the small table and inspected the dishes that remained where Tammy had carefully left them.

Her eyes narrowed. Cowbane. The woman had used cowbane to poison him.

She left the table and moved silently through the rest of the apartment, inspecting each room in turn. There would be nothing here to help her, she realised. The killer had seen to that.

She looked down at Don's corpse.

"Such a pity, Mr Stone," she said quietly. "Perhaps you deserved better."

She knew there was nothing more to be gained here. It was time to move on.

Anastasiya looked at her manservant, Lotho.

"There is only one avenue left open to us," she said. "And that is the priest. I think it is time we pay him a visit."

They left then, the manservant carefully wiping any trace of fingerprints before closing the front door behind them. It would be five days before Donald Stone's corpse was discovered—five days left to decompose in the LA heat. An ignominious end to a man who enjoyed playing the odds but who'd simply run out of his quotient of luck.

22

The people of the city greeted the new day, going about their respective morning rituals in the certainty that this day would be much like the day before and the day to come. Few people ever contemplate death, reasoning perhaps that any such thought is enough to invite that most unwanted guest into their lives.

Samuel O'Connor was under no such illusion. Much like the condemned man, he knew this day was to be his last. He hung, suspended from his arms, his feet only just touching the cold concrete floor. The harsh light provided by the single light bulb cast stark shadows along the basement's bare walls. He'd been stripped to the waist and his exposed upper body bled freely from dozens of well-placed knife cuts. The bruising on his torso also showed where Lotho's well-directed blows had cracked O'Connor's ribs and ruptured his spleen.

The priest's every breath was a torment. He'd long since lost the feeling in the bloody ruin of his hands and feet, Lotho having extracted the nails from each digit with excruciating thoroughness. Yet despite everything, O'Connor had not broken.

He drifted in and out of consciousness, the unsure footing provided by the slippery surface of the blood-soaked floor jerking him back to his reality each time, preventing him from gaining the respite he needed. He knew it was only a matter of time before he cracked. And when he did, the devil woman would finally know where to find his boys. What then? What would happen if she captured them? What inhuman torture would she submit them to?

No!

He could not let that happen. He would hold out for as long as he could. He would hold out in the hope Matthew and John would find out he'd gone missing and then they would disappear, as per their prearranged understanding.

The door opened behind him. O'Connor closed his eyes and offered up a silent prayer, bracing himself for what was to come. He could hear the sharp click-clack of the Countess' stilettos on the concrete, followed by the heavier footsteps of her manservant. He opened his eyes. Anastasiya smiled coldly at him.

"Ah, you are conscious," she said. "Good. I would not want you to miss appreciating Lotho's skill."

The big man loomed behind her, his granitelike face expressionless. O'Connor realised then there was no malice in the man's actions; he was simply carrying out the orders of his mistress.

"Come now, Father, there is no need for you to endure this pain," said Anastasiya reasonably. "Why not tell me where I can find your accomplices and I can put an end to all of this? And then you will have your peace."

O'Connor 's voice was barely audible as he spoke through his cracked and swollen lips.

"I...I cannot tell you what I do not know," he mumbled.

"If only I could believe you, Father," replied Anastasiya. "Alas we both know you are lying."

"No," rasped the battered priest. "I cannot lie. I do not know where they are."

He desperately hoped she believed him.

Anastasiya shook her head as though baffled by his insistence on maintaining the pretence.

"Come now, Father," she said patiently. "You are lying. You know these people. You are protecting them—these people, who entered my house and murdered my girls in cold blood. They shot them as though they were animals. You know who they are, these men and the girl. You are a man of the cloth, are you not? How can one such as you consort with murderous thugs such as these? How can you, a man of God, justify their evil?"

"They are not murderers!"

The words tumbled from the priest's mouth before he'd realised.

Anastasiya smiled grimly. She pounced on O'Connor's apparent slip.

"So," she said. "You admit then that you know these people?"

"No, I am only saying..."

"You are only saying what?" snapped Anastasiya coldly. "That you agree with killing? That these men had a right to murder my girls?"

She turned to the big man lurking nearby.

"Lotho, remind Father O'Connor why it would be better for him to confess."

She stepped away to allow Lotho access. He picked up a scalpel from a stainless-steel trolley and proceeded to slice the flesh from the priest's left side. At first O'Connor attempted to endure the searing pain, gritting his teeth as the knife sliced through his skin. But Lotho was too skilled at his work and soon the priest howled in agony. Lotho stepped back.

"It is you who are the murderer," cried O'Connor. "It is you who is murdering innocent people and drinking their blood! How many? How many have you murdered over your lifetime of evil? How many innocent lives have you cut short?"

He knew his words would only serve to incriminate him further, but he was beyond caring. Lotho's knife had seen to that. Every cut brought O'Connor closer to death, and with it the determination to fight back, even if only with words.

Lotho raised his blade to administer further torture, but Anastasiya stayed his hand.

"Innocent, you say?" she snarled. "Yes, I drink the blood of people, just as they eat the flesh of animals. Without their blood, I cannot survive. You talk of innocence, ha! It is you…"

Anastasiya pointed an accusing finger at O'Connor.

"It is you who have a choice. Like all of humankind, you can choose to turn from the meat of animals. I have no such choice. Nor do I care to. I am content in being who I am."

"You are a demon!" spat O'Connor.

Anastasiya smiled.

"No!" she said. "I am a god. I will endure long after you and your kind have turned to dust."

She nodded and Lotho stepped forward to continue his work. O'Connor howled again, blood flowing freely from the exposed muscle covering his ribcage.

"Life, it is said, is full of uncertainty," observed Anastasiya grimly. "But one thing I know is certain, Father: Before this day is past, you will beg to tell me everything I want to know and perhaps even more!"

◊ ◊ ◊

Faith lay against John, her head on his chest. The night had slipped away and now it was the morning. She raised her head slightly to look at the digital clock on the bedstand.

"Time's not gonna go any faster with you looking at the clock every five minutes," said John.

"I don't want it to go faster. I want it to stop," admitted Faith.

"Why? Are you worried about later today?"

"I suppose. But mostly I don't want this to end."

"What? You mean lying here?" He sounded mildly surprised.

"With you, yes," replied Faith quietly. "I'm happy. I know it sounds stupid, wanting to stop time. But I've never felt like this before, and I don't want it to end."

"Don't worry," said John confidently. "Matt and I have done this type of thing many times. I promise you, nothing will go wrong."

Faith moved then, propping herself up on an elbow so she could look into his eyes. She needed to know he understood.

"There's no way of knowing that for sure, John," she said earnestly. "The only thing I do know for sure is that I'm here with you now. That's what makes me happy. I know we can't stay here like this forever. But that doesn't mean I can't wish that we could."

"I want you to be happy, Faith. I know I shouldn't promise things will turn out the way I planned but that doesn't mean I'm not gonna give it my best shot. Besides, I haven't lost this moment. It's in here."

He tapped his head.

"It's locked in here forever. Believe me."

Faith smiled. It was the best she was going to get from him at this point. John's stomach growled.

He laughed out loud.

"And that's another reason we can't lie here forever," he said. "If I don't get something in my stomach soon, I might pass out from hunger!"

John got up, stretched contentedly, then strolled over to the chair to retrieve his jeans. He pulled them on and looked back at Faith.

"Are you coming?"

She nodded.

"I'll join you in a bit," she said.

John closed the door behind him on his way out. Faith lay back on the bed, her hands clasped behind her head. She stared up at the ceiling as she mulled over John's words.

'The way I planned.' That's what he'd said.

Did that mean she featured in his plans? Part of her so wanted that to be true. But another part of her hated the idea. Not because she didn't think she could rely on him, but because in some way, it threatened to undermine the very thing she'd so recently regained: her self-belief. She suddenly felt annoyed at herself for revealing all her feelings and thoughts to him. Had she sounded weak, like a cloying girl afraid to face the world on her own? She hoped she hadn't. It was the last thing she wanted—John thinking of her as someone who needed to be protected. She wanted John. She wanted to be with him but as his equal, someone he could rely on, rather than play the role of useless girlfriend/hanger-on. She sighed.

"Time to get your shit together, girl."

Faith spoke the words as though attempting to quell the unease she'd felt since waking that morning. Of course, she hadn't spoken to John about it—she hadn't wanted him to think she was afraid of the coming fight. The truth was she didn't know why she felt this way. Was it fear she felt? Maybe self-doubt? Or was it something else? A premonition?

She sat up. It didn't matter, she decided. There was no way around what needed to be done. She would see this thing to the end, and then maybe she and John could finally move on, someplace else. Some place far away. Maybe.

Faith rolled out of bed and proceeded to dress. When she'd finished, she took a final look in the mirror.

'Whatever you do, just don't get yourself killed today, girl.'

◊ ◊ ◊

O'Connor hung limply from his shackles. He'd finally passed out under Lotho's brutal torture. The big man moved to revive the priest, but Anastasiya stopped him, perhaps reasoning that the priest had now passed beyond the pain threshold and further torture would prove useless. Better, she thought, to allow O'Connor the illusion of rest so that when Lotho recommenced his ministrations, the priest would again feel each cut of the knife.

Anastasiya motioned Lotho to lower O'Connor. He unhooked the cable at the wall and the priest's body slumped to the ground.

The priest was stubborn, Anastasiya admitted to herself. But in the end, she'd get what she wanted. It was just going to take a little longer than she'd first anticipated. What would she do once he'd given up the location of his accomplices? She'd decided on three possible approaches. One, she and her acolytes could attack and kill the enemy in their hideout; two, she could send her acolytes to attack and kill the enemy without going there herself; three, she could send her acolytes to capture the three perpetrators and bring them back to her.

The first and second options were certainly the least complicated. Kill the enemy quickly and without hesitation. Rip the cancer out, root and stem. Then leave their bodies to rot and simply disappear into the night, like phantoms. The first and third options would allow her the personal satisfaction of gaining vengeance. She knew the second option to be the best, as this exposed her to the least danger. A casual observer might have reasoned that having lived for so long, Anastasiya would have had the apparent advantage of ancient wisdom, but the truth was that her seventeen-year-old self lurked ever-near the surface. That same blood-drenched girl who'd cut her way through those terrified soldiers those long years ago, ripping their limbs and heads from their bodies. That girl would be satisfied with nothing less than personal vengeance.

Anastasiya looked down at the crumpled form of the priest and was reminded of another time and place. She had chosen to strike then too, but 1920s Chicago had not been a forgiving town, and the mob had not taken kindly to the murder of one of their own—a high-level mobster who'd wanted to appropriate her brothel. The man had attempted to intimidate her into surrendering the business by brutally torturing one of her girls. Then as now, she'd vowed vengeance. She had killed him. But at what cost? The mob's retribution had been swift.

She closed her eyes. The terrified death screams of her acolytes burning in the inferno of their home carried across time to accuse her once more. It was one of the many terrible memories she kept locked away deep within herself. But like some unwelcome relative, these same memories had a habit of revisiting her uninvited, demanding resolution when none could be had.

Anastasiya breathed in deep. So many terrible memories. How many more was she to endure? She knew she could choose to step from this path of vengeance and so avoid the worst type of consequence. She could, but that was not within her nature. She understood that. Her only satisfaction would be in killing them. The quiet rage burning within could only be quenched with their blood. The murder of her acolytes demanded it.

"Lotho, give the priest another half-hour before you resume your work."

She nodded to the big man and walked from the basement.

As far as she was concerned, she had but two options: Trap them in their hideout and kill them quickly, like rats in a hole, or seize them and bring them back to the school where they might be made to suffer more. There would be time enough to choose before the priest finally broke, she decided.

23

I t was just past noon when the men in suits approached the back of the old house. At first, five heavily armed men had scaled the back fence. They had fanned out to maximize their arc of fire before going to ground, their weapons trained on the house.

Then it had been the turn of Dragan Millovic. He'd pulled his large frame over the fence with a curse before landing heavily on the far side. The men had risen at his signal and crept forward, past the old tree with its tyre-swing and onward up to the back porch. Dragan looked carefully about as they walked. He did not expect Matthew and John to be there, but was taking no chances. The men took up position at the windows and door and looked back at Dragan, awaiting his command. He gave another hand-signal and one of the men moved forward quietly to pick the lock. It opened easily, and within minutes, the men were inside. With their weapons at the ready, they moved expertly from room to room to ensure each was clear.

"No one is here," reported one of the men to Dragan.

Dragan nodded and walked into the kitchen. He looked at the solitary table with its red vinyl top and noted that the three of the chairs had been pushed back. He turned and looked at the dish rack. There were three plates and an equal number of mugs. Someone else was with the two men, he realised.

"Get in-position," he commanded. "I want no surprises."

The men took up appropriate positions whilst Dragan investigated for himself. He found what he was looking for in the second bedroom: a pair of cotton panties lay crumpled on the bed. He picked them up, held them to his nose and inhaled deeply.

'So,' he thought to himself. 'They have a woman with them. This will be good. This will give me something more to enjoy.'

Dragan smiled and tossed Faith's underwear carelessly to the floor before walking from the room. He went into the lounge room and chose to sit in the single armchair, turning it so that it faced toward the front door.

Placing his assault rifle alongside the chair, he sat back and thought about the young woman. Who was she? Why had Matthew not mentioned her? Not that it mattered, he decided. She would die just the same. But not before he'd had her, and better still, forced the two men to watch while he and his men took turns fucking her. Then he'd slit her throat before finally turning his attention to them. The place was well-isolated, so he'd be able to take his time.

'Yes,' he promised himself. 'They will die slowly.'

◊ ◊ ◊

It was late afternoon, the shadows growing progressively longer as the sun began to dip lazily beyond the horizon. John, Matt, and Faith had been watching the target house for most of the day with little to show for their effort. John had parked the car in an unobtrusive spot, but one which still allowed them a visual on their target. This cut both ways with the possibility of being spotted by their prey growing with every passing moment. Their unease increased as each hour crawled by, each of them having time to reflect on their chances in the coming fight.

"I don't think this is gonna happen today," mused John out loud.

"Why don't we give it an hour or so more?" countered Matt.

"We've been watching the place for most of the day and no one over there's made a move to leave yet, Matt," said John. "There's just too many of them. It's almost like they're expecting trouble."

"You think someone tipped them off?" asked Faith from the back seat.

"There's no way they'd know," Matt said, shaking his head.

"How could you be so sure?" asked John. "I've never questioned your sources, Matt, but you've got to admit this time the information seems way off."

"I say we need to give it more time. My source has always been on the money. Why would this time be any different?"

"There's always a first time," said John. "We've had it real easy till now. No point in taking any chances. That's what I say."

"I agree," blurted Faith before she could stop herself.

"What makes you the expert?" snapped Matt.

Faith gritted her teeth and glared at the back of Matt's head.

"No one's claiming to be the expert," said John. "But let's face it, it ain't happening today."

"Look, the information I got said today would be the best time to carry out the hit," protested Matt. "You wanna pack it in, then fine. Just don't go expecting it's gonna be easier the next time we come around."

"You don't think I understand that?" said John. "I just think that right now, it's too big a risk. The way I see it, we go in there, chances are one of us is gonna get hurt. I say we walk away and you go back to that source of yours and get better information."

"You know what?" snapped Matt. "Before this, you'd've been willing to take the risk or at least wait it out a few more hours. Now it seems you're looking for the first chance to run."

"Before what, Matt?"

"He means before me, John," interrupted Faith angrily. "I'm right here, Matt. You wanna accuse me, then grow a pair and come out and just say it!"

"You got some nerve, girl!" growled Matt. "We were a good team till you showed up. No one ever questioned anything, we just got on with the job. Everything always fell into place. It was like there was an order to it all. Then you come along, and it's all gone to shit. First vampires breathing down our necks, then O'Connor losing trust in us, then him."

Matt pointed at John.

"Questioning everything. You know what you are, girl? You're chaos. Nothing but trouble. You know what else? I reckon you enjoyed shaking that ass for Manny. I bet you—"

Faith slapped Matt hard across the face and cut him off in midsentence. He blinked, momentarily stunned at her angry response before quickly regaining his composure.

"You fucking little bitch," he growled.

He grabbed at Faith, but John moved quickly to intervene.

"Enough!" he shouted. "That's enough!"

He pushed Matt up against the passenger door.

"Both of you..."

He looked at Faith.

"Both of you just cool it."

John kept his hold on Matt and waited for the two to calm down. He felt Matt relax under his grip and let go.

"Good. Now we've got that off our chests, I think we'd better leave," said John. "Besides, you've got yourself an audience."

He nodded in the direction of the house adjacent their car. An old woman stood watching them from her gate, a picture of attentive curiosity.

"Any excuse to bail," sneered Matt. "Is this what we've become?"

"Give it a rest, Matt. We can talk all you want later."

He turned the ignition.

The car rumbled into life. He gave a cursory look up the street, then put the car in gear and pulled away from the kerb. They moved past the target house and turned out of the street a short distance later. It was time to head back home, though none of the car's occupants looked happy at the prospect.

◊ ◊ ◊

It was late. Dragan sat comfortably in the lounge chair, patiently anticipating the arrival of his prey. He was well-experienced in this approach and happy to let the hours tick by, confident that sooner or later they would walk into his trap. The early evening had been punctuated by the noise of the odd vehicle passing by on the nearby gravel road, but now it had become silent. He strained his eyes in the dark and could just make out one of his men standing near the front window. The man suddenly turned his head and hissed through his teeth. Someone was coming.

Dragan quietly picked up the automatic assault rifle at the side of the chair and sat up. Strange, he thought, there had been no sound of a car pulling up. He focused his attention on the front door, listening intently for his approaching victims. There! The sound of someone stepping softly onto the front porch. More careful footsteps. A moment's silence then the distinct sound of someone working the door's lock.

'Matthew is being very careful,' he thought.

Had he somehow lost the element of surprise? Dragan levelled his weapon and was rewarded with the sight of the door opening. Three figures were briefly silhouetted against the moonlit exterior before stepping inside and closing the door behind them.

This was the pre-arranged signal for one of his men to turn the lights on. He blinked. There before him stood three women dressed in sleek black leather.

What the hell?

One of the females hissed angrily and struck without hesitation, launching herself at the nearest man. He fired instinctively but missed as she ducked before spinning round to sweep his feet from under him. The man screamed as Lilith sank her teeth into his jugular, and with a quick jerk of her head, ripped out his throat. Dragan fired then, emptying a full magazine into the back of the vampire's head. Lilith slumped forward onto the already dead man, her head a bloody pulp. The Serb ejected the empty magazine and shoved in a new one as he moved back away from the fight which had erupted to his left.

Another of his henchmen already lay sprawled on the floor, his head twisted at an impossible angle. Andrej was struggling with a black-clad demon, the pair careening about the front room, furniture splintering in their wake. The powerfully built man was visibly weakening under the vampire's vicious onslaught, blood streaming from countless bullet wounds, but Meredith's fury, fuelled by the abuse she'd suffered from so many men, drove her on. Even now, she could feel the virus work its magic, methodically repairing her torn flesh as she moved in for the kill.

Effortlessly evading Andrej's desperate right jab, she was upon him, wrenching his head back to sink her fangs into his exposed neck. Dragan chose that moment to fire, deliberating that the vampire would be too engaged with the luckless Andrej to evade his shots. The fact that he was shooting one of his own men at the same time mattered little. The pair stumbled back as the rounds hit them and they fell over the lounge suite with a heavy thud.

Dragan discerned no movement from behind the couch but was taking no chances. He could hear the desperate struggle issuing from the kitchen as his two remaining henchmen battled another of the demons. He edged forward, confident that there'd be time enough to finish off any remaining life in the creature that had killed Andrej before going to the aid of his men. It was then that Anastasiya chose to attack.

Dragan heard the kitchen back door disintegrating, then a panicked cry as one of his men succumbed to the surprise assault. He spun around and ran toward the kitchen, crashing through the half-open door with his weapon raised. Anastasiya was crouched over the broken body of one of his men.

She looked up in surprise as he fired. The rounds hit her in the chest, driving her back against the cupboards behind. She howled angrily and leapt at the man, twisting to one side to spoil his aim. But Dragan had anticipated this and hit her again with another well-placed burst. Anastasiya stumbled back and lost her footing as she slipped on the blood-soaked vinyl floor. She landed heavily, then rolled to one side in a desperate attempt to evade Dragan's next volley. The vampire queen could sense her enemy closing in for the kill.

"Kuja!" spat Dragan.

He stepped forward and lifted the assault rifle, intent on finishing her with a shot to the head. A sudden movement to his right caused him to turn. He fired his weapon as he did, catching Eden full in the face with a burst of automatic fire. She dropped dead at his feet, her wound too severe for the virus to heal. But Eden's sacrifice had allowed Anastasiya the opening she needed and before Dragan could turn to face her, and she was upon him, ripping the weapon from his grasp as she threw him to the floor in one effortless move. Anastasiya straddled the helpless man as she pinned him to the floor, one hand maintaining a vicelike grip on his throat.

"Pathetic man! How I despise you," she growled. "So many times, your kind have tried to kill me. Each time you fail."

She looked over to where Eden lay and realised the true extent of the horrific wounds which had killed the one she loved. Anastasiya's lips pulled back from her pointed canines as she howled in rage. She looked down at the terrified Dragan, her eyes a violent red.

"Ty zwierze! You have murdered her! You do not deserve to die quickly. Instead, I will drain the blood from you. You will feel your life slip from you as I drink. You will die and then you will awake. But not as a human. No, you will be nothing more than a moving, rotting thing suffering the agony of your flesh devouring itself. I condemn you to the living death!"

Anastasiya grabbed Dragan's hair and twisted his head violently to the side before sinking her fangs into his exposed neck. The helpless man screamed then, his legs straining as he tried to raise his hips and attempt to shake the vampire from him. His shoes scarred the vinyl floor as his feet attempted to find purchase, the piston-like movement of his legs weakening visibly as she drained the blood from him. Once she'd finished with Dragan, she stood up and walked over to where Eden lay. Anastasiya knelt by Eden's corpse and held her hand one final time. The virus had already begun its desperate struggle for sustenance, and she watched as the body of her once-favourite began to wither.

"We will meet in another life," said Anastasiya quietly.

She looked up as Meredith limped into the kitchen, her black jumpsuit ripped and bloodied from the multiple wounds she'd suffered.

"Lilith is dead too," said Meredith solemnly. "I'm sorry that that I failed you, mistress."

"No, you have done well under the circumstances," said Anastasiya.

She stood up and offered her hand to her only surviving acolyte.

"Come, Meredith, it is time we return to our home. We will take our fallen with us."

The young woman looked to where Dragan lay writhing on the floor.

"What about him?" she asked.

They watched his limbs thrashing and twisting as cell-by-cell, the virus attempted to mutate his body into a vessel which could sustain it.

"Leave him," replied Anastasiya. "He deserves nothing less, and his fate will give the others pause to consider their own ends."

She knelt and lifted the desiccated remains of Eden in her arms. Meredith collected Lilith's body and they walked from the house and disappeared into the welcoming darkness.

◊ ◊ ◊

Two hours passed before John; Matt and Faith finally pulled up at the house. They'd had a frustrating end to a bad day with a punctured tyre and a flat spare, forcing them to walk six miles to the nearest gas station and back. No one had spoken for the remainder of the trip home.

"The lights are on," noted John suspiciously.

He looked over at Matt.

"Shouldn't be."

Matt reached for his pistol. John turned to Faith.

"Wait here," he said. "Matt and I will go on ahead and check it out. This could be nothing, but let's not risk it."

Faith nodded. She'd wanted to protest, but decided that it would've only caused more tension between the two men. Reaching down she pulled the shotgun from under the blanket that lay on the floor at her feet.

John saw the shotgun cradled to her chest.

"If things go to shit, get as far away from here as you can," he said softly. "I don't want anything to happen to you, understand?"

Matt and John got out of the car, pistols at the ready, and walked carefully toward the waiting house. Faith watched as they moved stealthily onto the front porch, John slightly to the rear and side of Matt to cover him. They stood to one side of the front door, John continuing to provide cover as Matt moved forward and opened the door.

The light from inside appeared to pierce the darkness, spilling out over the porch toward the girl in the car. The two men disappeared inside. It looked to her as though they'd been swallowed by some evil living thing. Long minutes passed, and to Faith, each felt like an hour. When she felt she could endure it no longer, she exited the car and crept forward, the shotgun raised with the butt pressed comfortably into her shoulder as John had taught her.

She climbed stairs of the porch and moved to the side of the open door, as she'd seen the others do. Faith peered around the door frame and gasped involuntarily. Furniture lay upturned and smashed amidst the gore-spattered lounge room. Her eyes followed the blood to where the body of a man lay. His throat had been ripped out. Her eyes widened.

Jesus!

She gripped the shotgun tighter to quell the fear rising within her and forced her legs onward. John had told her to wait in the car but the idea of sitting idly by while they exposed themselves to danger was not within her nature. She ventured farther into the room, picking her way through the scattered furniture and gore and found another mangled body.

Faith resisted the urge to call out. The fact that she couldn't hear either John or Matt concerned her. She quickened her pace and moved through to the kitchen. The sight of two more partially dismembered bodies caused her to hesitate by the entrance. The splintered remains of the back door hung from twisted hinges. Where had they got to?

She entered the room, sweeping the shotgun from left to right. Still no sign of the two men. Faith turned to leave but a sudden movement from beyond the shattered door made her stop. She aimed at the figure emerging from the dark, her finger restless on the trigger.

"Hold it!" hissed John.

He looked at once annoyed and relieved.

"Sorry," she said softly.

Faith lowered her weapon.

"Who are these guys?" she asked.

"I've no idea," John shrugged. "Probably looking for us, which isn't a good sign. By the looks of things, they weren't the only ones come to pay us a visit."

"The vampires?"

John nodded.

"Can't think of an alternative," he said. "I think we'd best be—"

John was cut short by Matt's scream, then a ragged burst of gunfire.

"Matt?" shouted John.

There was another scream. John sprinted down the passage toward the sound with Faith close-behind. The pair found him in the third bedroom.

"Oh, God!" exclaimed Faith.

A horribly wounded Matt lay on his back, feebly attempting to fend off the creature that tore at his exposed entrails. The thing looked up at the interlopers, its jaws chewing mechanically on a length of Matt's intestine. The creature that had once been Dragan Millovic gurgled hungrily as it shuffled toward the pair, dragging a fistful of intestine after it. John flicked the Glock to auto and fired a long burst into the advancing ghoul. It stumbled backward momentarily, then continued its shambling advance.

"Just die, you motherfucker!" screamed Faith.

She fired, pulled back quickly on the slide action of the shotgun, and fired again.

The shotgun rounds disintegrated the creature's skull in a spray of gore and splintered bone. The creature's headless body stiffened, then dropped to its knees and keeled over. The pair stepped carefully past the motionless corpse to where Matt lay. He moaned in agony as he attempted to push himself up, but his gaping wound was too severe. John knelt by his partner and took his hand.

"It's bad, isn't it?" groaned Matt.

"Yes. I'm sorry," replied John quietly.

"Oh, Jesus, I don't want to die. Not now!"

"Don't worry about that. We'll get you outta here, back to Father O'Connor," said John earnestly.

"I don't think so. Not like this," said Matt.

He choked on the blood rising in his throat.

"Oh, Christ," he groaned. "I had it all so well-planned."

His eyes glazed and his head fell limply to one side. Matt was dead.

"It's not the way any of us planned, brother," said John softly.

He remained kneeling with his head bowed next to the body, still holding Matt's hand.

"John…" began Faith.

She started to reach out to comfort him but then she stopped, unsure of whether he needed her to.

He looked back over his shoulder at her.

"Matt and I had our differences, but he was still like a brother to me," he said. "I just can't help thinking that somehow or other, we've fucked up."

"How?" she asked.

"I'm not sure," he said, shaking his head. "I'm gonna have to figure that out later. Right now, we must get away from here. Those men had silenced weapons, we don't. Someone's probably called the cops by now."

"What about Matt?"

"We'll have to leave…" began John.

Faith's startled expression alerted him to the new danger. He turned to look at Matt as the limp hand in his suddenly tightened like a vice.

"Holy fuck!" he yelled.

John tried desperately to pull away as the reanimated Matt pulled him closer.

Faith screamed in horror. She grabbed at John's shirt to pull him away. He fell back against Faith and sent her sprawling to the floor, the shotgun spinning from her hand in a lazy arc before hitting the floor and skidding a few feet across the blood-slick floorboards.

She looked back to see John struggling to free himself from the thing that clawed at him. Faith scrambled to her feet and ran for the shotgun. It took only seconds but felt like hours. She picked up the twelve-gauge, worked the slide action, spun around, and brought it to her shoulder. She fired, narrowly missing John but hitting the creature in the bloody mess of its torso.

A few quick steps brought her close enough to make no mistake. She worked the twelve-gauge's slide action again, aimed, and fired. A headshot put an end to the undead thing Matt had become. John lay still for a moment, his face covered in Matt's gore.

"Are you okay?" asked Faith earnestly.

"Yeah, I think so," answered John slowly.

He took a few moments to gather himself, then got to his feet. The far-off sound of police sirens drifted through the room.

"If we don't get out here now, we're gonna have a whole lot more trouble."

He grabbed Faith's hand and pulled her from the room. John stopped in the lounge room.

"Quick, get those weapons!"

He pointed to the dead men's silenced assault rifles on the floor.

"I'll get the others," he added.

He ran back to the kitchen. Faith started to protest, but thought better of it. She picked up both weapons and slung them over her shoulder by the straps. Long minutes went by before John reappeared with the other weapons. The pair ran to the car and bundled the assault rifles onto the backseat.

"You got the spare magazines?" John asked as he slid behind the steering wheel.

"Magazines?" asked Faith in surprise.

"Never mind," he replied.

He turned the key in the ignition and revved the car's engine.

The sirens were clearer now. John gunned the accelerator, slammed the stick into reverse, then put his foot to the floor, turning the steering wheel hard as he did so. The car spun round on the gravel, then John rammed the stick into gear and hit the accelerator once more. A moment later, the pair were hurtling along the dark road away from the house of death and the approaching police.

◊ ◊ ◊

An hour passed before John felt they were far enough away and pulled into a side road. The pair sat silently in the dark, wondering how quickly their circumstances had changed.

Faith was first to break the silence.

"What now?" she asked.

"We'll have to go back to that school," replied John grimly.

"Why?" she blurted.

"The more I think about it, the more I keep coming back to the same conclusion."

"Father O'Connor?"

John nodded.

"Yes," he said. "The vampires were at the house. There's no other explanation for what happened to those men. Only one person knew we stayed there. Only he could've told them."

"Maybe it was those men?" said Faith hopefully. "Maybe they're connected to the vampires somehow."

The possibility was remote, but she did not relish the thought of venturing back into the vampire's lair, least of all for someone who'd had so little regard for her.

John shook his head.

"Nope," he said. "There's no logical connection between the vampires and those dead men. Those men were gangsters, and from the looks of things, we were their target. Thing is, they didn't look part of da Silva's crew and that's what I'm trying to figure out."

"Maybe da Silva hired them," offered Faith.

"No, that's not his style. He would've come after us himself given the opportunity. Something Matt said, though. I just—"

"What?" asked Faith. "You mean just now?"

"'I had it all so well-planned.' That's what he said, and that makes me believe he was involved somehow."

"I'm not going to pretend I liked him much, John," said Faith. "But do you really think he was capable of double-crossing you?"

"Each of us struggles with our own inner demons, Faith," replied John grimly. "He was no exception. He'd had a rough time in foster care before coming to the Home. He'd seen some pretty fucked-up things. He used to talk about it from time to time. Maybe those demons just got the better of him in the end."

She nodded thoughtfully.

"Maybe," she said.

There was a moment's silence. A car went by on the main road. She looked over at John, trying to gauge his expression in the dark.

"You still want to go back to that school?"

"I have to, Faith," he answered.

"But why? After what you've just seen, you think they'd keep Father O'Connor alive?"

"It doesn't matter either way, Faith. I'm going there to take out those things. If he's alive—and I pray he is—then so much the better."

"This isn't a game, John," she said. "There's no hitting the reset button if things go wrong for us."

Her voice was choked with fear.

"Someone once said to me that our lives are just a series of connected random events, and that there was no real meaning or plan to any of it," said John quietly. "No heaven, no hell, just us. Just us stuck on this fucked-up little planet, lost amongst all the other planets. Floating in a sea of infinity. Going nowhere, just existing. I hated the thought of that—our lives having no meaning."

"You think going after those vampires is going to give your life meaning?" she responded angrily.

He shrugged. "Maybe."

"What about me, John? What about us? Doesn't that have any meaning?"

"You know it does, but this is different."

"Different how?"

"It's my destiny. It's what I was meant to do."

"What? Rid the world of a few vampires?"

"More than that. I'm going to rid the world of a plague. You saw what their bite can do to us. Imagine if that infection spread," said John in earnest. "Where would it stop? What if it got out of control?"

"I don't know, John. Maybe because those things know it would mean the end of everything. They wouldn't let it get out of control. If we're all dead, then what? How would they survive? I think they want to live just as much as we do, don't you?"

"We can't say for sure, can we?" said John. "All I know is, I don't want to leave that kind of power in their hands."

There was finality in John's tone. The pair sat in silence, each grappling with their own thoughts.

"You know I won't let you do it alone," said Faith finally.

"I understand that, and I'm sorry," said John candidly. "I'm sorry that I'm putting you in this kind of danger. If I could do it any other way I would. You know that."

"I know. But it still doesn't make it any easier knowing what we're going to face."

"You can still change your mind, you know."

Faith broke the ensuing silence with an exasperated groan.

"Fuck it," she said. "No one lives forever anyway. Let's just do it."

The pair set about preparing their weapons with a grim determination, topping up the magazines of two of the assault rifles and taking the other magazines as spares, filling them with the remaining rounds. Next was the twelve-gauge and then John's G18C.

John placed his hand on the ignition key.

"You ready?" he asked.

Faith nodded. "Ready," she said.

John turned the ignition, put his foot to the accelerator, and completed a U-turn to bring the car back toward the main road. Faith looked out the window into the night sky as they hurtled along. Out here, away from the city lights, she could see so many stars—they appeared like beacons of hope, promising life as they shone out from the dark, pitiless void. She was under no illusion about what they were going to face, and she wanted to take in every detail one last time.

24

A lone figure dropped from the top of the stone wall and crouched low to the ground. The full moon cast its wan light over the mansion's grounds, distorting trees and shrubs into an ominous mass of shape and shadow.

John scanned the deeper shadows, his assault rifle at the ready. When he felt sure the area was clear, he whistled softly to Faith waiting on the far side. A short while later he saw her figure silhouetted at the top of the wall. She passed the shotgun and other assault rifle down to him before swinging her legs over the wall and allowing gravity to do the rest. She took the twelve-gauge, slung it over her shoulder then picked up the assault rifle and crouched down beside John.

"You ready?" he whispered.

"You asked me that before, remember?" she shot back.

"Just checking," he said, smiling.

He moved forward, Faith following close behind. They crept along, training their assault rifles on every shadow as they moved toward the waiting mansion. Had Faith the time, she would've reflected on how different she was to the frightened girl who'd traversed these grounds a week ago. Now her every step took her further still from that past life, yet toward what destiny? The pair stopped at the edge of the tree line and looked at the silent mansion ahead. No lights were on.

"They know we're here," said Faith.

"Maybe," said John, "But we can't know that for sure."

He'd come to the same conclusion but hadn't wanted to panic her further.

"What now?" she asked quietly.

"I suppose we'll just use the same way as before," he said. "Cover me."

John started moving across the open ground toward the side-entrance before she could reply. She watched as he disappeared around the corner of the building. The minutes dragged by, and for a moment, Faith worried that he'd been discovered. Then he reappeared and signalled her to follow. She stood by him at the open side-door moments later. John placed a hand on her shoulder as she made a move to enter.

"Wait," he said.

She turned to look at him quizzically. "What?"

He kissed her softly on the lips.

"I know this is gonna sound lame right now," he said. "But I'm gonna say it anyway. Whatever happens in there, just know that I love you."

"I love you, too," said Faith weakly.

She knew her feelings for him were more complicated, but knew at that moment it was the only thing she could say.

He kissed her again and smiled.

"Let's do this," he said.

Then he stepped through the doorway with the assault rifle raised to his shoulder.

She hesitated a moment.

"Just believe you'll get through this, and you will," she whispered to herself.

Armed with a renewed resolve, she followed.

The moonlight filtering into the dark hallway from the adjoining rooms was enough for them to make out their surroundings. It occurred to Faith then that this might have been purposely done as a way of enticing them further into a trap.

The pair moved carefully down the hall. They stopped and searched each room as they went. When they reached the large entrance hall, they stopped. Three possible routes lay ahead—they could continue straight on to follow the front wing of the mansion, they could turn immediately left up the stairs to the first floor and the rooms there, or they could turn left just beyond the staircase to follow the hall to the back part of the building.

"Which way?" whispered Faith nervously.

John hesitated, annoyed with himself for allowing his need to be the hero cloud his judgement. He had no real plan, and worse, he and Faith were now on ground of the enemy's choosing.

Faith tugged urgently at his shirt.

"John," she hissed.

"Wait, I'm thinking," he snapped, trying not to sound annoyed.

'You could always walk away. The front door's right there,' whispered a voice inside his head. 'Go on, what are you putting your life on the line for? Humanity? You really think they're worth it? Take the easy way. A few steps, a turn of the handle, and you just keep on walking. Just you and her, walking away to a new life. A better life.'

It was tempting, but he knew he'd never be able to live with himself if he abandoned Father O'Connor. Besides, what if the vampires never let them be? The thought of being the hunted rather than the hunter was not appealing.

Just then, he detected movement down the hall that led to the rear of the house. Was it his imagination or perhaps a lure to get them further into a trap? He realised he had no way of knowing for sure.

"This way," he whispered.

He moved past the stairway and turned left down the hallway toward the back of the mansion, with Faith following close behind.

The hallway appeared identical to the one they had just been through, but there was less ambient light to guide them. They checked the first room. It was empty. They moved on.

Lotho chose his attack as they approached the second room, stepping out into the corridor and firing a bolt from a crossbow. The steel-tipped missile cut a furrow across John's cheek before slicing part of his ear away as he ducked, instinctively firing at the same time. The rounds from his weapon appeared to hit the big man, who stumbled and fell back into the room.

Faith watched in horror as John fell to his knees.

"John!"

She knelt beside him, momentarily forgetting the danger.

He grimaced in pain.

"I'll be okay," he said. "Just keep your eyes on that doorway. I don't know if I got the fucker."

Faith hesitated. The blood flowing from John's wounds worried her.

He noted her concern.

"Don't worry, it's just a flesh wound," he said.

"You sure?"

"Positive. Come on, now, we've got to keep moving."

He stood up.

Faith followed his lead and the pair edged forward with their assault rifles trained on the open doorway. John noted the blood spattered against the door.

"Thought I got him," he muttered.

John peered into the room, his rifle leading. Moonlight spilled in through the ceiling-high windows to fill the room with an eerie frostlike luminescence. A high bookcase covered the far wall, and apart from a few antique chairs, appeared to be the only furniture visible. He ventured into the room, Faith following. There was no sign of his attacker and no hint as to where he could have gone.

"Where—" Faith started to say before John stopped her.

He pointed to the blood on the floor.

"There," he said.

Faith nodded and followed as John moved on, scanning the floor for more signs of blood. They passed the painting O'Connor had studied a few days before, each droplet of blood luring them deeper into the room. The trail ended at the foot of the large wall-length bookcase.

"There has to be a secret doorway here or something," observed John.

He ran his free hand along the rows of books and soon was rewarded with a metallic click. Part of the bookcase swung inward suddenly.

"Just like in a movie," Faith said.

"You got that right."

He stepped inside.

A spiral staircase led down to what looked like a dimly lit passageway. He hesitated once more and looked back the way they'd come.

'The blood trail is too obvious!' his inner voice urged. 'You're being lured into a trap. It's not too late. The way back is clear. Turn around now and get the fuck away! Who the fuck knows what's waiting for you both down there?'

But then something occurred to him: Whatever was waiting for them down there did not feel strong enough to challenge them head-on, opting instead to run rather than attack. Perhaps, he reasoned, they'd not expected him to find their secret passage.

John's apparent indecision left Faith feeling even more apprehensive.

"John?" she asked nervously. "Are you okay? You think we should maybe go back?"

"Nope, just weighing up the odds." he replied. He was convinced the signs pointed in their favour. "This way."

He started down the stairs with renewed resolve. Faith followed.

They stopped again at the foot of the stairs. The passageway stretched out beyond them with its length marked by a series of lamps suspended from the darkness above. The stainless-steel doors set into the concrete walls on either side glinted malignantly, as though hinting at the horror lurking beyond each.

Their careful steps echoed loudly in the confined space, increasing the palpable tension in the air. They approached the first door. John turned the handle and pushed it open with his foot, careful to keep his assault rifle trained on the room beyond. The stomach-turning stench of blood, vomit, and human sweat hit them. Faith swallowed hard. They pushed on into the bare room.

A single light bulb provided the only light. Empty manacles hung from chains suspended from the ceiling above. A slick red pool of fresh blood covered the cold cement floor. John's eyes moved to where a figure hovered in the shadows just beyond the light.

"Father?"

John took a step toward the waiting figure, lowering the rifle as he did.

"John, wait," called Faith.

The figure lurched forward, jaws snapping open and shut as it moved with its arms extended, a mindless automaton driven only by the virus's desperate need for blood. John stared at the gruesome thing which resembled the once-living man he knew as Father Samuel O'Connor—a man whose obsession with righting the wrongs of his past had so consumed him that he'd sacrificed every principle he'd once held dear. A man who now lived a very different kind of hell.

The thing shuffled forward, its pace increasing as it approached. John lifted his assault rifle and hesitated. Pulling the trigger meant destroying a man he had loved and believed in.

A burst of automatic fire hit the creature in the chest. It stumbled back momentarily, then righted itself, apparently unaware that part of its abdomen had disintegrated under the impact of the bullets. The thing advanced, gurgling and hissing as it came. Faith fired again, this time decapitating the creature in a spray of blood and brain. The headless thing shuffled a few steps then toppled to hit the floor with a fleshy thud. The sharp smell of cordite hung in the air. John blinked, his ears still ringing from the proximity of the gunfire.

"I'm sorry, I tried to—" he started to explain.

"It doesn't matter. I know how you felt about him," said Faith softly. "What do you want to do now?"

"I know what he would've wanted."

"To finish it?"

John nodded grimly. "Yes, to finish it."

"Fine," answered Faith with fatalistic resignation.

What did it matter now, anyway? There was an even chance of dying, whether they chose to run or fight at this point, she realised.

John pointed at the assault rifle.

"You got any rounds left in that thing?" he asked.

She looked down at the open breach slide then ejected the magazine the way John had taught her.

"Nope."

"Guess it's down to the twelve-gauge then," he said.

"Guess so."

Faith dropped the assault rifle, unslung the twelve-gauge, and followed John toward the door.

"Okay, slow and easy," he said.

He pulled the door open carefully then edged into the passage with his assault rifle levelled. When he was sure it was clear, he motioned Faith to follow. The pair crept forward. The girl followed close behind as he continued toward the next door.

Meredith chose to strike then, dropping onto Faith from the darkness above. The impact knocked the wind out of Faith, causing the twelve-gauge to spill from her hands. John spun around at the sound, but it was too late—the vampire had latched onto Faith from behind, sliding her arms about the helpless girl in a suffocating combination of arm and rear headlock.

"Leave her be!" shouted John desperately, his finger restless on the trigger.

"Or what, lover?" hissed Meredith malevolently. "You're going to shoot me? Go right ahead and see which one of us survives!"

Her pointed canines were clearly visible.

"Faith, it'll be okay," said John.

Their predicament was obvious. If he fired, Faith would almost certainly be hit. He edged forward hoping for a clear shot.

"Careful there, lover," drawled Meredith. "I might just forget myself and snap her neck like a twig!"

She tightened her arm about Faith's neck.

"John—" Faith started to say before Meredith choked her words off.

The vampire backed down the passageway, dragging Faith with her all the while ensuring she remained out of the line of fire. John followed, reluctant to leave the girl he loved, yet all-too-aware he was being led further into a trap.

Meredith edged up to the third door along. She pushed it open, the girl still shielding her. The vampire's lips pulled back from her long canines as she laughed malevolently.

"Feel free to join us," she sneered.

Meredith quickly dragged Faith into the room, slamming the door shut behind them. John kept his cool, realising that panicking now meant certain death. He kicked open the door and stepped inside, aiming the assault rifle from the shoulder. The two women were in front of an ornately carved four-poster bed, the vampire still holding Faith tightly in the headlock. Another woman, clothed in a black leather jumpsuit like the vampire who held Faith, stood to one side. She held her tall, slender frame quite still. What struck John was not her natural beauty but the way she studied him—her ice-blue eyes boring into his, peeling back the layers of his soul.

"Finally, we meet," she said.

"Yes," was all John could manage, his finger never straying from the trigger.

"Your friend, the tall one, he did not come with you?" she enquired.

"No."

"Why? He was afraid?"

"Something like that."

"Something like that?" she repeated, smiling. "Why do you not just say he is dead?"

"Maybe because he isn't," John lied. "You think we'd come in here without backup?"

Anastasiya laughed coldly.

"You lie," she sneered. "I smell his blood on you. He is dead and I know how he died."

"If you're so sure about that, why ask?" retorted John.

"I was interested."

"Interested?"

"Yes, interested in how you would respond to my question."

"Doesn't really matter how I answered," snapped John. "The fact is, you murdered an innocent man!"

He realised the longer they talked, the less chance he and Faith had of making it out of the place alive, but all he could do was hope for an opening.

"Innocent? Which of those men was innocent?" challenged Anastasiya.

"Father O'Connor was. The man you tortured and left to die."

"I did not kill him," said Anastasiya. "You killed him."

"That's bullshit. That thing we just killed wasn't the man I knew. Father O'Connor died the moment you infected him with your bite."

"No," said Anastasiya. "Your priest was dead long before that. He had determined his fate the moment he ordered you here to kill. You say he is innocent of murder, but is the person who commands any less innocent than those who carry out his orders?"

"He didn't order us here to kill your people," protested John. "We were after someone else, the man your vampires were feeding on. Your people attacked us first. We had to defend ourselves!"

"So, an unfortunate error on your part."

"Yes," he responded simply.

A small part of him now wondered whether these vampires might be reasoned with. After all, had not both sides lost people?

"Yes, an error for which my acolytes paid with their lives," noted Anastasiya bitterly.

"We've both lost people in this," said John. "It could end here. No one else has to die."

"So you and your girlfriend walk away, and we all live happily to the end of our days?"

"It's a possibility."

He kept his finger on the trigger.

"It is a possibility," nodded Anastasiya.

She took a step toward John.

"I have lived for almost two hundred years and have lived in many different places. I have been hunted before and no doubt I will be hunted again. Do you think I have survived this long by forgiving my enemies?"

"This isn't about forgiveness," urged John. "This is about everyone walking away before more die. What do you say? We could end this right now."

He wanted to look at Faith and tell her that it was nearly over, but dared not take his eyes from the vampire woman, who took another step forward.

"Yes, I think it will end now," said Anastasiya.

She glanced at her vampire acolyte and nodded. Meredith smiled then sank her teeth deep into Faith's exposed neck.

"John!" screamed Faith.

John fired and missed as Anastasiya darted to one side. He quickly adjusted his aim and fired again, but she'd anticipated this, swivelling on the balls of her feet to deliver a high roundhouse kick that knocked the rifle wide. The rounds hit the wall behind and ricocheted wildly about the room.

The vampire queen struck hard, delivering a combination of blows that disarmed John and snapped his right arm. He fell back against the wall, reaching desperately for the pistol with his remaining good hand. Anastasiya moved in quickly, grabbing his left wrist whilst delivering an upward knee strike to his elbow that shattered the arm joint.

John grunted in pain, the pistol dropping from his useless hand. He tried desperately to twist away, but was too slow, and the vampire delivered another strike to his side. He felt his ribs crack under the blow and cried out as she executed a final downward strike with her heel to splinter his left knee joint. He sank to the floor, his unresponsive limbs unable to support him.

John watched helplessly as the other vampire continued to feed on Faith until finally her struggles ceased. Meredith looked up at him then, eyes as red as the blood which covered her mouth and chin. He glared helplessly at her but suppressed the urge to scream the obscenities which boiled up within him. John would not give the vampire women the pleasure of his torment. Anastasiya bent down and pulled him upright so that he was propped against the wall.

"Now watch as she is reborn," she said.

She nodded to her acolyte.

Meredith lifted the rag-doll limp body of Faith from the floor and placed her on the bed. The vampire women gathered up the scattered weapons and left the room, locking the door behind them.

An hour passed before the virus in Faith stirred. John watched impotently as her body began to writhe and twist within its chthonian embrace. He understood then that his fate had become inexorably entwined with hers, and knew that a choice would have to be made come the moment of her awakening.

25

The room was like a cocoon, effectively sealing off the evolving life within from the ignorant world beyond. John did not know whether it was morning yet. Time had been reduced to the progress of the virus as it wrought each genetic change within the girl on the bed. All he could do was watch and wait. How would she be changed from the girl he once knew?

The door opened suddenly and the lithe blonde he'd fought before entered. She ignored him and walked over to the bed. He noticed she'd changed from the leather jumpsuit and now wore a long, red silk robe. The woman proceeded to pull back the sleeve of the robe to reveal her pale forearm. She produced a small, curved knife from the folds of the robe and was about to cut into her forearm when she stopped.

She bent over the supine body of Faith, her face inches from the girl, as though to examine her closely. The moments ticked by. The woman suddenly stepped back from the bed, her back to John, appearing to be deep in thought. It was obvious that she'd changed her mind about something, but what?

John watched. The silence was broken when she finally said something in a language he did not understand. She walked toward him, smiling.

"The change is complete," she said. "When she wakes, you will need to make a decision."

John scowled.

"I didn't think I had any choice," he observed. "She's one of you now, isn't she?"

"Only if she chooses," replied Anastasiya. "That is where you fit into all of this."

"How is that?"

"I am going to tell you a story," she began. "It is a story of a young woman of noble blood. A young woman who lived a very different way of life. A life she had no choice but to leave behind once the plague and war had destroyed all she loved. Once you hear my story, you will understand why I give her the choice, and in this, know you play a part."

And when Anastasiya finished her story, John finally understood the way of it.

◇ ◇ ◇

Faith woke with a start. She lay staring up at the embellished ceiling and tried to remember how she'd come to be there. All at once, the horror of the previous night came to her and with it a flood of emotion which threatened to overwhelm her. Faith cried out and sat up quickly. She looked around the strange room and saw John propped against the wall opposite. He smiled weakly at her.

"John!" she exclaimed.

She leapt from the bed and ran to him.

"How bad are you hurt?"

"Pretty bad," he answered. "You feel any different?"

"Any different?"

Then she suddenly understood.

"I don't know," she replied.

She put a hand to her neck where Meredith had fed.

"I feel kinda strange. Like I've just woken from a weird dream. I saw myself bathing in a river of blood. There were these dead people floating in the river, their flesh rotting and pale. They were staring at me as they drifted past, their eyes cursing me."

Faith shook her head at the horror of the memory.

"But somehow, I didn't care. I loved the feel of the blood on my skin. Then I drank the blood. I drank and I drank, and it felt like I'd never want to stop."

Faith shivered as though repulsed by what she'd felt. She frowned and looked at John.

"Do I seem different to you?" she asked.

"She said it might take a little time," he answered quietly.

"Who did?"

"Anastasiya," he said. "This is her home."

"What did she say?"

"That the hunger within you would start soon, and that you would need to feed."

John looked in her eyes to see whether she understood the implication of what he'd just said.

She did.

"And if I choose not to?" she responded tearfully.

"Then you will die. You carry a virus within you that cannot survive without human blood. If you don't feed it, it will feed on you until both you and it die." He spoke the words plainly and without emotion.

"Then I choose to die," she said earnestly.

"I don't want you to die, Faith."

She shook her head vigorously.

"If I take your blood, you will die, John. I won't let you sacrifice yourself so that I can live," she said.

"I want you to survive this. One of us must. Don't you see that? If we both die, then our lives will have been for nothing."

"Who said our lives mattered anyway?" responded Faith petulantly.

She immediately regretted her words, if only for the hurt she saw flash in his eyes.

"I do," replied John solemnly. "Everything we do in life matters. Don't ever believe differently, Faith."

"I want to believe in that," she said. "But here we are, trapped in this room. Nothing we do is going to change that. They could leave us here to rot no matter what."

"Not if you take my blood."

"How do you know that for sure?"

"If you take my blood, you will be welcomed as one of their own. She gave me her word and I believe her."

"I don't know if I can do it, John. I don't know if I care anymore."

Faith was crying now, the tears streaming down her cheeks.

"I think you do care. Besides, I don't think you're ready to give up on life just yet. Do you?"

She gave a noncommittal shrug. How could she answer him? To say yes meant she agreed to killing him so that she might live. She hated herself because deep-down, she knew she still wanted life.

He could sense her self-doubt.

"You're stronger than you think, Faith," he said softly.

She hugged him then and wept, and together they waited.

◇ ◇ ◇

Afterwards, when it was over, she kissed him. Then, she stripped a red silk sheet from the bed and draped it over his corpse.

Faith went over to the bed and sat down. She could feel the vitality of the virus as it coursed through her veins, and sensed instinctively the new powers it granted her. Was this what it was like to be one of them? To be something other than human? She could not deny the thrill of it, the sense of absolute control over her own destiny. Although the door had not yet opened, she reminded herself. When it did—for she was certain it would—what would she do then? She could attack and strike at her new sisters in vengeance for John's death. She would probably die in the attempt, but not before she killed the leader, Anastasiya. Yet how would that change anything? John's death would mean even less.

Or she could embrace her new life. Embrace it as he would have wanted her to and see where her path in life would lead. Then it suddenly occurred to her: Within her also lay the means of destroying all of humanity. Her victims would be infected with the virus, and if allowed, they would attack and infect others. If left unchecked, the virus would spread. Could it mean the end of everything? Did some part of her want an end to this world? Faith realised she had more pressing matters to concern herself with for the present, but knew instinctively that someday, she would consider the option again.

It was in her nature.

◊ ◊ ◊

Anastasiya sat in front of the console and watched the young woman on the bed. There was something alluring and yet unsettling about this girl. Faith's genetics had adapted to the virus more completely than Anastasiya had anticipated. She would not need the constant blood infusion from Anastasiya that the others required. How, then, would she control this new acolyte?

Perhaps it was best the girl did not know the true extent of her power. At least for the present. Anastasiya had always considered herself unique, the only one to achieve full union with the alien virus. Was this young woman her true sister? An equal? Or was there something more sinister in all of this? Had the virus decided upon a new queen to lead the chosen? She smiled to herself.

An interesting time certainly lay ahead.

SHAUN GRIFFIN
240

Paris, 1910

The years had passed, and despite the night terrors he suffered every so often, George could almost say he'd enjoyed them.

"Well?" enquired Robert. "Was it everything you'd imagined?"

"Everything and more," sighed George as they pushed through the crush of people leaving the auditorium.

They paused at the top of the Grand Staircase.

"Robbie, I want to stand here awhile," said George. "I want to take it all in one last time."

He looked up at the high ceiling with its ornate decorations and paintings inspired by the Greek myths—the triumph of Apollo, the gods of Olympus. Apparently, Isidor Pils, the artist, had had to complete the paintings in situ. An astonishing feat by any measure.

"I thought we were going to enjoy a late dinner, George," grumbled Robert. "With all these people about, one might never find a cab in time."

"Tell you what," said George. "Why don't you run ahead and find us a cab? I'll be out in a moment."

"If you insist," replied Robert petulantly. "Only don't take too long or I might decide to leave without you."

"Yes, yes, now run along," said George.

He watched Robert descend the stairs and disappear into the crowd. The young man had grown rather tiresome of late, he thought, and realised sadly that their relationship was nearing its inevitable end.

He looked up again, his eyes tracing the elaborate architecture, following the line along the ceiling and then down the stately marble columns to the floor. His gaze drifted idly over the gay crowd of people on the balcony opposite.

George froze. A familiar face stared back at him, her ice-blue eyes piercing his soul. It was the young woman from the ship. The stuff of his nightmares. He felt himself transported back in time to the deck of the Servia. The woman started making her way through the crowd toward him, her cold eyes never leaving his. He hesitated, unable to move, a mouse caught in the hypnotic gaze of a snake as it moved in for the kill.

George uttered a strangled cry and then he was running, pushing through the crowd as he forced his way toward the exit. Men cursed as he charged blindly through bewildered couples, forcing his legs on, and then he felt the cool night air on his flushed face.

He looked about wildly and spotted Robert waiting beside a taxi-cab. It was one of the new motor vehicles, a Renault Type AG. George barged past Robert and tumbled into the back of the cab.

"Drive! Drive, damn you! Aller! Aller!" he yelled at the startled driver.

Robert clambered in after him, perplexed at the sudden change in his friend.

"George! What's gotten into you, man?" he demanded.

"I saw her, Robbie, I saw her!" shouted George.

"Saw who?"

"No time to explain," replied George. "But we're leaving. Tonight."

"What? What about dinner? I'm famished! You promised!"

"Not now, Robbie. There's no time for this!" snapped George.

He turned to the driver.

"Chauffeur, le Majestic. Depechez-vous!" he urged.

Soon they were back in the hotel room. Robert watched his friend with growing concern. He'd been both surprised and annoyed at his friend's sudden change of mood, especially when George had refused to speak about it on the way back. When he had finally spoken, it was to tell some wild story of a woman who fed on men's blood, and who he'd just seen at the ballet.

"Don't look at me that way, Robbie!" exclaimed George, and gesticulated wildly. "I'm telling you the truth, for God's sake. She was there! The woman from the Servia! The one who killed those men."

"I'm trying to believe you, George," replied Robert. "But you have to admit, it all sounds rather fanciful. Like something out of that novel by Mr Stoker."

"Stoker be damned!" snapped George.

He turned back to shoving clothes into his portmanteau.

"This is not fantasy, this is real life!"

"George, I..."

The words died on Robert's lips as Anastasiya grabbed him from behind, wrenched his head to the side and sank her fangs into his exposed neck.

George watched Robert's futile attempts to break free, horrified. The woman was too strong, and slowly, inexorably, she drained the blood from his lover. George tried to run but found his limbs unresponsive. He tried to shout but his voice failed him. In the end all he could do was watch and await the inevitable.

The blonde woman allowed Robert's limp body to slump to the floor when she'd finished. Her lips and chin were red with his blood. She smiled, revealing her long, pointed canines.

"I knew this day would come," gasped George, finally finding his voice. "When you would eventually hunt me down and kill me."

The woman laughed.

"Hunt you down?" she replied with a hint of amusement. "You think you are that important to me? It is true that I remember you from the ship. But I was not hunting you. This is merely coincidence. The hand of fate, you might say."

"All those years ago, you let me live," said George weakly. "Even though I could have exposed you. Why would you want to kill me now?"

The woman looked at him quizzically.

"You ask me why?" she said.

She advanced slowly, her blood smeared lips curled into a malevolent smile. George backed away as she did, and then his back was pressed against the unyielding surface of the wall behind. All too soon she was up-close, her face inches from his, the metallic scent of Robert's blood on her breath.

"Don't you know never to question a god?" sneered the woman. "Foolish man, your life is done only because I choose it so."

Anastasiya struck then, pinning George to the wall as she sank her fangs into his jugular. He did not struggle, but surrendered to the fangs which drained the life from him, a look of serene acceptance on his face.

When it was over, Anastasiya lifted his corpse and carried it over to the other body and laid it down. She then wrenched the heads from the two dead men. In the morning, the staff would discover two desiccated, headless corpses—a gruesome discovery which no doubt would cause a morbid sensation in the press but was preferable to having the corpses rise as undead.

She had no need for unwanted attention. Now, or ever. She would finish out the week in Paris before travelling to Vienna. From there, it would be back to America.

The land of endless opportunity.

END BOOK ONE

THE STORY WILL BE CONTINUED
IN BOOK TWO
OF THE AMERICAN NOIR TRILOGY

You reap what you sow—the old adage will prove no less true for Anastasiya, self-styled vampire Goddess. She allowed Faith, the young woman turned vampire, to live. But as Faith's powers continue to evolve Anastasiya must decide—is the girl a potential ally or a rival to her position of power?

As Anastasiya contemplates her next move she is unaware of an even deadlier threat. Goran, professional assassin and brother to Dragan, the man she killed, is out for revenge. His hunt will lead him to Anastasiya and her acolytes. Will they survive the deadly retribution he has planned?

Throw into the mix a corrupt biologist on the trail of the alien vampire virus, two FBI agents moonlighting as guns for hire, a cop investigating the suspicious death of his friend and you have the ingredients for an explosive showdown in book 2 of the American Noir Trilogy – Hera's Scream.

HERA'S
SCREAM

Shaun Griffin is a structural engineer currently working in Australia. He and his wife live in a small coastal town where they share a house with their spoiled pet Cavoodle. The children having moved out to follow their own careers, Shaun divides his spare time writing, reading history, collecting comics and in the gym.

HERA'S CURSE
Survival Is A Matter Of Choice
Book1 of the American Noir Trilogy

written by Shaun Griffin
cover by Nessgraphica

ISBN 978-0-6481701-4-3 (print)